SWEET NOTHING

#1 NEW YORK TIMES BESTSELLING AUTHOR

JAMIE MCGUIRE

NEW YORK TIMES BESTSELLING AUTHOR

TERESA MUMMERT

DEDICATION

To Michelle Chu, thank you for your unwavering support.
To Misty Horn, thank you for reminding me that people can be
kind without expectation.
~Jamie

To Joshua, my own lucky penny. Together we make cents. ;)
~Teresa

PROLOGUE

Josh

As I pulled up to the light at the intersection of Holly Road and Jackson Avenue, all I could think about was a hot shower and grabbing a beer with my partner, Quinn. We'd earned it after the day we'd had, helping rescue thirteen passengers from an overturned bus.

My phone lit up in my hand as I flipped through my contacts to find a woman who might want to join us. I could use a little company to take my mind off everything else. I paused and hovered my finger over Cara, a bleach-blonde with a smart mouth, who happened to be very flexible. I'd hooked up with her a few times in the past, and I knew I'd have to delete her soon before she thought our get-togethers were something more serious.

A birthday card from Quinn still sat on my dash, tossed there the week before. Twenty-six years was plenty of time to find love, settle down, and grow up. I spent my work hours in a meat wagon, more than just witnessing some of the most horrific and tragic events around Philadelphia—most nights, I was elbow deep in them. I'd earned the right to blow off steam, even if it meant using someone else to help me forget. I'd been ignoring the pang of guilt that accompanied the thought of a meaningless fling since I'd moved to Philadelphia.

I glanced at the comically ugly Prius to my left, locking eyes with the uptight nurse who had given me hell only hours before. Quinn and I had delivered four patients to her ER that day, and her first words to me were telling me how to do my job.

"You've got to be fucking kidding me." I smirked at her, even though my body struggled to make even the simplest movements after my long shift in the back of the ambulance. "Jacobs, right? St. Ann's?"

Her face screwed into a disgusted frown. "Don't pretend you didn't know."

Readjusting my grip on the worn steering wheel of my sixty-nine Alpine White Barracuda Fastback, I stepped on the gas pedal to allow the Mopar to purr.

Jacobs curved up her lips. I could tell the day had dragged on just as long for her in the ER. The meticulous bun I'd seen hours before was now hanging in sun-kissed wisps, framing her tired face. Her pink scrubs still held the brown stain near the collar from when she had run into me, sending her pudding flying and expletives exploding from her plump lips. She had berated me for not watching where I was going without a second of flirtation. She didn't like me, and I liked it—a lot.

I opened my mouth to speak again, but she did her best to rev her baby-shit-green Prius, its sorry excuse for an engine barely making a sound.

My window complained as I cranked it down further, motioning for her to do the same. Her window slid smoothly the rest of the way inside her doorframe as she cocked her head to the side, listening.

I have her attention. The nervousness I felt surprised me. Jacobs had intentionally and successfully ignored me since the first time I had brought a patient to her ER. Now that we were alone and she was speaking to me, I wasn't thinking about the usual smut running through my mind. Instead, I found myself embarrassed. Thanks to the ER break room gossip and my penchant for nurses, Jacobs likely knew about half my trysts.

"You got something to say to me?" Jacobs asked.

"I don't know what that noise was, but I think your car just soiled itself," I joked.

She pretended to be angry. "I'll have you know my car gets great gas mileage and has a minimal carbon footprint."

"Seriously? Was that your best attempt at talking shit? I'm disappointed, Nurse Ratched."

Jacobs showed me her middle finger but was unable to contain her giggle. It was fun to watch her unravel from her uptight shell.

"Oh, come on now. At least let me buy you dinner before you proposition me." I glanced at the red light ahead of us before looking back at her.

Her mouth hung open, unable to form a witty retort.

After recouping from the level of self-satisfaction only a Prius owner could understand, I smiled. "Me and some friends are hitting O'Malley's. Why don't you tag along?"

"Are you asking me out?"

My memory flashed to the first time I'd seen Jacobs in the ER as she tried not to stare at Dr. Rosenberg. Everyone else seemed oblivious, but I couldn't help but notice her lingering gaze, and the thin silver band on his left ring finger. Jacobs, however, wore no jewelry.

I couldn't compete with a guy like Doc Rose, even if he was out of reach for her. Jacobs wasn't the gated-community type, but she had her bar set high. She was attracted to the white lab coat and tie—the stable, sophisticated type. I was the guy who'd always done just what I needed to get by, no more and no less. If I was honest, my father had pulled strings to make sure I had a career at all. I had been too busy partying and spending the small savings my grandfather left me when he'd passed away.

I had been a cliché, and a pathetic one at that. Rarely came a night when I didn't take home a college freshman only to kick her out hours later with some lame excuse of having to work in the morning. I didn't make connections or share my feelings—I had no reason to—but graduation changed everything. I'd been thrust into the real world, alone. Part of me liked it that way. If you didn't get close, you couldn't get hurt when they left you.

"It's not a date," I said, rubbing my palm against the back of my aching neck.

I struggled not to look like a desperate douchebag. I didn't do dates, and she was way out of my league, but there was something about this girl I wanted to explore—and I didn't mean just her panties. "I just thought ... maybe you could use a drink."

"I could, actually."

My gaze dipped to her mouth, my foot accidentally pressing down on the gas pedal again. Jacobs was the fucking unicorn—the one we all talked about but could never seem to capture. She was smart, knew her shit at work, and didn't resort to dumbing herself down for guys who showed her attention. Instead, she walked with confidence, knowing she was the kind of woman who could hold out for the right guy. Unfortunately for her, the guy she thought was right for her was married to someone else, and she wasn't a woman who would take what wasn't hers.

Her giggle cut through the loud roar of the engine.

"Yeah? So, you wanna go grab a beer?" I asked.

She tucked the honey-colored wisps of hair behind her ear. Even disheveled and shiny from day-old makeup, she was beautiful. "Thank God I have a bottle of wine at home waiting for me."

"Is that an invitation?" I asked.

"Nope."

"At least give me your number," I begged as a car behind me honked. The driver waited just seconds before swerving onto the shoulder, leaving as quickly as he had arrived.

I glanced up at the green light and cursed under my breath, hoping my time wasn't up. Like my prayers had been answered, it switched to a dark yellow, and I returned my attention to her, instantly deflated. She couldn't have been less impressed. I needed to try harder.

"Give you my number," she repeated, amused. "So I can be added to your little black book of shame?" Her teeth dug into the plump flesh of her lower lip. "Do you really think the nurses don't talk?"

I chuckled, feeling nervous, watching her smile fade into a scowl. She was getting more annoyed with me by the second, but I couldn't stop myself. As long as she was talking to me, I was still in the game.

"Are you *laughing* at me?"

"No, no, Jacobs. I'm laughing at myself. I should have known better." I bent down, picked up a penny from the floorboard, and tossed it into the ashtray. Running my hand over my short, dark hair, I noticed the tension in her expression hadn't eased. "You're just too uptight."

"I guess you'll never know," she said as her whisper-quiet car pulled out to cross the intersection.

I reached out, already seeing what she would see just a half-second later, but that would be too late. The light had already turned red. She stiffened her hands on the wheel, watching helplessly as the tractor-trailer approached her driver side at forty miles per hour. Her expression turned to horror as the sound of metal twisting and cracking under impact filled the air.

My fingers gripped the steering wheel so tightly, my bones felt like they could snap under the pressure. I watched as glass exploded and the crumbled remains of her Prius launched toward me. The semi's brakes whined in protest and Jacobs' name ripped from my chest in a warning that had come too late. It was all too late.

I was used to saving people after tragedy struck, but it was easy to remove yourself from their pain when you didn't have to witness the shock and horror of the event.

The last words Jacobs had spoken to me tumbled over and over in my subconscious as I scrambled to back my car away from the wreckage barreling toward me.

I resigned to my fate as my car propelled backward, my neck slamming against the headrest. When the semi finally came to a stop, the world stilled. The silence was more deafening than the horrific accident. It took me a few tries to open my door. Using my shoulder, I shoved my way out, rushing over to Jacobs' mangled Prius. The sound of stones under my boots turned to broken glass. I was going to save her. I was going to save us both.

I sat in the waiting room down the hall from her room, biting at my thumbnail, my knee bobbing up and down. Nurses, doctors, and family members passed by without acknowledgment, oblivious that my entire world had shifted on its axis. Everything had changed.

"Josh," Quinn said, appearing above me. He sat in the chair next to me and patted my shoulder. "You okay?"

I didn't answer, staring at the floor.

"It's going to be all right. Just hang in there, buddy."

"She was there. She was right there, and then she wasn't," I said finally.

Quinn watched me, waiting for me to continue.

"I've been trying to get her attention since the first time I brought her a patient. She was finally talking to me, and ... I can't explain it."

"That had to have been hard to see. It's a miracle you're okay."

I cringed. "Even at the stoplight, when she was talking to me, I was thinking of ways to get her into bed." I shook my head, disgusted. "Avery has been this un-gettable get, you know? She's sitting there, smiling, finally acknowledging I exist, and my mind defaults back to the same douchebag shit."

"Don't be so hard on yourself, Josh." Quinn shrugged. "Avery's a beautiful woman. All the guys at the station talk about her. She's confident, feisty, and those eyes ..."

I glowered at him.

He cleared his throat. "Sorry. Everyone knows you've had a thing for her, too. I'm just saying that just because taking her home crossed your mind, that doesn't mean that's all it would have been."

I didn't want a *would have* or *should have*. My story had no more room for regret, yet I had watched it take physical form right in front of me.

I grazed my nose with my knuckle. "This is my fault."

Quinn shifted in his seat. "Don't go there, Josh. You can't take the blame for this one."

"I was there. If I hadn't been talking to her ... I've told you that when people get too close—"

Quinn blew out a frustrated breath. "You've got to give that up, man. The universe doesn't have it out for you."

I shook my head. "I couldn't get to her fast enough. She was hurt, I ran as fast I could to get to her, but my whole body was moving in slow motion. And then—against all my training—I cradled her in my arms and held her. That's all I could do." I felt Quinn's fingers press into my shoulder. "I've only felt that helpless one other time in my life. I'm tired of being too late."

"All paramedics get that way, buddy. It's why we do what we do."

"No, this was different. I wasn't doing just my job. I needed her to be okay, Quinn. I *need* her to be okay. I have to see her again."

"She'll be okay." Quinn said the words slow, watching me intently. "Are you? Okay?"

"I'm fine. And I know what you're thinking."

"That you hit your head harder than I thought? A little," he admitted.

"I saw her get T-boned by a semi. I thought I'd lost her." Heartbreak and loss were a part of life. Those of us who worked hand in hand with death learned early to appreciate those few precious moments we had before it was all taken away. I recoiled from Quinn's expression. "Don't look at me like that."

"I get it. Sometimes I think about the people I've lost, and it makes me work that much harder to bring people back," Quinn agreed.

"That's not it. I made a decision in the ten minutes I listened to the sirens get closer."

"What kind of decision?"

The possibility of losing something before it was even mine was something I'd never imagined. Watching what could have been slip away before it was in your grasp was enough to break a man. But it had also given me the chance to redeem myself, make myself worthy of her, in the event we finally got our moment.

"You'll see."

CHAPTER ONE

Avery

My muscles hurt even before I opened my eyes. I hadn't dreamed, nor could I recall the moment of impact. My only memory was the pain. But when the room around me came into focus, it all but went away.

The hideous brown and mauve wallpaper was peeling in the corners. The fake plants and watercolor prints were meant to resemble a nineteen-eighties living room, even though anyone would know by the smell alone where they were.

Nurse Michaels walked in with a stethoscope hanging from her blue floral lab jacket. She had the same dark circles I'd had when looking in a mirror mid-shift. Michaels typically worked in ICU but sometimes moonlighted in the ER with me, not that she was any help at all. Being in her care was unsettling.

The tiny catheter wiggled a bit beneath the thin skin of my hand while she fussed with the tape covering the entry site of my IV. I frowned and peered up, seeing Michaels' infernal, frizzy orange hair, and then my surroundings. *Yep. I was definitely in Step-Down.*

Unfortunately, it appeared Step-Down, the hospital wing for stabilized patients adjacent to the ICU, was short staffed, and Michaels clearly had hours to make up—as usual.

"Looking good, Jacobs. You hang in there. We're all worried about you," she said, pulling at the tape again.

"Jesus, Michaels. Take it easy," I said. My voice sounded like two pieces of sandpaper rubbing together, and my throat burned.

She startled. "Oh." With her finger, she pushed her black-framed glasses up the bridge of her nose, her tone more surprised than excited.

"If you're here, who's taking my shift?" I asked.

"I'm just going to—" She reached for the tape again.

I pulled away from her. "Would you fucking stop?" I snapped, already feeling guilty. It was true: nurses were the worst patients.

Dr. Rosenberg's Italian leather shoes clicked across the tile. Concern hummed from his throat, and my chest fluttered. His ocean-blue eyes sparkled, even if he was seeing me in a sack-like hospital gown. My face probably looked like a misshapen tomato, but I still reached up to flatten the rats in my hair, hoping a decent hairdo would distract him from the rest of me.

I refused to let out a sigh, or stare too long at his perfectly thick eyebrows or squared jawline, or snarl at Michaels when she did everything I refused to do. After all, Dr. Rosenberg wasn't mine. He belonged to Mrs. Rosenberg and their teenaged daughter. But, unlike Michaels, I didn't have to fantasize that Dr. Rosenberg cared about me. He did. He was standing right next to my bed, scanning over my embarrassingly thin hospital gown and looking rather upset, even though he worked three floors below in the ER.

Dr. Rosenberg touched my hand, and I tried not to let a squeal spill from my mouth. His warm fingers traveled up my palm to my wrist, and then he waited quietly while he checked my pulse. "Strong, considering. We can probably—"

The PA system paged him, and he nodded to Michaels. "Take care of her."

"Of course," Michaels lilted.

My blood boiled at her flirtatious tone. He was gorgeous and smart and charming, but knowing he was married didn't calm my instant and irrational jealousy, even if Michaels flirted with everything with testicles and a PhD.

After the doctor disappeared down the hall, I pushed up to sit higher on the bed. "What is today?"

"TGIF," Michaels said with a sigh, checking my monitor.

"See if you can expedite my discharge, would you? I'm too late for today's shift, but I can't miss tomorrow. I'm supposed to cover for Deb."

Deb Hamata and I had gone to nursing school together and had the same hire date. We had been through a lot together in St. Ann's ER. She was the only colleague I referred to by first name, and the only nurse I wouldn't annihilate for calling me Avery.

Michaels leaned in to gently push back a stray hair from my face. I recoiled. "You don't worry about a thing. I've got you covered, sister."

I crossed my arms and huffed as she walked away. Michaels was usually a lazy, unprofessional brat. She was just a few years younger than me, but her parents still paid her bills, leaving her without motivation for a solid work ethic. If a Bruno Mars concert were within driving range, she would call in sick. I had been burned enough times to know not to like anyone. At the moment, Michaels was compassionate and patient with my foul mood, making it very hard, but not entirely impossible, for me to dislike her.

I ran my fingers over my teeth. *Thank God. All present.* Felt my face. *Whoa. Better than I imagined.* I wiggled my toes. *Yes. I'm walking out of here.*

Not long after I took stock of my injuries, Michaels gave me the green light along with the few pieces of personal property that had been gathered from the wreckage. I hobbled from the sterile C.diff-and-bleach smell of the hospital to the sweaty mildew odor of a cab.

The driver looked unsure as I retied the second gown around me that I'd used as a robe. "You sure you can go home just yet?" he asked.

"That bad, huh?"

I tried to ignore his curious eyes in the rearview mirror as I struggled to secure my seatbelt.

"You okay?" he asked.

"Fine."

"You sick? You're not gonna puke in my cab, are ya?"

"Car accident. I feel fine, thank you."

"Your family couldn't pick you up?"

"No family," I said. Until that moment, it hadn't occurred to me to call anyone. I'd been alone for so long, family was a foreign concept to me. There was an aunt and a few cousins in Florida, but I didn't know them. Certainly not enough to let them know I'd been in a minor accident.

I kept busy enough with work that I barely noticed I was alone, but family was good for situations like this. Family kept you from having to ride home in a cab wearing two hospital gowns and oatmeal-colored non-skid socks.

"Where's your clothes, kid?" he asked.

"In my closet."

"Don'tcha have someone to bring you some? Anyone?"

I shook my head, giving him the address of my building. The driver finally pulled away, and after he learned the answer to the expected *what do you do*, he talked over jazz radio about his bunions, a life-long aversion to raw vegetables, and his two-pack-a-day Pall Mall habit. For some reason, when people learned I was a nurse, they felt the urge to confess their health sins. I guessed it was so I would either absolve them or diagnose them, but I had yet to do either.

"Is this the one, sweetheart?" the driver asked, pointing with his fat, tar-stained finger. "I think one of my ex-girlfriends lived here once."

"I thought everyone your age married the first person they dated?"

He made a face. "Nah. I would have, but she wouldn't wait for me." He pointed to his embroidered hat that read veteran. "Navy."

"Thank you for your service."

He nodded in acknowledgment. His yellowed nails were lined with grime, and he had at least a day's worth of silver scruff on his weathered face. He'd served our country and, by the looks of his hands, had worked harder jobs than driving a cab, compelling me to give him an extra-nice tip. I had no purse or pockets, and definitely no money. I opened my hand, revealing a few wadded up dollar bills and my keys.

"Let me just run up to get some more cash," I said, my sore muscles complaining as I pushed open the door.

He huffed. "The hospital fares never pay."

"No, I'll pay you. Please wait here. I'll be right back. Keep the meter running. I'll pay you for your time, too."

His eyes softened and he smiled. "Pay me next time, kid. Most people don't even offer."

For half a second, I'd forgotten there would be a next time. No telling what salvage yard my poor little sea-green Prius was in. It had crumpled around me as we cartwheeled together across the intersection into a patch of grass on the other side. I had somehow made it out in one piece, but there would be many more taxi rides in my future. That thought made my heart hurt. The Prius had protected me, and now it was spare parts.

"Thanks," I said, looking at his license on the dash. "Melvin."

"It's just Mel." He handed me a bent, smudged card. "Call me if you need another ride, but no more freebies."

"Of course. I will. Thank you."

He left me standing on the curb in front of the stoop of my building. I waved and then padded up the steps and pulled open the door, glad my apartment was only on the second floor. After just half a flight, my body slowed, barely able to put one foot in front of the other. I slid the key into the lock and turned it, shoving open the door and then leaning back against the wood until it closed.

"TGIF," I said with a sigh, sliding down to the floor.

Almost two years in the same apartment, and it still looked like something a property manager would use to entice a potential renter. Nailing holes into walls that didn't belong to me just didn't feel right, but that didn't explain why I hadn't bought real plates, either.

I looked over at the door-less kitchen cabinets, exposing my collection of paper plates and plastic cups to match the plastic cutlery in the drawers below. Just one glass casserole dish, a skillet, and one pot were sitting in the space beneath the countertop gathering dust. Eating out had been more of a pastime than a necessity until that moment.

I pulled myself up and forced my feet across the room in order to rummage through the medicine cabinet for an old bottle of Lortab. I rolled the tiny robin's-egg-colored pill in my palm before tossing it to the back of my throat, chasing it with a gulp of flat Mountain Dew.

The Formica felt cold against my backside as I waited for my veins to carry the hydrocodone and sugar through my body.

Once I began feeling human again, I showered, slipped an off-the-shoulder sweatshirt over my head, and stepped into my favorite royal-blue cuffed sweatpants. As I piled my still-damp hair on top of my head, it crossed my mind that I would probably meet who might be the love of my life while dressed like a colorblind cat lady. But I had to eat, and I would rather make the walk across the street without a bra than try to scrounge up something to cook—not that I had any groceries.

I glanced in the mirror and paused. My face was not the frightening mess I'd imagined. Instead, I looked ... normal. Tired, maybe, but otherwise fresh-faced and not at all like a mushy tomato.

Keys in hand, and gripping the railing the whole way down, I headed back downstairs, pausing just long enough to check for traffic before crossing against the light to JayWok, my favorite Chinese eatery in Philadelphia.

The soy sauce and grease filled my nose before I even opened the door, and I smiled. The takeout line was long, so I sat at my regular table and waited for Coco to take my order.

Within moments, she was standing next to me in a maroon apron over skinny jeans and a name tag that read *Cocolina* pinned to a too-small white polo shirt. She was holding a menu I didn't need and filling a glass with water I wouldn't drink. "The usual?" she asked.

"Probably," I said.

She frowned. "Did you quit the hospital? I don't think I've seen you without scrubs on."

"I have the day off."

"Sick?"

"Not really," I said.

She turned on her heels, knowing I wouldn't expand on my answer.

I cupped my chin in my hand. Dozens of people of all shapes and sizes passed by the large window next to the booth I'd made my own since I'd first walked through the door twenty-three months ago. Summer break was in full swing, and now that the sun was out, tourists grouped in families and crowded the sidewalks, making an old wound throb in my chest. I was an adult, but still, I missed the feel of my father's large hand around mine. I envied the little girls who passed by with wide grins and impatient, pointing fingers, either being pulled by or tugging their daddies along. By now, I knew it would never go away. I would always miss my parents and mourn every moment they couldn't experience with me.

A white sack crinkled when it was set in front of me, bearing the simple JayWok logo on the front: a cherry-red medallion with thick, mirrored lines and spaces. I always wondered what the mini-maze meant, but I was distracted by the knuckles covering the rolled-down top of the sack.

"Eating alone?" the man asked.

His hands were sexy. *Yes, sexy.* Thick, just the right size, and muscular. *Yes, muscular.* When a woman had been single as long as I had, we began to notice certain things, like hands, that others may not. The tiny dark hairs on his fingers, his freshly cut nails, and the scar on his right index finger. Most important was what his hand was missing: a wedding band. The only thing worse than a wedding band was the dreaded tan line on the ring finger of a man looking to stray. He was missing that, too, and I couldn't help but smile.

I looked up, seeing a familiar pair of gray eyes belonging to a guy I knew was definitely single. "Excuse me?"

"Are you eating alone?" he said again, this time enunciating.

"Uh, yes." His assessment was more than a little embarrassing. "I know. It's kind of pathetic."

"I don't know," he said, sitting in the chair across from me. "I think it's kind of romantic."

I narrowed my eyes. *Romantic?* That didn't sound like the obnoxious paramedic who flirted with every nurse in my ER.

He let go of the sack and held up his hands. "I'm glad to see you're okay. If you'd taken off a few seconds earlier, it would have been a lot worse."

"It's all pretty fuzzy."

He frowned, lost in thought. "Not for me."

"Well, keep it to yourself if you don't mind. I'd rather not know."

"You're welcome."

"For what?"

"Digging you out of the crinkled can of a car and calling nine-one-one."

I blinked. "Oh. I mean ... thank you. I didn't realize."

He waved me away. "That is not my coolest act of heroism. I have way better stories."

I raised an eyebrow. "I'd like to hear them sometime. Just to know what I'm up against."

The break room gossip had circulated that the new paramedic was also new to Philadelphia. I wasn't sure what he was running from, but it was obvious what he was chasing: tail. Tall, thin, short, voluptuous, and any combination in between. He loved to conquer, and until that moment, I wouldn't have dreamed of giving him the time of day. Knowing what he'd done—even if it was a normal thing for him—his eyes seemed a little softer, and his smile a little sweeter. It was easier to see him, not as a predator but as having the potential for more than a one-night stand.

He chuckled. "I know what you're thinking. I didn't follow you here or anything. My shift is in an hour and I was grabbing something to go."

The hydrocodone made it more difficult to process everything he was saying, and I was more than just a little aggravated he didn't respond to my pickup line.

After a short pause, I finally found an appropriate response. "I didn't think you were stalking me. I can't see you putting in that kind of time."

"That's not true."

"You have the attention span of a toddler."

He grinned, his eyes bright. "What's your name?"

"You know my name."

"Not your work name, Jacobs. Your first name."

I hesitated. We kept to last names at work to keep things professional. I sometimes had to work with this guy. Even if the accident had changed certain things, I had a hard time believing he was someone I could trust with my first name.

Maybe it was because I had remembered how alone I was more than once that day, or maybe I had no reason at all, but I chose to give it to the flirty paramedic who had sexy, ringless hands. "Avery."

He shot me a dubious look. "Avery."

I nodded, unsure if I had, in a Lortab-induced haze, mispronounced my own name.

"Avery?" he said again in disbelief.

"Yes, why? Is that okay?"

He pointed to his chest. "Josh Avery."

"Oh!" I said, finally understanding. "Maybe we're related." I was proud of myself for managing humor in my current state.

He turned up one side of his mouth, and a dimple sunk into

his left cheek. "I hope not." His thoughts were anything but innocent as his gaze bore into me.

He reached across the table, extending his hand. I barely tapped it with my fingers, but he held on to them a bit longer as I pulled away.

Even before I knew his name, I'd known Josh as Quinn Cipriani's new partner, the charming, bed-hopping paramedic who had come out of nowhere to seduce every nurse under thirty-five in the ER. Even aware of all that, I had no choice but to be flattered.

Josh had all the traits of the modern, attractive male: the square chin, strong jaw, a celebrity smile, long lashes, and *I-could-fall-in-love-with-you* eyes. He always smelled like fabric softener and cheap but pleasant cologne, even nine hours into a shift—not that I'd made a point to notice.

Now he was sitting across from me, somehow still looking attractive in a worn T-shirt and mismatched athletic shorts. He watched me with a new spark in his eye, no doubt the infamous, undeniable charm I'd seen him exhibit a hundred times before. He nodded at Coco as she passed, and then turned his attention back to me, his eyes the most beautiful I'd ever seen. He was enjoying watching me squirm, shamelessly flirting with me when we both knew I looked like hell. I tried to retain my game face. It would be too embarrassing to admit to Deb that I'd giggled like one of a dozen new nurses we'd watched him win over.

"Don't be late, Josh."

"Are you working tonight? Maybe I'll run into you."

I shook my head. "Not tonight, but I'm sure we'll cross paths again."

The sack crackled in his hand as he scooped it up. He stood and smiled. "Cross paths? I was thinking more along the lines of dinner and movie. Maybe not a movie. You can't talk during a movie."

"I hate when people talk during movies."

"Me too," he said. "I bet we hate a lot of the same things."

"Sounds like a good time."

"Doesn't it?" He flashed his dimple again and then walked past me. The door chimed, and he continued down to the stoplight, turning the corner. Even though my forehead was pressed against the glass, I lost sight of him.

"Chicken fried rice and low-sodium soy," Coco said, setting down the white sack with a red circle.

I rolled down the top of the sack and held it close, unable to stop smiling.

"Guess your bad day isn't so bad?" Coco chirped.

I bit my lip, annoyed at how happy the last five minutes had just made me.

"Josh Avery," Coco cooed. "I'd let him take my temperature, if you know what I mean." I arched a brow, but she continued. "He lives three blocks down. I'm surprised you haven't run into him here before."

"How do you know where he lives?" I asked, still staring out the window, ignoring her crass comment. I couldn't blame her. I'd seen countless women reduced to a puddle of mush in his presence.

"We deliver, Avery. Remember?" She sighed. "He's cute. With all of that dark hair and the light eyes, he reminds me of the prince from *The Little Mermaid*. But, you know, beefier. Ooh, if you married him, you'd be Avery Avery." She giggled and pulled at one of her tightly curled spirals. It bounced back into place.

"Marry him," I muttered. "How absurd." I stood and clutched the bag to my middle. A wide grin spread across my face, and despite the aches and pains from being tossed inside the Prius like a penny in a vacuum, the feeling lasted the rest of the day.

CHAPTER TWO

Josh

I gripped the paper sack in my fist as I jogged across the street, puddled water splashing over the toes of my sneakers. I didn't have much time before my shift started, but I hadn't slept at all last night and was dying for a few minutes of shut-eye.

I rubbed my empty hand mindlessly over my stomach as it growled in protest from skipping breakfast. I'd opted to spend my morning in the gym down on twenty-seventh instead of letting my imagination run wild with thoughts of Avery in the wreckage.

I took the stairs up to the second floor of my building two at a time, relishing in the burn of my calf muscles.

The key had just turned and the door had barely cracked open before Dax, my scraggly, sad excuse for a puppy, was jumping on my leg, clawing for attention.

I'd saved him from becoming another spot on the highway two weeks before. We had become fast friends, if I ignored the fact that he liked to piss on the kitchen floor more than a drunk frat guy.

"You want some lo mein, little man?" I tossed the bag on the counter before rummaging through the cupboard and grabbing two paper plates.

The bag crackled as I dug my hand inside and pulled out the single container of food, dividing it evenly before setting the extra plate on the ground.

Dax wasted no time pushing his brown nose into the plate, shoving the food onto the dingy linoleum.

"You're welcome." I stepped into the living room and sunk down on the secondhand love seat with a groan.

Grabbing the remote, I clicked on the television to fill the room with a little background noise, in hopes to keep the worry that had plagued me at bay.

From day to day, I saw some horrible things: families ripped apart, lives cut short. If you didn't learn how to cope with it, you wouldn't last long in my line of work. My way of dealing with loss and suffering was to block it out and pretend it didn't bother me. After a while, it didn't. My heart had hardened enough that I could lie to myself and say I didn't care—and it was almost believable. Almost.

I unrolled the sack and pulled out the JayWok box, letting my vision go unfocused. The people on the television blended into colored blobs as their voices began to fade into the background.

I swallowed a large bite of my food, thinking of Avery and her crooked smirk. She was the complete opposite of my type, meaning there wasn't a hint of glitter on her face and her clothes wouldn't need to be soaked in baby oil to be peeled off her body.

Dax pawed at my arm as I shoveled in another bite.

"You had yours," I said, pushing from the couch and making my way to the kitchen.

Hard as it was to admit, I couldn't take bumps and bruises like I could as a kid when I rode dirt bikes. I felt every scrape and muscle strain from the fender bender. Pulling open the fridge, I grabbed the half jug of milk and twisted off the top to chug the contents.

Mid-sip, I turned around to see the rest of my food being devoured by the dog.

"Damn it, Dax," I barked, twisting the cap back on the jug and putting it back into the fridge.

The time on the stove clock made my jaw clench. "I don't have time to pick anything else up, shithead."

He whimpered with guilt as I approached him, but I wasn't the type to raise my hand to an animal. I ran my palm over his wiry hair before pulling my T-shirt over my head and dropping it on the floor.

"You're lucky you're cute," I called out over my shoulder. I stepped into the bathroom and turned on the cold water, hoping a shower would wake me up for another long shift.

I kicked off my sneakers before sliding my basketball shorts and boxer briefs down my legs. I could hear my cell phone going off from the kitchen counter, the faint sound of Tom Petty and The Heartbreakers crooning a private concert.

I slipped behind the glass door, cursing under my breath as the icy droplets of water hit my back. "Shit." I spun the knob, groaning as warm wetness slid over my achy shoulders. I lathered up the weird poofy sponge thing Talia, a waitress from Buckin' Bulls, had left for me.

That gesture alone was enough to keep me from calling her back. Regardless of how flexible she was, clingy was not my thing.

I dumped a blue glob of liquid soap onto the mesh mass and rubbed it over my tense stomach muscles while singing *It's Good to Be King*. I hurried through my before-work routine and was out of my apartment only fifteen minutes later, hungry but reenergized.

The sun was blinding on my walk to work now that the sky had cleared, and the warmth was almost sickening. Pulling my cell from my pocket, I clicked on the voicemail icon and listened as Sloppy Joe yelled loudly into the receiver.

"You screenin' your calls now, J? Look, man. I know you're out there starting your new life in the big city and all, but you can't just forget about everyone you left behind. Call me, man." The line went dead and my finger hovered over the number nine before I clicked it, erasing the message.

I hurried my pace as I shoved the phone back into my pocket, promising myself I'd call Joe later, even though I knew it was a lie.

The past needed to stay just that: the past. I wasn't ready to deal with home. Not yet, anyway.

"Hey, man. You look like shit," Quinn called out. He pulled open the ambulance door and tossed a small black bag inside.

"Your mom didn't think so," I shot back, rolling my head from shoulder to shoulder to ease the tension in my neck.

"That's fucked up, man."

"What's fucked up is that thing she did with a beer bottle."

Quinn shook his head. "I'm telling her not to cook for you anymore. You're a twisted asshole." He held out a can of soda for me and I took it with a grateful nod.

"Twisted asshole. I think that's what she called that other move." He shot me a warning glare and I shrugged. "It's part of my charm."

By the time my shift had ended, my eyes felt burned open. The night had been relatively calm compared to most, but that didn't mean it was easy. I'd dealt with a choking victim and a lost child before things kicked up a notch and we helped a man who had suffered a tragic table-saw incident. Usually, flirting with the nurses in the ER made the night bearable, but I was far too exhausted to mutter any one-liners as we flew in and out of the hospital.

I hurried home and took Dax out for a walk before crashing from exhaustion.

My self-induced coma only lasted a few hours before my phone began to ring. I answered it while rubbing the sleep from my eyes.

"This better be important," I groaned, rolling onto my back.

"Twins."

I sat up, blinking open my eyes. "What the fuck are you talking about, Quinn?"

"Fucking twins, Josh. Blondes with some tig ole bitties. Get down to Corner Hole, bro. They told me to call a friend."

I glanced at the bright red numbers on the alarm clock beside my bed before stifling a yawn.

"You owe me a beer," I grumbled.

"You help me seal the deal with these chicks, I'll give you my firstborn."

"I'll just take the beer." I clicked to end the call before tossing the phone next to me on the bed. "This better be worth the time," I mumbled to myself. I slipped out of bed and padded my way down the narrow hall to the bathroom. Even splashing ice-cold water on my face did little to snap me from exhaustion.

I dressed quickly, not bothering to double-check how I looked before heading out into the cool night air.

Corner Hole bar was located almost exactly halfway between my building and St. Ann's. Because of the location it was the bar of choice for hospital staff, making that horrible little dive perfect for fraternizing.

Being a weeknight, the place was practically empty, but a few familiar faces popped into view, one of which made me smile. Avery looked shocked when her gaze settled on mine, but she quickly worked her way through the crowd toward me.

"Thank God you're here," she said as my chest puffed out from the surprise greeting.

"It's good to see you too."

"I need you." Her thin, long fingers circled around my wrist as she pulled me toward the bar. I zeroed in on the door to the backroom. It would be the perfect place for us to fool around.

"Whoa, Avery. I'm into you too, but I didn't think you were that kind of girl," I joked.

She didn't find it funny, instead glancing back over her shoulder to glower at me. "No, pervert. There is this guy over here who won't leave me alone. I figured you could help a girl out?" She cocked her eyebrow and waited for my response.

"Lead the way. I'll teach the asshole a lesson."

Avery pulled me toward the bar. Her friend was waving at her with a forced smile plastered on her face, and standing next to her was a very sloppy-drunk Quinn.

"You've got to be fucking kidding me," I mumbled, stopping in front of him. Two very pissed off women were waiting for me to do something.

"I believe you know Quinn, the asshole." Avery swooped her hand out in his direction dramatically, fighting against a smirk.

Clearing my throat, I struggled to appear serious. "What's going on, man?"

"Fucking twins," he said too loudly as he pointed to the women. I stifled a laugh as I noted the distinct differences between Avery and her friend. Quinn had to be wasted to think they were in any way related. The friend had dark hair that hung just past her shoulders and huge tits. Her curves were a contrast to her sharp features, and to Avery's blonde hair and athletic build.

I patted his shoulder. "I don't think they're twins, buddy."

"No, no, no. Listen," he slurred as he put his arm around the brunette's shoulder and pointed his finger in her face. "This one is Bed. How great is *that*?" He waggled his eyebrows suggestively.

She smacked him hard across the chest. "My name is *Deb*, you asshole."

Quinn nearly fell over before rubbing his chest as if he'd been violently attacked.

"You think that's bad? This is the nice one. That one—" he extended his arm toward Avery "—is into slavery."

"Avery," I corrected. "Her name is *Avery,* and we know her from work, remember?" I couldn't contain my laugh at his serious expression.

"She doesn't like me. Can you believe that?"

"I can." I grabbed Quinn's arm and looped it over my shoulders, pulling him from Deb's side. "Come on, buddy. I think it's time we go home."

"But I want to hang out with the twins."

"I think they've had about enough of you." I winked at Avery, and she smiled, appreciative.

"But I owe you a beer," Quinn whined.

"Yeah, you do. But I think we should go back to my place. You can sleep on the floor where Dax pissed this afternoon." I helped Quinn through the front door of the bar and let him lean against the brick veneer exterior as he drank in the fresh air.

"It's so hot out here." He tugged at the collar of his blue polo shirt, stretching the fabric. "I think I'm going to be sick."

"You have it coming." I turned around at the sound of the door creaking behind me.

"Make sure you keep him hydrated and maybe feed him a banana or something," Avery said.

"Yeah, ahh … thanks for being so cool about him." I shoved my hands deep into my jean pockets. "He's not normally like this." I glanced over my shoulder at Quinn, who was doubled over and dry heaving loudly, his shirt lying on the ground at his side.

"I sure hope not. His mother would be very disappointed."

"He told you about his mother?"

"He all but bribed us with her homemade pie to sleep with him." She covered her mouth as she struggled to contain her laugh. "It was an interesting strategy."

"I'll let him know you were impressed with his pickup lines tomorrow. Better yet, I'll let his mom know." I winked and she focused on the space between us.

Conversation stalled as I tried to think of something to say to her over the sound of Quinn emptying his stomach. I wanted to ask her out, desperate to stick around and spend more time with her, but there wasn't a line in the world that would work in this situation.

"I should get him home." Rubbing my hand over the back of my neck, I decided then that I was going to make tomorrow a living hell for Quinn.

"Thanks again." Avery pulled open the bar door and slipped inside to join her friend.

"Come on." I helped Quinn stand upright, tossing his shirt over my shoulder and guiding him down the darkened street to my apartment.

It was going to be a long night.

CHAPTER THREE

Avery

"So let me get this straight," Deb said, standing by her locker in just a scrub top and striped, neon-colored socks. "He pulls you out of a burning car—"

"It wasn't burning," I deadpanned.

"—and calls his ambulance buddies to bring you to safety, probably cradling your head in his beautiful, buff arm while sniffing your granny panties."

I shook my head, revolted. "At what point in this story did my panties come off?"

She stared at me with a blank expression. "This is Paramedic McPanties we're talking about, right? He probably took them off to fashion a tourniquet like a sexy MacGyver."

I exhaled. "McPanties is an awful, horrible nickname."

"You laughed the first time I said it. Now you're defensive. This is bad." She dropped her shit-soaked sneaker into a plastic bag and tied the top, tossing it into her locker with a *thud.*

"You're going to just throw that away, right?" I asked, rubbing the beginning of a headache from my left temple.

"Throw my shoes away?" she asked, appalled at my suggestion.

She spun around, stepping into the tiny bathroom across from the lockers, and scrubbed her hands until they looked raw.

After ripping a paper towel from the dispenser, Deb turned off the faucet and then took a few towels to dry her hands before throwing away the wet paper. She reached back to tie her dark hair into a tiny ponytail at the nape of her neck. "You must have hit your head harder than I thought."

I smiled, watching Deb step into a fresh pair of scrubs and then slide into her Crocs. "At least keep it in the bag until you know if your patient tests positive for—"

"Bleach kills everything," she said. "Anyway, if I get C. diff, I might lose that last fifty pounds I've been trying to get off since the eighties."

"You were born in the eighties."

"My mother had gestational diabetes. I was husky." She closed her locker, snapping the combination lock and twisting the dial.

"Better twist it again," I said. "Don't want anyone taking your shit shoe."

"I don't want those skinny bitches from radiology stealing my pudding."

Andrea from X-ray glanced over her shoulder at us.

"That's right," Deb said with wide eyes. She pointed at her. "I see you staring at my chocolate vanilla Super Snack Pack."

Andrea pushed through the door, suddenly in a hurry.

"Jesus, Deb. You're going to get written up again."

"My shit shoe could end up under your pillow tonight. I have a key to your apartment. Hey," she said, pointing at my head. "You've been doing that a lot today. What's up with that?"

I dropped my fingers from my temple. "Just getting a headache. It's nothing. I'll take something when I get home. C'mon, we're clocked out. I already feel bad that you came in on your night off. Let's get the hell out of here before a code comes in."

She followed me out of the women's locker room and into the hall. I waved to the night shift, pausing when Dr. Rosenberg gestured for me to wait.

"A ... he's going to ask you to marry him," Deb whispered as he approached.

"Shut up," I said through my teeth.

"B ... he's going to say that he likes your tits in that scrub top all romantic-like and shit."

"I will punch you in the vagina," I hissed just as the doctor came closer.

"On your way out, ladies?" Dr. Rosenberg asked.

"C ..." Deb began.

"See?" Dr. Rosenberg repeated, blinking his fantastically long eyelashes. His eyebrows pulled in, forming twin lines between them.

"C. diff," I blurted out. "She was wondering if that last patient has tested positive for C. diff."

"Oh. Well, I don't need the results to know it's negative. It has that unique smell and—"

"Weird pillow talk," Deb muttered.

"Pardon?" Dr. Rosenberg asked.

I said the first thing I could think of. "She said we're going to walk. To her car. She's giving me a ride home. Did you need something before we leave, Doctor?"

"Oh, that's right. You don't have a vehicle. I hope you have insurance."

Deb opened her mouth again, but I elbowed her hard in the ribs.

She yelped and rubbed her side, frowning at me.

Dr. Rosenberg watched our exchange with curiosity, but he continued, "My commute took twice as long because of the construction on I-95 North. If you're going that way, you might want to find an alternate route."

Deb chuckled. "You live in Alapocas, right, Doc?"

He smiled warmly. "I do, Hamata." He looked down, embarrassed. "I didn't realize that was common knowledge."

"Yeah ... we're RNs," she said. "We drive up I-76 West to our shithole apartments, but the traffic is clear, so there's that."

"Well," Dr. Rosenberg said, amused. "Enjoy your night, then. Good night, Avery."

I nodded. "Good night, Doctor." I turned on my heels, stiffening when Deb hooked her arm around mine. "I hate you, I hate you, I hate you, I hate you ..." I chanted all the way down the hall.

"He is going to be thinking about you while bathing in his champagne-filled bathtub tonight, so you can't be too mad at me," she said, chuckling.

"No, he's not. He's going to be thinking husband things because he's married, and you're an asshole for plotting things like that."

"I'm not plotting. I'm pulling the strings of your life like a puppeteer because it amuses me."

"Your honesty is my favorite thing about you, but it also makes me want to squeeze your throat between my hands until your eyes bulge. Just a little. Not a lot."

She tightened her grip on my arm. "Aw. I love our little talks."

A blue blur rushed around the corner, nearly knocking me to the floor. Hot liquid instantly soaked my scrubs and splashed up my neck and down my arms. I held my hands out to my side, in shock.

"Oh, Christ," Josh said, holding his nearly empty Styrofoam cup of coffee. "I'll go find some cold water. Did it burn you?"

"Yes, the boiling-hot coffee is burning my flesh, Captain Obvious," I said, feeling the dark liquid drip from my jaw.

Raising his chin, he sniffed the air before his face twisted in revulsion. "What's that smell?"

"Be right back," Deb said, rushing down the hall and through an unmarked door. I shook my head, trying not to laugh at the thought of her shit shoe.

Josh barely glanced down at the stain on his own shirt and cargo pants before looking around, desperate to find something to wipe his coffee off my scrubs. The heat was already subsiding—hospital coffee was rarely hot enough to scald. He resorted to using his hands, clumsily brushing his fingers over my stomach, arms, and breasts. It was more awkward than getting felt up by Bobby Lawson in the tenth grade.

I tried to turn in an attempt to deflect the impromptu pat-down. "It's okay, really, I—"

"This coffee was meant for you ... Not exactly like this, though," Josh said, ignoring my efforts to stop him. He used his thumb to gently brush my wet chin as he looked down into my eyes. He sighed, frustrated.

"W-what? I ... um." I swallowed. "I guess this is my fault?" I asked, still trying to sound tough while completely captivated. Dr. Rosenberg had an effect on me, but he'd never looked at me the way Josh was at that moment. It was a combination of awe, anticipation, and regret. Being that close to him, it became very clear why all the nurses melted in his presence.

He took a step back. "The coffee." He held up the cup. "I saw you when I came in earlier, so I thought I'd bring you some. I wasn't sure how long your shift was, so ..."

One side of my mouth turned up. "That was very un-McPanties of you, Josh."

His nose wrinkled, and his head turned to the side a bit like a confused puppy. "Huh?"

"Um … thoughtful. I meant it was very thoughtful." I took the almost empty cup from his hand. The cooled drops of coffee on the outside of the Styrofoam dampened my palm, matching the rest of me. "I'm off work, actually."

"Here!" Deb said, pressing a cold towel on my neck. "I brought wet and dry towels from housekeeping and Dermoplast spray. Did he burn you?"

I shook my head, still smiling at Josh. "Not yet."

He teetered after letting me shoulder past him. I glanced back to see him smirking at the floor. This was a fun game I was sure he had played many times, but not with me.

I pulled Deb along, and although she was confused, she followed.

She looked back to Josh, and then at me. She frowned, repulsed. "Ew, Avery, really? You were just all nervous and goo-goo-eyed at Doc Rose."

"I'm more single than Rosey," Josh called. "And I'm probably *more* in other areas, too."

I cackled, far too loudly. It wasn't that funny. He had the humor of a twelve-year-old, but I was in full flirt mode. I'd seen Josh Avery around the ER before, but back then he was just McPanties. Now, he was *The Guy Who Pulled Me from the Wreckage*. That had meaning. We now had a unique connection. I wanted him to save me again. I just wasn't sure from what. *My thirteen-month dry spell, maybe?*

"I am!" he yelled. "And I'm still holding you to an evening of whiskey and lists of things we hate!"

I turned, pushing my ass against the exit. "No coffee?"

Josh held out his hands. "I can bring coffee, sunshine. I'll bring whatever you want."

"Give up, Josh," I said. "I'm not your type."

"Exactly," he said, standing tall, wholly satisfied with himself. Quite the turnaround from the upset, fidgeting doof from a few minutes before. His sudden resurfaced confidence had caused mine to waver.

I paused and then pushed my way out into the humid summer night air. My scrubs were soaked, and even though it was at least ninety-five degrees outside, goose bumps formed on my skin. I pulled my hair into a messy bun and waited while Deb searched her huge purse for her keys.

"I know what you're thinking," I said, waiting next to the passenger door of her red Kia Rio. It was only a year old but had already suffered a love pat from the back. The rear fender was hanging down a bit on one side, and the corner was still bruised where it had traded paint with the white Buick that hadn't stopped in time.

"Are you ever going to get that fixed?" I asked.

Deb looked up at me, her almond eyes lifting with her eyebrows. "Do you want to talk about what your Prius looks like right now?"

"Touché. Carry on," I said, glancing around the parking lot." I heard a jingle, and then the doors unlocked in unison.

We sat together in the tiny confines of her compact car. Deb shoved the key into the ignition, but paused before turning on the engine.

"I haven't told you, but I'm glad you're okay. You scared me to death."

I smiled, touched by her uncharacteristically tender moment.

"I mean, who would cover my shifts?" she asked. My smile vanished. "Who would fetch me ice cream when I'm sick? Who would make fun of Michaels with me?"

"You're a bag full of dicks," I said.

"Yeah, but I'm going to buy you a six-pack of beer to celebrate your return from the dead and your new found infatuation with McPanties."

"Please stop calling him that," I said.

"Where does this leave the doc?"

"What is with everyone? I realize my crush on him wasn't as secret as I thought, but ..." I sighed. "Yes, I like him. But I don't want him." My eyes bulged at the word *want*. It was embarrassing to think anyone would believe I would act on my silly infatuation. "It's just a safe, harmless crush. Exactly the kind I'm comfortable with."

"Until McPanties came along and cradled you in his arms, fighting Death himself until the cavalry arrived with full lights and sirens."

"You've got to stop calling him that."

Her theatrics faded as she backed out of her parking spot and headed toward the road. "Yeah ... but I won't."

CHAPTER FOUR

Josh

The night shift during a full moon had irritated my achy muscles more than I'd admit, but instead of going home to rest, I found myself walking into St. Ann's ER. Even if every step was agony, it was worth the pain to see Avery. She didn't seem to be suffering at all. In fact, our collision was a turning point neither of us had seen coming.

Once the ambulance bay doors swept open, I saw Avery right away. She was scribbling quickly with her left hand in a chart. She glanced at the cheap watch on her small wrist and then jotted down a few more lines. Her hair was pulled back into a single braid cascading down the back of her turquoise scrubs, moving to the side when she turned to see who was approaching.

"I thought that was you," she said, shoving the chart into a cubbyhole.

"It was the boots, right?" I asked.

She looked down, chuckling.

I scanned her face, noting the braid had fallen over her right shoulder, and the way her mascara lightly clumped around her lashes. It was morning, her makeup was still fresh, and her scrubs hadn't met with anyone's bodily fluids, yet. Either way, she was stunning.

The accident had given us something that only we held in common, but appreciating that felt wrong. Avery had almost been killed.

"Avery," I said.

She looked up, and I saw something in her smile I hadn't seen before. She wasn't only happy to see me—she'd been looking forward to it.

"Have lunch with me," I blurted out.

After a half-second of surprise, Avery scanned my face, looking for something. She didn't trust me, and who could blame her?

She twisted her wrist to look at her watch, and then pushed away from the counter in front of her. "Nope."

"*Nope?*"

She glanced over her shoulder toward the waiting room and then leaned in, looking straight at me—no running her fingers nervously through her hair, no shifting her weigh from one leg to the other, no looking up at me from under her lashes. She wasn't intimidated by anything, and I had to know why.

"It's Jacobs."

I grinned. "So, does that mean you're going to call me Avery? Because that's just weird."

She blinked and then stumbled over her next words. "Fine. First names. But I'm still not going out with you. At least, not for lunch."

"Not for lunch ... then dinner?"

Someone called her last name, and then Avery went into action. "If you'll excuse me ..." Avery slid by, leaving me standing alone at the nurses' station.

"Ouch," Ashton said, resting her full cheek on the heel of her hand.

Carissa Ashton was a charge nurse in the ER, and one of my easier conquests when I had first moved to Philadelphia. Ashton couldn't let our one evening together go, and she seemed to be fully enjoying the sight of me getting shot down by Jacobs.

My nostrils flared, and I gritted my teeth to keep my mouth shut.

"Doesn't look like you're taking that one home tonight. Did you say you were heading to lunch? What about brunch? I get off in fifteen minutes."

"I can't, Ashton. Go f—have a pleasant rest of the day."

She frowned but said nothing else as I made my way back out to the parking lot.

I drove home half confused, half pissed. I'd never had to work this hard for any girl, and it was even more maddening because I could tell Avery wasn't totally opposed. She was waiting for something. A gesture, maybe? Or was she still wrapped up in Doc Rose? Avery wasn't the type to care about the white coat or the title. Maybe the stability, the assumed dependability. He at least appeared to have his shit together. He'd settled down, and Quinn had mentioned the doc had a house in Alapocas. I could never give Avery that, but I was one ring-less finger better than Doc Rose.

I jogged up the stairs of my building and turned the key. Stale beer and bad breath infiltrated my senses, and I frowned at the sight of Quinn, who was still sleeping off his hangover on my couch. I knew he was partially to blame. The little stunt he'd pulled at the bar had less than impressed Avery, and it was hard to look like I was winning at life while hanging out with sloppy people.

Quinn was a douche, sure, but he was a loyal douche. I hadn't met any friends like him since I'd moved to Philadelphia. He knew my shit and wanted to be my friend anyway.

Grabbing his ankle, I pulled him until his body rolled to the floor with a thud.

"Fuck! What was that for?" he asked with his right eye barely opened to stare up at me.

"Get up. Party's over."

With a groan, he pushed to his hands and knees before standing on unsteady feet. "I feel like I've been hit by a car."

"That's funny. You know who *has* been hit by a car?" Shoving my finger into my own chest, I winced at how even such a small movement caused such unbelievable pain. I wasn't a small guy, spending most of my spare time in the gym. I'd learned in seventh grade after an after-school brawl that weight training was a healthier way to vent my frustration than picking fights and ending up in juvie. "This guy. I still managed not to drink myself into a stupor, humiliate myself, and sleep away an entire day."

"Maybe you're just not applying yourself." After shooting me a crooked grin, Quinn padded his way to my kitchen and opened the fridge. "You really need to get groceries, man. This is no way to treat company."

"You're not company, and if I lived in my mom's basement, I would have my shelves stocked, too."

"I live in her apartment building, not her basement. Totally different."

"Does she wash your underwear?"

"That's irrelevant."

"Yeah, whatever. Let's go down to Tootie's and grab some eggs after I change my clothes."

"You buying?"

My teeth clenched, and I threw my coffee-stained shirt in the dirty laundry hamper. "Just get up."

"All right, all right. Jesus, you're cranky today," Quinn said, pulling on his jeans.

"Just—" I sighed "—try not to say anything stupid to anyone with tits today."

"Oh. You're still pissed about Jacobs."

I ripped my belt from the loops and folded it in half, glaring at him.

He held up his hands. "Okay. You're right. I fucked up. It's been a while and I was nervous, so I might have tried for liquid courage."

"I'm pretty sure you drank liquid jackass instead."

"I wasn't that bad."

"You introduced Jacobs as *slavery*, and then you puked sushi and raisins all over the ground."

Quinn looked around, trying to remember. "Damn."

"Yeah," I said, remembering the look on her face when she walked away from me at the hospital. She had the upper hand, and she knew it. "Get dressed."

I'd consumed enough food to feed a small village, and all I wanted to do was sleep. Instead of going back to my apartment, Quinn used his mom's apple pie as a peace offering. We walked back to his place and then helped his mother move a bedroom set she'd found from a secondhand store to the third floor of her apartment building.

"You sure you're all right, man?" Quinn was leaning back against his mother's counter, polishing off a thick piece of pie.

"I'll live."

He shook his head but didn't press me any further. I didn't

need anyone looking over my shoulder, and Quinn understood that. Despite his frequent fuckups, he was a good guy.

"You boys have plans this evening?" his mother asked as she handed Quinn a napkin and a glass of milk. I shook my head, struggling not to laugh at how helpless he became in the presence of his mommy, a spitfire Italian.

"I got something I gotta do." I walked toward the door with a wave. "Thanks for the pie, Mrs. Cipriani."

Quinn lifted his chin in acknowledgment as he continued to shovel food into his mouth.

I was practically running on fumes by the time I slipped out of the old brick housing unit and made my way down to Tit for Tat, a small tattoo joint I saw on my way to work every day. I'd hoped I wouldn't be seeing the inside of one of these places for a long time, but it had become a superstitious ritual now. A bell chimed overhead when I pulled open the door. A man with a Mohawk and more ink than a paperback glanced up at me through dark-rimmed hipster glasses.

"Just finishing up here, man. Check out the flash on the walls. It will just be a second." He wiped a towel over the arm of the woman he was tattooing, smearing a small stain of ink across her milk-colored flesh.

I nodded, glancing over the drawings hanging on the walls. There were a lot of traditional pieces and some new age tattoos that looked like they could be in a gallery somewhere. But I wasn't up for something fancy. My tattoo was more of a scoreboard—a death cheat sheet.

Shoving my hands deep into my jean pockets, I roamed around the lobby area, averting my eyes from the woman's breast now in clear view as she showed one of the employees her nipple ring she was worried was becoming infected.

The cash register slammed closed, and the tattoo artist called to me. "Sorry about the wait." I turned around, approaching the front desk. It was made of glass with various body jewelry and morbid décor inside. "Can you give me an idea of what you're looking for?"

"No problem." I reached behind my head, grabbing the back of my basic cotton T-shirt and pulling it off. The ball chain necklace holding a single penny fell against my chest. I ran my fingers over my left ribs, tracing the nine tiger stripes that cut across my skin. "I earned another stripe."

The man stepped from around his counter and bent down to get a closer look at the work before standing back up to his full height. He was much thinner than I was but several inches taller than my six-foot frame.

"I hope this isn't a body count. Most guys just opt for a tear drop or a few dots."

I laughed as he tilted his head toward his station. "No, just a few times death got too close."

"I thought cats only had nine lives. You're pushing your luck. Have a seat and tell me about it."

I sank down on the black cushioned seat that reminded me of a dentist chair and described the moments before impact. It paled in comparison to some of my other close encounters, but this time we'd all walked away relatively unscathed, leaving me waiting for the other shoe to drop. I shuddered at the thought of Avery almost losing her life right before my eyes. As if having those memories of my sister on loop weren't hellish enough, now I had Avery's close call to torment me. Since I had been young, it had seemed like I was a magnet for bad things. Guilt flooded my gut as I thought of how selfish it was for me to continue to pursue Avery knowing that fact.

I'd earned my first stripe at just seven, although it wouldn't be branded on my body until years later. For the first time, my curse had made itself known, taking from my life one of the most important people to me, shaping me into the aimless mess I was now.

"Can I take Kayla fishing?" I asked Mom as she finished mixing the batter for my sister's birthday cake. She was turning three years old, and half our family from across Liberty County was coming over to celebrate.

"Kayla?" Mom yelled as she wiped the back of her hand across her forehead, leaving a powder-white residue.

My baby sister came clunking down the stairs from her bedroom, her yellow teddy bear, Oliver, clenched in her little fist.

"Cake?"

"Not yet, sweetie. Go out back and play with your brother. I'll let you know when it's ready. Josh, you make sure you watch her." My mother's firm stare met mine and I nodded, grabbing Kayla's free hand and tugging her toward the back door. I didn't need to be reminded to watch my little sister.

We slipped into the yard and both broke out into a full sprint as we made our way to the small boat dock at the edge of our rural Georgia property.

Kayla stopped with the toes of her tennis shoes on the first slat of wood.

"Come on, Kayla. You're a big girl now. I have to teach you to fish. Dad is too busy, so it's my job." I grabbed the two sticks I'd spent the day working on. Tied to the ends were some old fishing line and plastic bait. I held one out for my sister, who beamed from ear to ear.

"Come on." I turned and walked to the end of the dock with the pitter-patter of her small feet not far behind me.

We sat on the edge, our feet dangling over the water as we soaked up the hot southern sun. We didn't catch anything because I knew mom would freak out if I took any of Dad's hooks for my new poles, but Kayla didn't mind. She had fun just the same.

"I'm hungry." Kayla pouted as a warm breeze pushed her dark, shoulder-length curls across her face.

I looked back at the house just beyond the trees. It wasn't that far. She could sit on the dock alone for the couple of minutes it would take me to run to the pantry and back. "I'll grab us some crackers if you watch my line."

Kayla nodded in agreement, and I handed her my stick. I stood, brushing the dirt from my bottom. "Be still, Kayla. No dancing or nothin' until I get back. Just hold the poles."

She nodded, peering up at me with her big, sparkly eyes, looking happy and tiny and a little pink already from the sun.

"I'll get you a hat, too," I said. I hurried back across the yard and into the kitchen, excited the family would all be there soon.

"No junk food," my mother warned, her eyebrow raised as she continued prepping for the party.

"I know, Mom." I grabbed a box of crackers and pulled open the fridge as the front screen door squeaked on its hinges. Dad was home from work.

"Where's my birthday girl?" he yelled. I could tell in his voice he was tired, but he smiled for Kayla anyway.

"She's out back playing," my mother replied.

Dad leaned in and kissed Mom on the cheek before glancing out the kitchen window.

"Where? The swings are empty."

"She's on the dock, Dad. I took her fishing." I walked over to my father, pushing up on my tiptoes to point out the wooden walkway. My smile slowly fell as I looked for my sister. The dock was empty. Only her yellow teddy bear remained.

"John...?" Mom said Dad's name like she was asking a question. Her voice was thick with worry.

"I told her to be still," I said. "That I'd be right back."

"Oh, God," Mom said.

Dad was already out the door. "She's not out there!" he screamed as he rushed across the backyard toward the water.

Cake batter splattered up the sides of the cupboards when my mother dropped the bowl she'd held in her hands. She chased after my father while I stood helplessly, watching from the window.

It felt like a lifetime had passed since they'd sprinted out the door. Boy, Kayla was going to be in trouble for not listening to me.

Nerves twisted my belly into knots as I waited to see the mess of dark curls that sat atop my sister's head. I hoped Dad would still let her eat her cake tonight. I would tell them it was all my fault if they didn't. I didn't want to ruin her birthday.

My father's head broke the surface of the pond, dark circles of water rippling from his body, expanding outward. That was when I saw her. Her tiny body in my father's arms made her seem like she was still just a baby.

Mom's bare feet nearly slipped from the dock as she took Kayla from Dad's arms so he could boost himself up onto the old planks of wood.

Lying her body down on the ground, Dad began to frantically push against her chest. Once in a while, Mom would stop crying and lean down over Kayla's face. Chills rushed through my body, and I began to shiver, recognizing something was wrong. Kayla wasn't pretending. Mom and Dad were afraid. I'd never seen Dad scared of anything, not even when the Radleys turned their garage into a haunted house two Halloweens ago.

"Come on, Kayla," I mumbled to myself. Unable to wait, I rushed to the back door and fumbled with the handle.

I hurdled toward them, feeling like I had to do something, anything, to help her. By the time I reached them, Mom was sobbing and covering her face. Dad was slouched over, looking at my baby sister with his hands on his knees and lake water dripping from his chin.

"Is she okay, Dad?"

He didn't answer.

"What can I do?" I asked, feeling something awful surround me. "Dad? What can I do?"

Dad broke down, his cries harmonizing with Mom's. I knelt down to hold Kayla's tiny, cold hand in mine.

"It's going to be okay, Kayla," I said.

Mom wailed.

I sat in silence, wishing I could do more. But I had no idea what it was she needed. We were all helpless, sitting around Kayla. Her pretty curls were wet and splayed out on the grass. Tears burned my eyes while I waited for her to wake up, because deep down I knew she wouldn't.

"Kayla?" I said one last time, wiping my eyes with the back of my hand.

Not knowing why we couldn't save her, and next to my sister on the ground, I promised myself I would never feel helpless again.

With cellophane taped to my freshly inked ribs, I dragged myself back to the apartment, desperate for a few hours of sleep.

I knew I wouldn't have long before Quinn was calling me again, wanting to party, and truth be told, I welcomed a break from reality. The past few days had begun to stir some repressed memories inside me. Kayla's death was hard enough to relive; the last thing I wanted was for the rest to come back full force.

Falling back on my double bed, I closed my eyes, groaning as Dax jumped across my stomach and snuggled into my side.

I'd gotten a full four hours of shuteye before the heat from Dax's puppy belly began to make me sweat. It was crazy how such a tiny thing make me could feel like I was under an electric blanket. I tugged off my clothes and groggily made my way to my bathroom, rushing through a warm shower.

As I smeared some ointment on my newest stripe, my phone chimed with a message from Quinn. He texted me a picture of the sign from Corner Hole Bar, and then a second picture. It took me a moment to figure out what it was: the back of Avery's head.

Smirking to myself, I typed out a quick response, letting him know I'd be right there before changing into a fresh T-shirt and jeans. I headed out into the night, walking faster than I'd ever admit. One thing I loved about the North was the bars were open on Sundays, although Pennsylvania was a weird state where you could only get your alcohol from bars and state stores. It wasn't like back home in Georgia where I could pick up a six-pack at the gas station.

Corner Hole was full of the usual suspects: doctors and nurses fresh from their shift and a few other third shifters peppered alongside local alcoholics. I nodded at Quinn, who held up a beer before looking to his left. I followed his gaze and locked eyes with Avery, who was laughing at something her friend Deb had said. She tucked her hair behind her ear, her teeth sinking into her lower lip to suppress her wide smile.

I stared at her for a moment, unable to look away. It wasn't until Quinn stepped into my view that I let the connection be broken.

"I don't want to be a dick, but I call dibs on the brunette."

I glanced around him to Deb, who was still engulfed in her conversation with Avery. Avery wasn't as invested, still sneaking glances in my direction.

"She's all yours, buddy." I patted his shoulder before I walked toward the bar, struggling to suppress a laugh. Deb was a fireball, and she would eat Quinn alive, but she may have been the only kind of woman who could put him in his place besides his mother.

Leaning against the bar, I held up two fingers to Ginger, the barmaid. She nodded as she grabbed two Budweisers from the cooler and popped off the caps.

"You gonna keep an eye on this asshole tonight?" she asked as she tilted her head toward Quinn.

He mumbled something inappropriate under his breath as he picked up his beer. His grin widened as Ginger flicked her artificial auburn hair behind her shoulder.

"I'll do my best." I pulled my wallet from my back pocket and fished out two twenty-dollar bills, slapping them on the bar. "Can I get a round for those ladies? The usual."

Ginger raised her eyebrow before pouring out two Cowboy Cocksucker shots.

I held up my beer to Avery as she smiled appreciatively. Deb picked up her glass and winked at Quinn before she ran her tongue over her lips and downed her drink.

"I'm hittin' that tonight. How about you and her friend?" Quinn said, his words already slurring.

"I already hit her the other night, remember?" I laughed, and the fresh stripe tattoo on my side rubbed against the material of my shirt, reminding me the situation wasn't funny at all. Not before, and not now. Getting involved with Avery was dangerous—for both of us. She could get hurt—even more seriously this time—and I had a feeling that would wreck me.

CHAPTER FIVE

Avery

Deb was chattering in the background, going on about the way Quinn was looking at her from across the Corner Hole bar. My ears only caught every other word, between the live band and Josh Avery's form fitting T-shirt and five o'clock shadow drawing my attention. He had bought me a drink, and any moment, he would walk toward me with the *fuck me* smile I'd seen him offer to other women so many times before.

It was shameful, the way I could anticipate his every move before he made it, yet I was playing along. Like so many before me, I would believe this time was different. Something about me would change his whoring ways, and he would be deeply in love and loyal to me until one of us died—and maybe even after that. It was a vicious cycle that kept us perpetually single and in desperate need of our next connection, however brief.

I looked over at Deb. I had kept a small, faithful circle of friends my entire life, but that circle was ever changing and grew smaller as I aged. I wasn't sure if that meant something was wrong with me, or I was just growing wiser.

"Thanks for being here, Deb."

She snorted. "I asked you here, remember?"

"You know what I mean."

After my parents died, I didn't seem to have anything in common with my high school friends. I couldn't hear complaints about Shari's mom not buying that dress for an upcoming rush party or how overbearing Emma's dad was. I was trying to figure out how to juggle funeral arrangements and death taxes along with rent for an apartment and applying to nursing schools.

Deb and I had been part of a tight group since nursing school, and we'd grown closer once we were both hired on at the ER. The other nurses had fallen away for one reason or another. Heather had cheated on her husband and, once caught, blamed her single friends for her wild ways. The result was only spending their free time with married couples. Elizabeth liked designer clothes and expensive cars on a student's budget, then borrowed money to pay her bills. Deb and I had decided it cost too much to be her friend. Shay made us laugh and was always up for a good time, but every week some absurd drama plagued her: pregnancy scares, stalker ex-boyfriends, and friends who had wronged her. Life seemed to be complicated enough without complicated friends, so we'd cut them loose. But I'd kept Deb, and she'd kept me.

After I had been forced to let go of my parents, any feelings I had about losing anyone else were barely noticeable. I worried letting go had become too easy.

"Stop, or I'll tongue punch your fart box," Deb said.

My expression twisted into disgust. "You are fucking offensive."

"Yeah, but you're here instead of there."

"What does that even mean?"

"I won't let you punish yourself for whatever fucked up thing in your past you couldn't control."

I smiled. Deb knew I was losing myself in a sad memory and

used one of her shocking remarks to snap me out of it. It always worked. Deb got me, and for some odd reason, I got her.

As predicted, Josh left Quinn at the bar to wade through the maze of people and high-top tables to the charcoal velvet love seat where Deb and I were seated. He tapped the neck of his beer to mine and then shot me a charming grin before taking a sip.

I was different. Josh just didn't know it yet.

Since the day I had woken up in the hospital, everything was different. The old Avery wouldn't have given someone like Josh a chance, but things like ego and how I should or shouldn't behave didn't feel so important now.

Josh sat in front of me, pointing his beer toward the short tower of empty shot glasses stacked on the table in front of us. "How was the shot I sent over?"

"I've had better," I said.

Josh made a face. "Why are you always so mean? I never have to try this hard. Ever. It's damaging my already fragile ego," he joked, placing his hand over his heart as if he were injured.

I smirked. "That's why."

Josh had earned his nickname. McPanties would take me for the night, but Josh and I had walked away from that horrible accident for a reason. I wasn't exactly sure what that was, but we definitely hadn't survived a high-speed collision with a tractor-trailer for a one-night stand. Call it fate or kismet or maybe just plain dumb luck, but I wanted to know, why *us*?

Josh settled in next to me, clearly intrigued. "So, you're saying I've got a shot."

"I'm saying this shot," I said, holding up an empty glass, "was mediocre. You better up your game."

His gray irises sparkled. "Challenge accepted."

I giggled, lifting my bottle to take another sip. The bottle never made it to my mouth. Dr. Rosenberg was standing at the bar with Michaels. She was still wearing her scrubs, a ball of orange frizz seeming to hover above her head. When she spoke, her wild bun wobbled.

Dr. Rosenberg barely acknowledged her, looking trapped and uncomfortable. *Good.* Michaels had likely talked him into grabbing a drink after work. She wasn't known to take no for an answer, and Dr. Rosenberg had been catching a lot of hell recently for not being approachable. I sighed, hating that I was making excuses for him. If I wasn't careful, he would topple from the pedestal I placed men like him on.

Josh stopped and turned to see what had drawn my attention. When he faced me again, I felt my cheeks burn.

He gestured toward the doctor, clearly annoyed. "What is your deal with him? Are you having an affair?"

"No. God, no. He's married," I stuttered, not anticipating him being so direct. Josh wasn't the type to sugarcoat anything, no matter how bitter the truth was to swallow.

"So?"

I frowned.

He held up his hands and shrugged. "I'm not saying I agree with it, but a doctor banging a nurse isn't the craziest thing I've heard."

"Dr. Rosenberg is a good man. He would never cheat on his wife."

"So, that's it," Josh said as the skin between his eyebrows smoothed and he visibly relaxed.

"What?"

"Why you like him so much. He's safe. You think you don't have to worry about him returning your affection."

I turned to him and narrowed my eyes, leaning my shoulder into the cushion. "Well, Dr. Avery, continue your analysis."

"You obviously have daddy issues."

"Oh, please. Who doesn't?" His assessment was spot on, and I tried to count the years it had been since I'd even spoken to my aunt.

He didn't hesitate. "You like me."

"False."

"Bullshit." His eyebrow rose as he tipped the beer bottle to his lips.

"That certainly falls in line with your initial belief that I'm addicted to unrequited love."

"You're in *love* with him?" He didn't try to hide the disgust in his tone.

"No. That's not what I said. At all."

"Then stop staring at him," he said.

I blinked, realizing I was watching the doctor again. "I wasn't. I was ... I'm watching Michaels."

"Because she's with the doctor, and you're jealous."

"I'm not jealous. I'm revolted. I might have a tiny crush on him," I said, watching Josh squirm at my confession, "but I would never act on it. Michaels *would*."

Josh observed Michaels for nearly a minute before he made a judgment. "Yeah, she would. But Rosey is a big boy. You can't make his decisions for him."

"He would never," I said. "He loves his wife."

"Then why isn't he at home with her right now? Even husbands who love their wives cheat. Men are animals, Avery. All it takes is fucking the same woman for seven years and a little extra attention from the right barely legal blonde."

I sneered. "Maybe for you." I looked at Dr. Rosenberg with a new respect. "But not him. He's one of the good ones."

"Get a few shots in him and see if that's the case. He's only human."

The multi-colored lights flashed over the bar, highlighting Deb giggling and pawing at Quinn. I hadn't even noticed she'd left the love seat. Corner Hole was packed. The ten-by-ten wooden dance floor was shoulder to shoulder, couples were laughing and kissing, meeting for the first time and falling in love, and sitting next to me was my knight in shining armor, advocating adultery. I peered into my longneck bottle, wondering if maybe he was just a cynic in a tinfoil hat.

My eyebrows pulled in. "Not every man shares your lack of morality."

He balked, almost offended. "I have never cheated."

I shot him a dubious look. "Because you've never been in a relationship."

"Exactly. I wouldn't commit to someone if I wasn't ready. That's much different from those who are willing to leap but still stray."

I put down my beer. "I did ... like you. For about two seconds. Then you started talking."

Josh put down his beer, too, only more determined. "That's because you're not listening. You're the type of chick—"

I glared at him and he rephrased.

"You're the kind of *woman* who listens to reply, not to understand. But I can't fault you for that. I've come to learn that is the way most women are. It's in your genes or something."

"In my genes?"

"You know ..." Leaning forward, he lowered his voice. "If you let me into your jeans, maybe I could get to know you better?"

I burst out laughing, and Josh's arrogant smirk faded. "Does that usually work for you?" I tried to make eye contact with Deb, hoping she'd be ready to leave, but she was turning out to be an awful wingman.

"Dance with me," Josh said.

I looked at him, waiting for him to admit he was joking, but he was serious. For once, I didn't have a witty retort. He stood and then held out his hand.

"We can't dance to this," I said, referring to the band's cover of Ellie Goulding's *Halcyon*.

Josh looked at the lead singer and put his thumb and middle finger in his mouth, filling his lungs and then blowing a loud whistle that cut through all the loud talking and music. He pointed to me, the singer nodded to her band, and the music transitioned seamlessly into a slower song.

"You know her?" I asked.

He shrugged. "I know everyone."

I stood, following him to the dance floor. He slid his arm around my lower back, his fingers pressing against the thin fabric of my blouse. The heat from his hand warmed my skin as he pressed me against him. His other hand gently enveloped mine, dwarfing it in his palm, and he began to sway slowly to the beat. As she began to sing the opening lines to *At Last* by Etta James, I relaxed into him.

"I like this song," I said just as Josh touched his cheek to my temple.

"Good, because it's our song."

I smiled. "It is?"

"It is now."

I looked up at him, not wanting to let go of this Josh, who looked at me like he was searching for forgiveness and I was the only woman who could give it to him. "If you were like this all the time, I could like you."

"Same."

I pressed my lips tighter, trying to suppress a smile.

He opened his mouth but hesitated.

"What?" I asked. When he shook his head, I prompted him again. "Oh, c'mon. Be brave."

He sighed, and then he turned his head an infinitesimal amount, just enough that the side of his lips brushed my skin as he spoke. My eyes fell closed at the simple touch.

"I was just thinking ... we could just make it easy on each other and play nice."

I leaned back to scan his face, noting the tiny bit of vulnerability behind his eyes. "You first," I said, dubious.

He stopped dancing and looked down at me, pondering his next words. "Dinner tomorrow?"

"What, like strippers and hot wings?"

He looked up to the ceiling before sighing loudly. "I prefer mild wings, but I guess I can make an exception for you."

The corner of his mouth twisted up into a grin, and as much as I wanted to scowl, I couldn't help but grin back.

"Okay."

"Yeah?" he asked, clearly expecting a different answer. I was stubborn but no fool. Josh may have been a notorious whore, but his surprise in that moment was all I needed. He was different now, too.

I smiled. "I get off at eight." I left him standing on the dance floor alone, signaling to Deb that I was leaving.

"Avery," Dr. Rosenberg said, stepping in front of me with a smile. He looked relieved to see me.

"Hello, Doctor."

"You can call me Reid here," he said, looking around. When he looked back at me, there was something in his eyes, but now that I'd experienced the way Josh looked at me, Dr. Rosenberg's attention wasn't as charming as before. "I was hoping you'd be here."

I peeked back at Josh, who was fixed on my exchange with Dr. Rosenberg, his lips pressed into a hard line. I nodded and smiled politely. "It was nice to see you, Doctor," I said. I walked away, still feeling Josh's touch on my skin.

Deb hooked my arm with hers. "Josh is smiling. *Super* cheesy. He looks like an eight-year-old boy on Christmas morning."

I grinned, unable to help myself.

"Is Quinn watching me leave?" she asked.

I glanced over my shoulder to the bar, seeing the disappointment in Quinn's eyes. "Yep. He's devastated. You should have left your shit shoe behind like a deranged Cinderella."

"He gave me his number. Slap me in the tit if I try to drunk text him later. Where are we going now?"

"Home," I said. "I have a ten-hour shift tomorrow and a date after. I need to get in a full eight hours of sleep."

"Home?" Deb asked. "But I'm not even buzzed." She pressed her key fob, unlocking our doors.

I didn't pull the handle. "How much have you drank?"

She shrugged. "Just the shot Josh sent over. Is he your date, or does the doc want to plant his seed in your bush?"

I cringed. "I agreed to a date with Josh, just to … I dunno … get him off my back." I downplayed our plans, trying not to grin like an idiot.

"Get him off your back? I'd let him put his hands on me like a gorilla scaling the Empire State Building." She began thrusting her hips and I looked away, embarrassed. "You really like him," she said, half teasing, half surprised. "That's great, I think, but I thought you couldn't stand him."

Slipping inside the car, I waited for her to get inside before resuming our conversation.

"I don't know. Something about him fishing me out of my wadded up car and holding me until the ambulance arrived made me rethink his character."

"I mean ... I guess," she said, unimpressed. "His tight ass probably doesn't hurt either."

"Why are we still here? I need to get home and figure out what the hell I'm wearing."

"Why? You're going to bail. You always bail." She started the car and tapped the buttons on the radio.

"Not this time."

She wasn't convinced. "Twenty bucks says you'll call him by seven thirty and tell him you're sick. You *hate* dates, and you're going to come to your senses about McPanties by quittin' time tomorrow and develop a sudden case of the Hershey squirts."

I lifted my chin. "Fine. Twenty bucks. I'm going on this date, even if my anxiety goes nuts."

She clicked her tongue, backing out of her parking spot. "You should just give me the money now."

CHAPTER SIX

Josh

I was too amped to sleep after scoring a date with Avery, so I began to prepare.

Behind my apartment, in a brick shack that leaned slightly to the left, I stared at my battered and bruised car, Mabeline.

Compared to Avery's matchbox car, mine had stood up against the small impact. Muscle cars were built that way, to be tough. Cars today crumbled like a wadded up tissue. I saw it every single day, and most people weren't nearly as lucky as Avery. That girl was her own rabbit's foot or ... I reached up and gripped the penny beneath my shirt that I had found on my floorboard right before our impact.

Sinking down on my haunches, I wiped my hand over the baby-shit-green paint that had marred the front left fender.

"What did she do to you?" I did my best to brush away the flecks of paint before standing, blowing out a heavy breath. Avery's Prius was part of Mabeline now. They couldn't be more different, but now they shared the same story. I could buff the hell out of it and repaint, but I kind of liked the smudge from Avery. She'd left her mark on me, too.

"Looks like I need to make a trip down to the junkyard and find you a new headlight. You are in no shape to take on a date."

Digging my phone from my pocket, I swiped my finger over the screen so I could check the time. The junkyard wouldn't be open for a few more hours, and if I knew Bud, he wouldn't be pulling parts until he walked his partner, Dusty, down to Emerson's Country store to get his morning coffee.

If I left early, I could grab us some joe on the way and maybe get Bud moving with a breakfast sandwich. I only had one day to get everything in order.

I wasn't worried, though. I had practically built Mabeline with my own two hands over the past six years. She had been my dream car since I was a boy, and I knew every inch of her frame. I could have her looking as good as new in no time. I'd always enjoyed working with my hands and fixing things, people included. As an added bonus, it was cheaper than therapy. There was hardly anything a little grease and hard work couldn't cure.

I rolled my neck from shoulder to shoulder, relishing in the relief from stretching my tight neck muscles. I was still sore from the accident, and I wondered why Avery didn't seem to be in any pain at all. I was actually looking forward to figuring her out.

The hardest part would be planning our date. Avery probably hadn't set the bar very high for me. Like any confident, sensible woman, she had taken one look at my scruffy face and grease-stained hands and seen trouble. But she was wrong about me.

Pulling open the driver side door, I slipped inside my car and turned the key. Stepping on the gas pedal, I made her roar, relieved that the only damage seemed to be cosmetic.

The drive across town was peaceful. Bud owned a large swath of property just outside Philadelphia, and even though the city was close by, it felt like another world. Amish buggies clogged the roads as they made their way to their vegetable markets, the relentless summer heat failing to slow them down.

I waved as I passed an older man who held the reins. Nodding, his beard rubbed against his plain, hand-sewn shirt.

The horse didn't startle as my engine roared louder, thanks to its blinders that kept it focused on the road ahead.

Slowing as I crossed three small hills, I turned down the old dirt drive to Bud's junkyard. I hadn't lived in Pennsylvania long, but Bud was one of the first people I'd met when I'd arrived in town with an oil leak and no place to stay. He had let me crash on his couch until I was able to find an apartment and a new start.

"Didn't think you'd be up." I closed my car door behind me before I crossed the dusty lot.

Bud was inside a rickety carport, wiping the grease from his hands onto an old rag. "Timing's off." He pointed to the old beat up Chevy in front of him. "Get in and let me use the timing gun."

Slipping inside the car, I turned the key, revving the engine while I waited for Bud to give me the signal. After a few curse words, he slammed the hood closed and I got out, shaking my head.

"What brings you to my neck of the woods so early?" He didn't even glance up at me as he spoke.

"Mabeline has seen better days." We both walked toward my car, and I leaned into the driver's window, pulling out the two coffees and fast food breakfast.

"Aw hell, son. What did you do?" He snatched a coffee from my hand and began to drink the scolding liquid without as much as a thank-you. I stifled a laugh as it dribbled down his three-day scruff and blended into the stains of his old gray T-shirt.

"Got in a fight with a Prius."

Bud's eyes widened before he shook his head. "I'd hate to see how that faired against this beast."

"You think I can pull a headlight?"

"I'll have Russel grab it for you and you can pick it up when you stop by again."

"Actually, I need it today. I have ... plans later."

"She must be something special if you're fixing to pick her up in Mabeline."

I didn't answer, trying to hide my smirk by drinking a sip of coffee, and burning my lip in the process.

"You know where everything is," he mumbled as he grabbed the bag of food from my hand and retreated to the dilapidated single-wide trailer at the edge of the lot.

Hours had passed, and my body was coated in sweat and grime, but Mabeline was parked outside my apartment, finally looking like her old self. I slipped into my shower, moaning as the cold water cascaded over my tired, tender muscles. Avery and our date drifted into my thoughts as I scrubbed off the hard work of the day. I expected her to give me shit about every detail throughout the night, so everything had to be perfect.

I'd already picked out a royal-blue button-down and dark blue jeans. I didn't own Italian shoes like Doc Rose, but I could still clean up pretty nice. After shaving my face, I almost looked like the type of guy a girl could take home to her mother. *Almost.*

I hurried through getting ready and put down a plate of food for Dax before heading out the door.

I knew Avery would be exhausted after her shift, so dancing was out of the question, no matter how badly I wanted to feel her body pressed against mine again.

Damn it. I pulled into the lot twenty minutes early. The sun had already vanished behind the tall buildings, and the muted wail of an ambulance in the distance helped muffle the hammering of my heart. *Am I actually nervous?* I'd never cared about impressing a girl before, and the feeling was so foreign, I contemplated calling the entire thing off. But when Avery stepped outside the hospital in jeans that hugged her slight curves and a fitted white tank top, I knew I couldn't back out. Leaning back against my car door, I shoved my hands into my pockets and waited for the moment her gaze met mine.

When she noticed me, the dimples deepened in her cheeks. A few of my buddies from LifeNet had described feeling a bolt of electricity, and I had made fun of them, but that was exactly what I was experiencing. Her steps faltered before she continued toward me, as if she was thinking of bailing, too. She adjusted the strap of her purse on her shoulder, looking at me for a few moments before blinking and looking at her feet.

A few steps behind Avery was her friend Deb. The moment Deb noticed me, she tapped Avery on the shoulder. Avery chuckled as Deb whispered something, and then laughed out loud as her friend placed money in her hand. Avery's heels clicked against the pavement. She strode confidently toward me, but her expression told a different story. Deb veered off toward her own car, and Avery took one last glance at her friend before stopping a few feet away from me.

"I wasn't sure you'd come," she said as she looked up at me, her nose scrunched as if regretting her words.

"Deb bet against me?" I asked, glancing down at the wadded up bill clutched in her palm.

"Me, actually. She thought I'd back out."

I nodded, trying to figure out what that said about Avery. "Well then, we better go before you make a run for it." Placing my hand on her lower back, I guided her to the passenger side of my car and pulled the door open.

"Who knew you were such a gentleman?" She slipped inside and I closed her door. I tried not to jog to my side, but I was anxious to begin our night.

I started the car and cringed as AC/DC blared through the speakers. "You can change that," I mumbled, reaching out and turning down the volume knob.

"No, it's fine. I like it."

I felt her watching me as I backed out of my parking spot. I shifted into drive and glanced to my left to see Deb dragging her finger across her throat in warning of what was awaiting me if I hurt her friend.

"So ... where are we going?"

I cleared my throat as I looked down the street before pulling out into traffic. "Are you hungry?"

Avery glanced into the back seat, and her smile faded. "Please tell me you didn't cook."

"I still have my eyebrows, don't I?" I said. She didn't seem amused, so I cleared my throat, suddenly nervous. Avery was the type of woman who was attracted to a guy like Doc Rose. She was right; I was going to have to step up my game. "No, ma'am, I didn't cook. Not tonight."

We drove out of town to back country roads, winding over small hills. I pulled into the back entrance of Bud's junkyard. Avery stiffened at my side, craning her neck to glance over the rows and rows of dilapidated cars.

"I knew it. You brought me here to kill me."

I laughed, pulling my car into line with the other vehicles, and cut the engine. As my headlights faded, a bright light from overhead shined onto the old white sheet that hung haphazardly on a stack of twisted metal.

"Come on." I pushed my door open and grabbed the mystery

box from the back seat, along with a fitted sheet that matched the one hanging in front of us.

Avery hesitated before following.

Spreading out the sheet on the patchy grass in front of my car, I sank down on my knees and waited for her to join me.

"I figured since we both hate people who talk at the movies, this would be the next best thing. We're thirty acres from anyone in every direction."

"Said the serial killer," Avery deadpanned.

My lips formed a hard line, but it was hard to be frustrated when she was looking at me like that. "No one is going to talk through this movie."

She winked, nodded, and then glanced around. "This is ... really thoughtful of you, Josh." We fell silent for a moment as we listened to the crickets chirping in the distance.

"Wait," I said, chuckling. "I'm not done, yet." I began to pull the wrapped plate from the basket, my stomach growling at the sight of Mrs. Cipriani's pie. "After the movie, you're going to pick a car."

"What?" She scrunched her nose as she glanced around the mass of rusted and broken vehicles.

"Don't worry about what they look like. I can make any one of them look good as new. These cars have been through a few drivers, but show them a little love, and they are reliable. You need something that can keep you safe. Not expensive and unreliable."

"We still talking about cars here?" She raised an eyebrow.

The last thing I wanted was to remind her of Doc Rose. I knew how I looked compared to men like him. He was mature and had his shit together. I had yet to commit to a car payment, much less a girlfriend.

"Of course ... and things we hate, remember?"

"That's easy." She laughed. "Next on my list is Christmas."

"You hate baby Jesus's birthday?"

She giggle-snorted. "No, I just hate the whole build-up. It never ends up the way it's planned, y'know?"

"Life rarely does," I agreed. "But now you need to explain, because this confession has traumatic childhood written all over it."

"After my parents ..." Her smile faded, and she slipped a mile away into her own thoughts. "Christmas is just a really lonely time for me. Probably not first date conversation."

I realized I was right, and it felt like all the blood had drained from my face. "Fuck, I'm sorry." She waved me away, dismissing my apology. "How about, um ... how about before?"

"My mom was Jewish. The kids at school used to go on and on about their tree. Maybe I was a little jealous," she confessed. She pressed her lips together, but then her laughter escaped and echoed throughout the salvage yard.

It was contagious, and soon my cheeks hurt from smiling so much.

I opened my mouth to ask more questions, but the movie began, and we both turned our attention to the makeshift screen. I lay back, propped on my elbows as Avery sank down on her side and pulled the cellophane from her plate. Her eyes danced over the homemade apple pie before her smile stretched from ear to ear. She kept weird hours like me, and being single, that meant a lot of TV dinners and takeout.

"Thank you for this." She took a bite and hummed in satisfaction. I'd never seen a woman quite so beautiful as Avery sitting on a worn sheet in the middle of a junkyard, looking perfectly content.

"Quinn promised you a piece of his mom's pie for a piece of ass. I thought it was only fair that you get to try it. Just make sure you return the plate or Quinn's mom will kick my ass," I joked.

She covered her mouth as she chewed and giggled, her laughter chiming along with the crickets' chirping.

CHAPTER SEVEN

Avery

"Stop," Deb demanded.

"I can't help it."

"Stop, or I'll shave off all my body hair and mail it to you."

I turned around in my chair, noticing her annoyed expression as she waited by the microwave. The break room was full of a strong medley of smells, none of them appetizing. I was chomping on my PB & J and apple slices, the only thing in my cabinets that would keep until lunch. Deb was heating up what looked like a plastic replica of broccoli, chicken, mashed potatoes, and gravy, and Michaels was sipping on a Diet Coke in the corner.

I hadn't seen outside in over an hour, but the last time I'd looked, the sky was dark and rain was soaking the parking lot and pouring off the awning that hung over the ambulance bay like a waterfall. I wondered if Josh was working out in the weather, and if he would feel like seeing me after being out in the muggy wet all day.

"I can see you thinking about him," Deb said in an accusatory tone.

"He's helping me with a car." My frown turned into a wide grin. "Who does that? I'm going to have transportation again in a month, maybe two. Until then—"

"You dirty little slut," Deb said, sitting across from me at one of the five round tables in the west break room. The wallpaper reminded me of Step-Down and waking up after the accident. That only made me think of Josh more. I was annoying *myself*.

She leaned in like I was going to reveal a juicy secret. "That's why you didn't call me for a ride. He took you to work today, didn't he?"

"I ... none of your business."

"Road head?"

My face screwed into disgust, and I peeked over at Michaels. She was pretending not to eavesdrop, but everyone knew she had been one of the first nurses in the department to welcome Josh to Philadelphia ... with her vagina. "Deb. Jesus."

She rolled her eyes. "How did I befriend such a prude? At least a good-night kiss?"

"No."

"*No?*" Her voice went up an octave. "Give me something. You're boring me to death. I can't even have a decent sex life vicariously through you."

"What about you and Quinn? Did he call?" I asked, hoping she'd change the subject.

"Maybe," she said. It was a pitiful segue into a detailed reproduction of their phone call, complete with inappropriate jokes and innuendo. The longer she talked, the more I knew they were made for each other.

In truth, I was glad I didn't have to recount the last moments of my night with Josh. Deb wouldn't have understood, anyway. It had been wonderful, and quiet, and exciting, and from the moment we left until he walked with me to the stoop of my apartment building, a million butterflies had burst from their cocoons and fluttered around in my entire body, hairline to toe polish. In one night, Josh Avery had transformed from the hospital hustler into what I had been waiting for. We hadn't had time to kiss because we'd hugged, his cheek had touched mine, and words had tumbled out of his mouth like he couldn't keep them in any longer. Seven words that would change everything.

I need to see you again. Tomorrow.

I'd said yes, and then he'd turned around, got in his car, and pulled away. He had seemed just as surprised by his request as I had been. When I'd finally processed what had happened, his brake lights had already turned the corner.

Josh hadn't said he wanted to see me. Anyone could say that, and it would be sweet. No, he *needed* to see me, just like he'd needed to say it before it burst out of him like water from a broken levy.

"So," Deb said, "I told him he was a narcissist. I could shart on stage at the Merriam Theater in front of the entire hospital board and it would somehow be about him. But I dunno, I kind of like it," Deb said, resting her chin on her hand.

"Romantic," I said.

"Speaking of romantic, did you fuck him?"

"Deb!"

"Spill it!"

"No," I said through my teeth. Thankfully, Michaels was only on her fifteen-minute break and on her way out.

"How many times did you have to slap his hand away?"

"None."

"*None?*"

"No, Deb. He was a perfect gentleman."

"Man. That sucks, Avery. I'm sorry."

I sighed, already regretting my next question. We were alone, so it was a good time to pick her perverted, twisted mind. "Why would you be sorry?"

"Well," she hesitated. "I know you're sort of into him, and ..."

"And what?"

"He doesn't ... You know I tell you straight, Avery."

"Just say it!"

"He doesn't seem to be that into you," she blurted out.

I sat up. "What makes you say that? Did Quinn say something to you?"

"No, but he didn't even attempt to sleep with you, and he's slept with Carissa Ashton. I mean, dear God. That's like dipping your stick into a rancid whale. It's not even that she's fat, because—" she ran her hands over her own enormous breasts "—you know I feel sorry for you skinny bitches with no curves. But Ashton's a heinous bitch *and* fat. Do you know why McHale was fired? Ashton told McHale she'd take her shift and then didn't show and claimed not to know what McHale was talking about. McHale just smiled at Josh. Just *smiled*. Ashton got her fired for that. She's a jealous, weeping, rotten cun—"

"Deb! Stop!" I snapped.

She was taken aback. "I call people names, Avery. You know it's my thing. I enjoy it. I—"

"*No*. Stop talking about Josh and the other nurses."

"Wow, I mean ... I'm sorry. I didn't realize how much you liked him. Already."

"We're going out again, okay? Just because he didn't *one-night* me, doesn't mean he's not interested. Can we please just drop it?"

She grinned. "He asked you out again already? That's good, right?"

"Yes," I breathed. "Yes. It's very good."

A deep voice spoke behind me. "Well, that's a relief."

I winced. Josh's fingers cupped my shoulders and sunk in just enough to massage my sore muscles. I didn't dare turn around. My cheeks caught fire and my eyes glossed over. *How much did he hear?*

Deb nodded once and then looked up with her fakest smile. "We were just finishing up."

"Me too," Josh said. He didn't sound offended or creeped out, both good signs, but not enough for me to turn around. "Just thought I'd stop in and say hi."

I didn't respond. My brain couldn't form a single syllable.

"Pick you up at eight thirty?" he asked.

"Yes," I managed to say without vomiting all over my shoes. "Sounds ... sounds great." I closed my eyes tight, grateful he was behind me and couldn't see the mortification on my face.

He pecked the top of my hair and then Deb nodded, signaling he was gone.

Deb raised an eyebrow. "He seems awfully handsy for not even getting a good-night kiss."

"You couldn't warn me?" I whined.

She held up her hands. "I honestly didn't hear him. The door is propped open. Anyway, he looked absolutely thrilled about what you said. You should have seen the shit-eating grin on his face. And I was wrong. He definitely likes you. Josh Avery doesn't go looking for nurses. He ... shit," she whispered, sitting up and smoothing her face.

"He ... *shit?*" I asked.

"Doc Rose," she mouthed.

"Avery," Dr. Rosenberg said, setting a white box on the table. He removed a pair of chopsticks and a napkin from a long, translucent package.

He opened the box, and a waft of steam and soy sauce filled the room. Doctors had their own lounge, so it wasn't typical for him to be rubbing elbows with the peasants.

"That looks much better than the rubber chicken I'm having," Deb said, standing to retrieve her frozen entrée from the microwave.

"Have you noticed any soreness or experienced any headaches since the accident?" He reached over, gently massaging my shoulder near my neck. I stiffened. "You seem to be just fine, but I worry you're not complaining so you don't miss work."

He looked down on me with his big blue eyes, which set off the specks of silver in the patch of hair above his ears. He was so beautiful, like he just played a doctor on TV. Once I might have stumbled over my answer, but he didn't make me nervous anymore. I shrugged away from his touch. "Just the first week. Thanks for checking on me."

He glanced over his shoulder and then looked back at me, keeping his voice low. "I've been worried about you a lot, actually. I apologize if I'm overstepping, but I've heard some whispers that you and one of the paramedics have started spending time together, and—"

"Dr. Rosenberg," I interrupted. "I really don't think we should be—"

"I understand," he said with a wink. That move would have made me giddy once. Now it made me want to cringe. "But guys talk. I consider you a friend. We've worked together almost two years now, and ... I just don't want to see you get hurt. Josh Avery has built quite the reputation in his short time here. Just ... be careful. I care about you."

I realized my mouth was hanging open, and I snapped it shut. Dr. Rosenberg had always been on a friendlier basis with me than the other nurses, but this didn't feel friendly. "Thank you," I said. I blinked and righted my posture as Deb joined us.

Dr. Rosenberg checked his watch. "Oops. I forgot a meeting. Enjoy your chicken, Hamata." He stood, gathered his things, and left us alone.

Deb swallowed, clearly unsettled.

"What?" I asked.

"Ever notice that you're the only nurse he calls by your first name?"

"Yeah? So?"

"Never mind," she said, taking a bite. "It's just that," she continued with a mouthful, "he really seems to be interested in your new friendship with Josh, and he's been chatty since your accident, and when you were brought in he ..." She hesitated, and I raised my eyebrows. "He might have excused himself from the exam room because he was too upset."

"Too upset? Are you serious?"

"He's been weird. I think he's realized he has feelings for you, and now you're dating Josh."

I rolled my eyes and sat back in my chair. "You are way off, Hamata. No reason to make things up for the sake of drama."

She seemed hurt. "You know me better than that."

"Maybe the accident did make him realize we're good friends and close colleagues, and now that he knows I'm talking to Josh, he's concerned. And he *should* be. Josh does have a reputation. Dr. Rosenberg has teenage daughters, Deb. He watches out for me. I think it's nice."

"You have him on a pedestal, and he's going to fall on his ass and break your naïve little heart. But at least it will be amusing."

A few more nurses and an MRI tech came in, and Deb shoved the last two bites of her lunch into her mouth. "Break's over. Back to work."

"Don't share your theory with anyone, okay? Apparently, there is already talk about me."

"That offends me, Avery. Seriously," she said, walking out.

I stood alone, fidgeting. I'd never made Deb mad before. I didn't know it was possible.

She popped her head back in. "Just kidding. I'm glad you said something. I was gonna tell everyone that Doc Rose wants to put you in stirrups and bang you until you scream *Papa*."

"Hate you," I said, following her out.

The rest of the day dragged on. Josh and Quinn brought a patient in once, but the moment Josh and I were both free to talk, he got another call.

He kissed me on the cheek before he left, starting a fury of chatter from the other nurses. The moment Ashton got wind of it, she was immediately too far inside my personal space.

Just after I finished giving report, she was twirling her hair, trying so hard to be casual. "So," she said, a Cheshire grin on her face. "You and Josh."

"No," I replied.

"No? So it's not true? He didn't kiss you?"

"No," I said again.

She sighed, relieved. "That's good because, you know, we've been talking for several months, and I'd hate for you to have my sloppy seconds, if you know what I mean."

"I mean *no*, I'm not discussing personal matters with you. And, I hate to break this to you, Ashton," I said, scribbling on a chart. I slammed it shut and looked at her. "You were sloppy seconds. Every nurse in Philly who's slept with Josh Avery is sloppy seconds."

She puffed up and pursed her lips, her chubby cheeks reddening. "If you like him, I'm sorry. Josh is Josh. He is charismatic by nature, and it comes across as flirty. But we've been talking since he came here. You don't have to be a jealous bitch about it."

I narrowed my eyes. "Watch yourself, Ashton. You're at work."

"I'm your superior."

"You still can't call me a bitch at work."

The ER doors slid open with a *whoosh*, and Ashton's expression changed.

"Josh!" she said with a flustered smile, rocking back on her heels.

"Hey, Ashton." He smiled down at me. "You ready?"

"Yeah, just let me finish up this last chart," I said, pulling a large brown folder.

"Um ..." Ashton began, fidgeting with her hair. "What's going on?"

Josh didn't flinch. "I'm taking Avery out tonight."

Ashton blinked, her face taut. "What the hell do you mean you're taking Avery out tonight? We were just talking about going out last night."

Josh sighed. "No, *you* were talking about going out. I told you no."

"You didn't tell me about Avery," she whined.

"Wow, this is getting too *Days of Our Lives* in here," I said, shutting the chart. I looked at Josh. "Can we go?"

"Yep," he said, putting his hand on the small of my back as we walked toward the locker room.

He stopped just outside while I went in to retrieve my purse and wash my hands. When I came out, Ashton was standing in front of him, tears in her eyes.

"Really?" I said to Josh.

"Carissa, I don't know how more clearly to say it. I've been saying it for four months."

"Saying what? I don't understand."

"It happened once. If I'd known you couldn't let it go, it wouldn't have happened at all. I'm just going to say this one last time: I'm not interested in a relationship with you. Please stop contacting me."

Ashton puffed out her chest again, taken aback. Her mouth trembled, and then she glared at me before stomping off.

Josh raised his eyebrows and then formed his mouth in an *O* shape before blowing out. "She's different."

"Sounds like you broke her heart."

"I told her before we went to her place—which is filthy and smells like baba ganoush, by the way—that I wasn't looking for a relationship. She said she wasn't, either."

"No one has accused Ashton of being rational."

"You're rational, and sensible, and selective ... I kind of like that about you."

I chuckled. "That sounds so boring."

"Definitely not boring," he said, opening the passenger side door.

He drove us to an apartment building just three blocks from mine. When he shut off the engine, I reached for the lever but hesitated. "Is this your place?" I asked.

"It is. I just need to grab my wallet. I was in a hurry." He flashed what I was sure was his most charming grin, and then he pushed out of the car and jogged around to my side, opening my door. "You don't have to come in if it makes you uncomfortable."

"Does your apartment smell like baba ganoush?" I asked.

He laughed. "No."

He took my hand and held it until we reached the front

stoop, seeming disappointed to let go. He started to use his key, but the door swung open.

"Oh!" a woman said. She wasn't much younger than me, with a dirty blonde bob and thick glasses.

"Good timing," Josh said.

"Who's this?" she said, stepping aside so we could walk in.

"This," Josh said, gesturing to me proudly, "is Avery Jacobs."

"Nurse?" Cinda asked, pushing up her glasses.

Josh chuckled, looking down for a second. "Yes, she's a nurse."

Cinda nodded. "Nice to meet you. Your fur baby has been checked on thrice, walked, played with, and I'm sorry to report, he barfed in your kitchen."

Josh made a face. "What did you feed him?"

"I cannot confirm nor deny that I am now out of Cajun-style deli meat."

"Cinda, I told you he can't handle that shit."

She suppressed a giggle. "But he loves it so much! You can't even tell. I bleached your entire floor and ventilated your apartment. I also did your dishes, because ... gross."

Josh seemed confused. "I didn't have any dishes in the sink."

She thought about it. "Maybe that was someone else's dishes. You all run together. I'm heading out for work."

"Babysitting the Ramsey twins still?"

"They haven't killed me yet," she said as she passed.

Josh shut the door and grabbed my hand again, leading me up two flights of stairs to the second door on the right. He grabbed the knob. "This is me." He motioned across the hall. "That's Cinda. I always know she's home because of the kids screaming."

"*Her* kids?" I asked, alarmed.

"No." He chuckled. "No, Cinda is a professional babysitter. She's always busy. If she's home, she has somebody's kids with her. Even at night. She makes a *killing*," he said, pushing open his door. "She also sits for me because I'm gone so much. I probably shouldn't have gotten a dog, but Quinn didn't want him, and it seemed like a Good Samaritan thing to do at the time ..." His voice trailed off as he opened the door to his apartment.

His apartment was blank like mine, just a ratty couch, recliner, and hutch in the living room. I breathed in, and instead of chicken vomit or baba ganoush, I smelled bleach, mint, and Josh's cologne.

"Lived here long?" I asked.

"Nope. Just a few months. I had to find something quick so I could stop couch surfing."

"And why is that?" I asked.

"Why was I couch surfing?"

I nodded.

"Because I'd just moved to town."

"Why?"

"Damn." He grinned. "Didn't know this was going to turn into the Spanish Inquisition."

I clutched my arms. The air conditioning was on full blast. "I'm alone with you in your apartment. I think I'm entitled to the basics."

"You cold?" he asked.

"It feels like a meat locker in here."

"I sleep better that way."

"How do you afford the bill?" I asked.

Josh disappeared into a doorway and then came out holding a gray hoodie. He tossed it to me. "Put it on. It's really warm."

I looked down. "I don't think you want it against my scrubs."

"C'mon, like I don't get lathered in bodily fluids all day? It'll buff out. Put it on before you freeze."

"*Buff out*? That's an odd thing to say."

He shrugged. "Like buffing a scratch from a car. My dad used to always say it for everything. We're gearheads. I get elbow deep in grease on a regular basis. It relaxes me. Clears my head."

I slipped the hoodie over my head. A green Adidas logo was stamped on the front, and it happened to be the softest thing I'd even worn. "God, this is amazing."

"Isn't it? It's my favorite."

The gesture wasn't lost on me that he'd handed me his favorite sweatshirt to wear. "I'll get it back to you after I wash it."

"No rush ... There you are!" he said, grabbing his wallet off the hutch and stuffing it into his back pocket.

"Now we can go. Sorry about that." He called his dog, reaching down to pet him.

"That's an awful name. Sounds like a serial killer," I said.

Josh feigned offense. "You don't like it? Okay, you name him, then."

"What? No. I just meant ..."

Josh stood, crossing his arms. "I'm serious. Give him a better name if you don't like it."

"Like a nickname?"

"Yeah. I'm still calling him ..." Tiny whimpers came from the floor, and I bent over to run my fingers through coarse black and brown hair. "Didi," I said. "That's close enough to what he's used to, so I don't confuse him."

Josh wrinkled his nose. "He's a boy, Avery."

"Fine, just Dee, then."

"Dee it is," Josh said, bending over to ruffle the hair on Dee's head. "I'll be back later."

Dee whined when we approached the door.

My mouth curved down. He looked so lonely, and I knew exactly how that felt. "You just got home. Maybe we should stay here?"

"You sure?" he asked.

"Yeah, we can have JayWok deliver and watch a movie."

Josh shook his head. "No movies. I'm kind of enjoying the inquisition." He jogged back to the door, opened it, and then grabbed his phone. The dog wiggled its butt against Josh's ankles again, and then ran over to me. I picked him up and sat on the couch.

"Hey, it's Josh."

I smiled. Josh called them as much as I did. "The same for me, and Avery's over here. Yeah, chicken fried rice and low-sodium soy." He gestured to me, making sure that was all right. I nodded. "Delivery. Thanks, Coco."

"If I still had a car," I said, "I'd ask you to teach me to change my oil. That would save me a ton of money."

He shrugged. "I can do it. I don't mind."

I looked at him, unimpressed. "I need you to teach me, that way I can do it on my own when you tell me you're not interested in a relationship."

He looked around his apartment and then walked over to me, sitting on the cushion next to me. "Hadn't crossed my mind, actually."

"Right," I deadpanned.

I wasn't about to feign naïvety just to make Josh feel better. I had to at least protect my dignity, if not my pride. Knowing what the other nurses were thinking, seeing us chatting and making plans when he delivered patients to the ER, was hard enough. I had been one of those nurses once, making bets with Deb on how many drinks it would take Josh to get a particular nurse into bed, and how many days she would cry after.

Work would be easier later if I played this right.

"I thought we weren't going to do that," he said, unhappy.

"Do what?"

"Play games."

"I recall you saying play *nice*. Technically, that's playing something."

"That's not what I meant. You know," he said, shifting uncomfortably. "Like you said, let's be brave. Balls out. No back and forth, no anticipation of the other person's next move. Let's cut through all the bullshit and just be honest without worrying we sound too … anything."

"Okay," I said, unsure.

"I like you," he admitted. "A lot. I was attracted to you before the accident, but since, everything's changed. I want to get to know you better, but I've been sort of a dick since I got here, and I'm fairly certain you don't believe a word that comes out of my mouth."

"No, but you oversharing is mildly entertaining. Tell me more."

He smiled. "You look exceptionally beautiful in my hoodie. Avery?"

"Yeah?"

"Can I kiss you?"

"Um, sure." I cringed at how awkward I sounded.

He raked his fingers gently into my hair at the nape of my neck and leaned in. I closed my eyes, and then I heard whimpering. Dee jumped up, licking and nibbling my chin.

I squealed, leaning back and wiping my chin with the hoodie sleeve.

"C'mon!" Josh said, chuckling while he set the wirehaired dog on the floor.

"He missed you," I said.

He shook his head, pointing to the ball of fur. "No, no," he said, trying not to laugh. He turned to me. "Ask me something."

"Anything?"

"Almost anything."

"What can't I ask?"

"Oh, c'mon!"

"You said to ask you something! At least answer that."

"I don't like talking a lot about my past."

"Join the club."

"Oh, sweet Avery Jacobs has skeletons?" He smirked.

"Everyone has skeletons. So, pretty much everything is off the table with you."

"Ask me. I can't promise I'll answer now, but I promise to answer later."

I thought for a minute. "Why did you move to Philly?"

"My grandfather got me a job at LifeNet here."

I nodded. "Does your grandfather live here?"

"He did when he first married Granny. They moved to Abbottstown when she found out she was pregnant. He had some connections here and said it would be good for me."

"Why?"

Josh squirmed. "Later."

I nodded. "Were you always so ... charismatic?"

"That's a nice way to say it. Y'know, it never occurred to me to be embarrassed about it, but sitting with you at the moment, I kind of am."

"You don't have to be embarrassed. It's not like I'm a virgin."

"You're not?" I couldn't discern the look on his face.

My shoulders fell, and I looked at him as if I were bored with his question. "Please. I'm twenty-four. Do you know anyone our age who's a virgin?"

"Just you."

I cackled.

He shifted in his seat. "How many?"

"Are you fucking kidding me with that? You don't ask a woman how many people she's slept with on the second date."

"If this were a date, I'd be ashamed of myself. We're hanging out ... getting to know each other. So far, I've learned I love it when you curse. It's hot."

"Good. My dad had a mouth on him. *Damn it* was my first sentence."

"How many?"

"You first."

"I don't know," he said honestly.

"I'm not playing this game if you're going to cheat."

He laughed. "I swear to God. I think maybe in the forties. Maybe."

"You're a walking STD," I said.

"Nope. I'm the safest bastard you've ever met. I get checked every three months like clockwork."

"More like a prostitute."

His mouth fell open. "Easy!"

"Yes, that would definitely qualify you as easy," I shot back. "Two," I confessed.

His smile vanished. "Two."

"Yep. What?"

"I don't know." He frowned. "I'm aware of how irrational it is, but I don't like the thought of you being with someone else."

"Really? You're bothered by my single-digit number?"

"I am. Who are they? I might want to Facebook stalk them."

"You don't get names. I'm not a pristine virgin. Deal with it."

His eyebrows pulled even more. "No. I'm feeling genuine anger over here. I'm going to have pretend you're a virgin."

I rolled my eyes. "Don't tell me you're one of those guys who have slept with half the city but prefer their women untouched."

"Not at all. I'm just now discovering I might be the jealous type."

"That was awfully truthy of you."

"Isn't that what we're doing?"

"I guess so," I said. "What's in the hutch? It's locked."

Josh looked over at the peeling white paint and thought about his answer. "It's my liquor cabinet. Only for emergencies."

"What qualifies as an emergency?"

"My mom's an alcoholic." He glanced to the hutch. "I've only opened that lock twice since I've been here. Both were wrecks involving kids. One shot of whiskey was over that car versus train with the toddler in May. I drank two shots for a van-full last month."

I frowned. "I remember that one. I drank myself to sleep. You only had two shots?"

He shrugged. "I made a deal with myself that I'd only drink in a bar. It sounds stupid, I know. But drinking at home is how it started with my mom."

"It makes perfect sense, actually."

Josh looked into my eyes, seeming to appreciate our conversation. He stood after someone buzzed the apartment. He walked over to the small silver square on the wall by the door and pressed the black button, letting them in.

Josh pulled out his wallet, talking to the overgrown puppy scuttling around his feet. A few seconds later, someone knocked on the door and Josh answered.

Jeremy from JayWok's delivery team stood in the hallway, handing Josh a large white sack. He leaned over, looking past Josh to wave at me. I waved back.

"Thanks, man," Josh said.

"Coco told me to tell you not to screw this up."

"Bye, Jeremy." Josh shut the door, kicked off his shoes, and then returned to the couch.

"You're two for two," I said, digging into my box of noodles. "Two great nights so far."

"My two best nights in Philly since I've been here."

I pressed my lips together, trying not grin like an idiot, and then nodded, looking down at my noodles.

"My turn," Josh said. "What else do you hate, besides movie talkers and Christmas?"

"Dating douchebags," I said without hesitation.

"I can fix that, too."

CHAPTER EIGHT

Josh

Water dripped from my chin as I hung my head, hands gripping my knees, struggling to catch my breath. *One. Two. Three. Four. Five. Six. Seven. Eight. Fuck, keep it together. Nine. Ten.*

We'd managed to save the toddler who'd fallen into the family pool, but now it was *my* chest that was aching, memories weighing heavily on me as the boy's dark hair was replaced with curls in the recesses of my mind. I rubbed my palms against my dampened shirt, struggling to keep my calm. The boy's mother flung her arms around my neck and, from the rudimentary Spanish I understood, was thanking me for being his hero.

I felt like anything but as Quinn pried her from my body, his voice fading in and out like a radio station that wasn't quite in tune. His pocket-sized flashlight was shining in my eyes like the headlights of a semi barreling toward me. The thought immediately brought Avery's sweet face and soft hands to mind as I batted him away and righted my body.

"I'm fucking fine. Just tired."

"Avery keep you up all night?" He smirked.

I broadened my shoulders, widening my stance. Quinn and I often joked about women, but it didn't feel right when it was about her.

"She isn't like that," I snapped. I pulled my shirt that clung to my skin over my head and tossed it on the vinyl seat of the ambulance. I rummaged through my duffel bag and pulled out a spare.

"She shot you down?" Quinn asked.

I glared at him and then pulled the fabric down over my stomach before turning to walk to the back of the meat wagon. "I didn't even try."

As soon as the words left my mouth, I regretted them.

"I'm sorry," he said, not really sorry at all. "Did you grow a fucking vagina?"

I stopped walking, turning to face him. He nearly slammed into my chest. Quinn wasn't a small man, but I towered over him, at least half a foot taller.

"I'm just saying, if you have one, you gotta show it to me. Sharing is caring."

Shaking my head, I shouldered past him to the driver's seat.

Quinn slammed both back doors and then jogged up to the passenger side. He slammed the door and leaned back, pulling his hat low on his forehead.

I turned the key in the ignition, and the ambulance rumbled as we pulled out onto the main road. "Looks like you have your hands full with Deb."

"That girl has the mouth of a sailor, only ... you know, tits and stuff, too."

I shook my head and breathed out a laugh. "Sailors can be women too, you know."

"You think she'd wear one of those sexy little sailor outfits for me?"

"Deb? I think she'd let you throw bologna at her ass if it made you laugh."

"You're right." He looked out his window, thoughtful. "She's perfect."

Work had been exhausting, but I was reenergized as I stood at Avery's apartment door. She always seemed to have that effect on me. I had dropped her off from work only an hour before, but gone were her dirty scrubs and messy bun. She had disappeared into her bedroom and reemerged wearing a strappy plum-colored dress that hung loosely from her hips and stopped just above her knees. I suddenly felt underdressed in my jeans and gray polo.

"What do you have planned for us tonight?" she asked.

"It's hard to top a junkyard and twenty questions, but I think I've found something you may like. This is for you." I held out a small box in my sweaty palm, hoping she wouldn't laugh in my face.

Her eyebrows pulled together as her delicate fingers wrapped around the blue velvet object.

"I hope you're not proposing, because I haven't packed for Vegas," she quipped, the dimples settling deeper into her cheeks.

"Not yet," I replied before I could stop the words from spilling over my lips. "I mean not *ever*." Vomit. Word vomit was cascading out of my mouth like I was starring in *The Exorcist*.

Her eyes widened and I put out my hand instinctively, as if she might kick me in the balls. "I didn't mean *any* of that," I groaned. "Just open the damn box already."

Stifling a laugh, she opened the hinged cube and lifted the delicate ball chain from its tiny satin pillow. The shiny penny that had caught my eye that night in my car hung in front of her sparkling green eyes. I could see her imagination spinning as she waited for me to explain.

"It's a good luck charm. You know, a lucky penny. I found it in my car the night of our accident."

"I think we may have different definitions of good luck." Her eyebrow crooked up as I took the necklace from her hands and unclasped the chain.

"You're standing here, aren't you?" I asked, waiting for her to turn around. She did, lifting her long hair from her neck. The skin beneath was soft and perfect. "And I'm standing with you."

I slipped the necklace over her chest and fumbled with the clasp, my fingers too big to snap it back together. I used the opportunity to lean closer, inhaling the honey scent of her hair. "I'd say that makes me the luckiest man on Earth," I whispered.

Her shoulders shook from a small shiver. After three attempts, the clasp finally locked in place. Avery let her hair cascade down her back, over my fingertips. It was as soft as silk, and I had to fight against the urge to slide my fingers through it.

Turning back around, she grasped the penny that hung against her chest. "That's really thoughtful of you, Josh."

I made a face, unsure if she was being sarcastic. "You've said that before."

"I mean it."

I shrugged, wondering if I'd made a fool of myself. "Flowers die, and we see enough of that at work. I thought this might help keep you safe, you know, when I can't be there to pull you from the wreckage."

She breathed out a laugh. I placed my fingers under her chin to raise her gaze to meet mine. "Penny for your thoughts?"

Her teeth raked over her lower lip. "You just ... you surprise me. You don't seem like this kind of guy."

"What kind of guy is that?" I tried to push down the twinge of jealousy. I knew what kind of guy she thought I was and who had caught her eye first.

"Well ... " She held up the penny and peered through the hole drilled into its center. Her eyebrows pulled together. "I just didn't see you doing arts and crafts. What's next? Scrapbooking? Painting happy clouds?"

My grip was so tight on the steering wheel that my fingers ached. I'd never been so worried about impressing a woman. Chancing a glance at Avery, I relaxed. She was mindlessly rubbing her penny between her thumb and index finger.

"You look nervous." I slowed to turn off Milton Avenue onto Broadbeck Street.

"Maybe I am," she admitted, causing me to sit taller. "Not like that." She sighed, rolling her eyes for dramatic effect.

"Like what?"

"I just ... I get that this is kind of your thing. I see the way the women at work look at you, and how many you've gone through."

"You think I'm just playing you? That this is all some sort of game to get in your granny panties?"

"Well, yeah—wait, what? I do *not* wear granny panties! Who told you that? Was it Deb?"

I chuckled. "I know I have a reputation. I'm not going to lie to you and say I didn't earn it." Putting the car in park, I turned to look at her as she wrung her hands together in her lap, visibly cringing. "I've never made any promises to anyone, Avery. Every one of those women knew what I was putting on the table."

"You haven't made any promises to me, either." Her voice was barely above a whisper, but I could hear the tiniest edge of hurt in her words. "I guess I'm just saying ... if this is all part of *the game,* I don't think I want to play. I'm not like the other nurses."

I reached over to her, hesitating before slipping her honey-colored strands behind her ear, my fingertips brushing against her soft cheek. She turned toward me, worry in her eyes. Whatever this was, she felt it too, and it was scaring the hell out of both of us.

"Avery, you think that bothers me? That's what I *like* about you."

I could see that she was still uncertain, but she was willing to trust me, to give me a chance. That's all I could ask for. Something changed the night I held her unconscious in my arms. I couldn't hurt Avery. If I had it my way, no one would hurt her again.

She looked out over the row of trees before us. "You brought me to ... the woods."

"Yes." I shoved open my door and made my way to her side of the car to open hers.

She hesitated before sliding her palm against mine and letting me pull her to her feet.

"I'm not really dressed for the outdoors. You should have warned me. I could have changed before we left."

"You look perfect. Just trust me, Avery." Lacing my fingers between hers, I pulled her through the greenery, pine needles crunching under our feet. Her grip tightened on my hand as twinkling lights began to peek out between the branches.

"What is this?" she asked. She began to walk faster, now the one pulling me. I couldn't wipe the smile from my face as her very own living Christmas tree came into view. I'd done my best to clear the area around the small pine. Finding the decorations in the middle of summer was the hard part. My family didn't celebrate much of anything after my sister passed away, and I didn't care to carry on any traditions when I moved out.

She gasped, and I smiled.

I didn't admit it to Avery on our last date, but I had reasons to hate Christmas, too. As much as I wanted to make all her old memories into happy new ones, I needed it for myself, too. Luckily, Quinn's mother had no shortage of twinkle lights, balls, and tinsel. She'd filled the box I'd brought over with every piece she could find, including a snowman made out of Styrofoam to add to the ambience. The rest took some creativity. I'd emptied damn near every shredder in the hospital to gather enough "snow" to lay on the ground around the tree. I promised to clean up every scrap of paper to be able to pull this off in Amos's Tree Farm.

I reached up and tugged on a string hanging from a branch, making a cardboard box with holes cut in the bottom shake out its contents. The fake snow concoction I'd learned to make online floated down around us. Avery marveled at the sodium polyacrylate I'd harvested from a package of value diapers mixed with water, making me feel pretty damn great. The snow wasn't perfect. Some of it fell in clumps, but she seemed to appreciate the gesture.

"Josh," she whispered. The sound of my name in her mouth made the hair on my neck stand on end. "This is incredible."

"I almost forgot." Pulling my cell phone from my pocket, I scrolled through my music before slipping an earbud into my ear and holding one out for her. She held the tiny speaker to her ear, and her eyes brightened as *White Christmas* began to play. She beamed from ear to ear as she slipped her free hand back in mine and leaned her head against my shoulder.

"Christmas isn't so bad," she whispered.

From the corner of my eye, I could see her eyes glisten, reflecting the colors from the hanging lights above us.

She looked up and then back at me, feigning disappointment. "No mistletoe?"

She was like gravity. My entire body moved toward her, and the only thing I could do was wrap her in my arms and touch my lips to hers.

Even with my eyes closed, I could see my future with Avery. Everything I'd heard about first kisses and falling for someone manifested in that moment: fireworks, electricity, music playing, ridiculous happiness, and even bells ringing. Her lips parted, and I slipped the tip of my tongue inside. She squeezed my hand, nearly sending me over the edge.

I pulled away, looking down at our fake-snow-covered feet. "Whoa."

She picked white flakes from her hair and then glanced around, looking happier and more beautiful every second. "I also hate the little wrinkle above my top lip when I smile," she said, smiling and pointing to it. "Are you going to change that, too?"

I shook my head. "I wouldn't change a damn thing about you. What else you got?"

"Road trips."

I leaned back. "Seriously?"

"Loathe them. I don't think it's possible to fix that."

"Make a list," I said without hesitation. Playing it cool or being aloof or hard to get wasn't fun anymore. Avery didn't want to play games, and there was no question I wanted Avery. I was all in, and I was hoping she meant what she said, or trying to wear my heart on my sleeve would blow up in my face.

"Global warming, the smell of coconuts and cigarette smoke, white ribbed man tanks, being the center of attention, overripe bananas, spiders, baseball, screaming children, bacon, drool, gagging, mucus, crumbs, Howard Stern, static cling, bad haircuts, leaving Costco without a churro, and the word *elbow*."

"Is that all?" I asked, straight-faced.

She cackled. "What happens when we run out of things I hate?"

A lot of things came to mind. I didn't want to ruin everything by saying even one of them. My brain was still buzzing from the way she tasted. I wasn't sure how anyone could think under this condition. "We'll make stuff up."

Tugging her hand, I pulled her toward the clearing.

"We're leaving already?" she asked, her bottom lip jutting out slightly.

I laughed at her pouty face. "I'm trying to be a gentleman, Avery, and a gentleman wouldn't end the night pulling pine needles from his date's ass, if you catch my drift." I winked, and her lips spread into a wide, knowing smile.

"I may have some hot cocoa at my place."

She raised an eyebrow as I concentrated on her soft lips. I wanted to be the good guy she needed, but it was becoming increasingly hard, in more ways than one.

A tiny gasp slipped from Avery's lips when I spun her around. The passenger door of my car popped as I pressed her against it, and she startled. We both laughed, and then I dipped down to capture another taste of her mouth, relishing in her sweetness.

I reluctantly pulled back, wondering if it was this way with everyone. The more time I spent with her, the more beautiful she was. I pressed my forehead against hers, hoping to never wake up from this dream. Heavy drops of rain began to fall on us, breaking the magic of the moment. Avery laughed and looked up. I scrambled to gather Mrs. Cipriani's belongings, and then Avery joined me. Our laughter grew louder with each item we put away.

"Here," I said, handing her the box. I reached up, unhooking the glass balls from the pine tree and tossing them gently. She beamed as she moved the box to catch each one.

After the final decoration was packed, I took back the box and kissed her forehead. "Hot cocoa sounds pretty great," she whispered. The air had cooled with the rain, and her hair and dress were sticking to her skin.

I brushed a damp, golden strand away from her eyes. "Let's go."

My stomach was in knots by the time I pulled up to Avery's building. She hadn't spoken the entire trip back to her place. I wasn't sure if she was having doubts about me coming inside, and a guy like me shouldn't chance assumptions with a woman like Avery.

Parking on the side of the road, I hurried to her side of the car and pulled the door open. She smiled shyly as she slipped from the seat, pushing down the silky fabric of her dress.

I could see the nerves eating away at her, so I slipped my fingers between hers, squeezing her hand gently as she led me into her building and up the stairs, guiding me to her door. Fumbling with her keys, she nearly fell as the thick metal gave way and she lunged forward.

"It sticks," she mumbled while I closed it behind me.

"I can fix that for you."

She blushed. "You don't have to do that."

"I want to."

I took a step closer to her, sliding my hands against her warm cheeks and pulling her face to mine. Her body stiffened, but as my lips met hers, she relaxed against me. She slid her hands up my chest, and I sucked in a breath, feeling the sensation of her warm palms pressing the damp fabric into my skin. I wanted to feel her flesh against mine as I explored every dip and curve of her petite frame.

Gripping my shirt from the back of the collar, I pulled it over my head and tossed it to the ground. Avery's eyes danced down my torso as her fingers ran over the tattooed stripes on my ribs. Her brows pulled together, and I could see questions forming on her lips, but I didn't want this moment to end. We had plenty of time to talk later. In that moment, I just wanted to fully enjoy every second without distraction before she came to her senses and realized she deserved so much better than someone like me.

Slipping my fingers to the back of her neck, I slowly pulled at the knotted purple fabric until it became slack and fell loose. I could feel goose bumps rising on her skin as I let the pad of my finger slide down her spine. Her lips turned rigid, and then she pulled away. Her hands shot up, holding her dress in place over her chest as she took a step back from me.

I reached out for her. "Jesus, Avery. I didn't mean to—" *Too fast. I always move too fucking fast.* The girls I typically spent time with after dark didn't care how many hours we had known each other before my hand was under their clothes, but I knew better with Avery. She didn't need to let me fuck her in hopes it would keep me coming back long enough to feel something. I was the one hoping for more time.

"No. It's fine. I mean, you ..." Her voice wavered as she raked her hair back with her free hand.

Closing the gap between us, I wrapped my hand around hers

and pulled it down to her side before reaching back to retie her halter top.

She didn't look away, but she breathed through her nose, crushed under her embarrassment.

I pulled the fabric until it caught, and then held the soft skin of her cheeks in my hands. "I don't expect anything, Avery. Not a fucking thing. Tonight was perfect, and if it ends here, we have ..." *Forever.* "... plenty of time. I don't want to rush if it'll ruin anything." I wasn't sure if it would be ballsy or stupid to tell her how I really felt, but tomorrow seemed too small for what I wanted from Avery. Even forever felt like it could crash down around us. Every second I wasn't with her was beginning to feel stretched, tearing gashes into the fabric of space and time.

"That sounds dangerously close to you planning to stick around a while." She attempted to smile, but failed.

"Hey." I lifted her chin. "You can talk to me."

"I'm just ..." She sighed, her smile fading as she struggled. "I've seen the women you chase, Josh. I'm not like that. I ..." She trailed off, wincing with humiliation.

It took a moment to wipe the confusion from my face while I tried to process her words. I laughed once. "Thank Christ. That's what I like about you, Avery." Caressing her jawline with my thumb, I watched as the rosy color of her cheeks deepened.

"I probably haven't done ... a lot of things," she said.

I shook my head, failing to stifle a laugh. Her expression turned from worried to pissed off. She pulled away from me, and I was learning quickly that I hated that.

"You're laughing at me?" she snapped.

"No. Jesus, Avery. Is that what you're worried about? A lot of this is new to me too, y'know. I'd rather be your first. And if I can't be your first in something ..." I gritted my teeth, willing myself to grow a pair.

"What?"

Her anger fizzled, but the worry in her eyes had returned. I would have to choose my words carefully. If I seemed like the old Josh, she was going to bolt. If I told her the truth, she was going to bolt too.

"No," I said with a sigh. "I'm trying to tell you that I ... I'm just going to fucking say it. I care about you, okay? And that is new to me and fucking terrifying. And I'm not really sure what to do if you don't feel the same way."

Her lips parted and she sucked in a tiny breath. After an eternity, she finally spoke. "I do. Feel the same, I mean."

"Yeah?" I asked, relief making my shoulders sink.

She nodded. "It scares me too. But something about us is different. I want this. I want *you*."

My eyebrows pulled together and I exhaled. My mouth crashed into hers, as if she were the only source of oxygen in a burning building. I wanted to be consumed by the inferno now raging between us.

The fabric of her dress fell away, and I scanned every soft curve of her skin. The only sound in the room was our breaths; the only movement was the reflection in her eyes as she watched me reach for her. I lifted her effortlessly, wrapping her legs around my waist. She kept her mouth on mine as I walked across the living room to the bedroom doorway. Reluctantly, I lowered her to the ground, until she was standing on her toes.

"What's wrong?" she asked.

"Something new for me."

"Which is?"

"A bedroom."

Avery bit her lip and giggled as I slowly slipped a hand behind her, fumbling with the small clasp of her bra before it snapped free and slid down to her waist. She broke her hold on me just long enough to toss the lace to the floor before pressing her body tight against mine.

My dick was painfully hard against the rough fabric of my jeans, but I didn't want to rush things with Avery. Her hands slid tentatively over the ridges of my abdomen, and they involuntarily flexed under her touch.

"Josh," she whispered against my lips as her fingers slipped under the waistband of my jeans. I quickly undid the button and zipper before shoving the denim to the ground and kicking them off my feet.

Giggling into my mouth, Avery gripped my shoulders. I lowered her back onto her bed, our bodies tangling in the mass of fluffy comforter beneath us.

There was no urgency between us. I wanted to savor every taste of her skin, from the valley above her collarbone to the soft curve of her breast.

I kissed my way down her stomach as it dipped and raised with her ragged breaths, her long, elegant fingers lost in my hair, guiding me lower.

Pressing my lips to the pale pink lace adorned by a small matching bow on the front of her panties, I felt her body tense. My rough, calloused fingers tugged at the edge of the fabric, sliding it down over her hips and the widening of her thighs. I dragged them down to her painted toes and tossed them into the darkness. I considered kissing the apex of her thighs, but I climbed my way back up her body, desperate to feel her beneath me.

Even though Avery was significantly shorter than I was, her legs seemed impossibly long as they crossed behind my backside to hold me tighter against her. Her soft lips, still sticky from gloss, settled on a patch of skin just below my ear. I grew harder as I rocked my hips, moving my length along her inner thighs.

She breathed in and then let out a sexy, soft moan.

I tensed. "You keep that up, this will be over before we even start," I joked, and she rewarded me with one of her soft giggles, a whisper's breath blowing against my ear.

Pressing my cheek against hers, I closed my eyes. I needed a moment to calm myself before I lost control and flipped her ass over to take her in one of the many dirty ways I'd dreamed about since we'd spoken at JayWok. Avery deserved better than that. With her, I wanted more than just a quick, dirty fuck. I wanted to look into her eyes. For the first time, it was just as important to see the expression on her face when I slid inside her as the sensation itself.

"Don't move," I said, more begging than warning. I crawled from her body and fumbled with the button of my jeans at the side of the bed.

I said a silent prayer, followed by a thank-you when a small foil packet fell from my pocket into my hand. It bothered me that it had been placed in my wallet with the intention of being used on any random girl I took home. Now, I couldn't imagine this moment with anyone but Avery. I couldn't have predicted us being there, in Avery's bedroom, but it didn't stop the guilt from consuming me. Even watching me behave like the kind of douchebag she hated, Avery Jacobs was somehow lying beneath me, completely naked and impatiently waiting for me to make love to her. Everything had somehow fallen into place, even though I knew the truth: my life had been a series of bad luck. It was just a matter of time before Avery walked away.

I tore the corner of the packet with my teeth, and Avery's hand wrapped around mine, stopping me. My heart sank, as if she could see through the façade. Did she just now realize she was making a mistake? That she was settling?

Taking the small packet from my hand, she pushed gently against my chest, guiding me back onto her pillow. Her smooth thighs straddled mine as I watched in awe, willing myself to be patient. Eager women didn't require a lot of self-control. I knew the purpose and the end result, and I'd always accomplished that. Letting Avery set the pace was so different from what I was used to, and arousing in itself.

I couldn't help but run my fingers along her silky flesh as she took the condom from the packet and rolled it down my length. I didn't think it would be possible to be any more turned on, but Avery smiled in a way I'd never seen before, her mouth only half turned up, mischievous, ready. She skimmed my stomach with her lips, tasting my skin in a dozen small kisses. As soon as protection was in place, I grabbed Avery's waist and flipped her onto her back, settling in between her thighs. I couldn't wait any longer. I needed to be inside her.

Without looking away, Avery sucked in a sharp breath. I pressed against her entrance, painfully slow, allowing her to adjust to my size. The bite of her fingernails into my flesh let me know this moment was real, and this girl I had dreamed of was now mine. The room was quiet, aside from the mattress shifting with my movements, our ragged breathing, and small whimpers from Avery's lips as I filled her completely.

"Are you okay?" I asked, already breathing hard.

She nodded as my lips found hers. Relief washed over me, knowing she wanted this as much as I did and feeling the trust we had given each other. For the first time—at least, for me— sex was more than just sex. I'd never allowed myself to be that vulnerable with anyone. It was terrifying, and exhilarating, much more than any one-night stand I'd ever had.

I eased back and then filled her again. My movements were slow, matching the pace of our kiss. I wasn't used to being so gentle. I was afraid the perfect image of Avery would break and dissipate beneath me, leaving me in a crumbled heap of regrets and past mistakes.

Her pelvis tilted to meet mine as she mumbled my name against my lips. With my forehead resting against hers, I saw the only thing still between us: a small penny pinned between our chests.

Our panting mingled and became deafeningly loud in the small space as Avery shook beneath me, our bodies coated in a thin layer of sweat.

I leaned down, kissing her hard, feeling the build. My intended lovemaking was turning into fucking, and Avery welcomed the pounding rhythm.

Her soft cries of pleasure pushed me over the edge, and I thrust into her one last time before growling my release. We both stilled, struggling to catch our breath.

I brushed her slicked hair from her face, tracing my thumb over the arch of her eyebrow. I slowly eased out of her, seeing the disappointment in her eyes mirror mine.

"If I add sex to my list of things I hate, can we do that again?" An impish grin spread across her face.

"That was you hating sex? What are you like when you're enjoying yourself?" I leaned down to pepper her cheek and neck with kisses, finally settling on her lips.

Avery exhaled, suddenly seeming vulnerable and embarrassed. I touched her cheek, trying to think of something to remind her I was different.

"Is it lame for me to ask to see you again right now?"

She relaxed, settling against the mattress. She shook her head, pursing her lips to ask when. Before the word slipped from her lips, I said, "As soon as possible. Tomorrow. In the morning. Actually ... is it cool that I just stay?"

"You want to stay the night?"

I shrugged. "Waking up next to you sounds pretty fucking amazing."

She pretended to think about it for a few moments and then leaned up to peck my lips. "Yes."

I scanned her eyes for a moment and then rolled off Avery and made my way to her bathroom to dispose of the condom.

Flipping on the bathroom light, my eyes instinctively squinted at the intrusion. I bent over the sink, splashing cold water on my face, avoiding my own reflection. Small hands slid around my waist from behind, causing me to jump.

Avery's reflection appeared in the mirror, her hair disheveled and sexy, her mascara smudged below her emerald eyes. Long, elegant fingers ran over my striped tattoo, and my muscles tensed as her nail dragged over the fresh ink.

"That looks new."

"It is. Still a little tender. I actually got it because of you." The moment the words tumbled from my mouth, I closed my eyes tight and gritted my teeth. *What the fuck, Josh? Why would you open that can?*

I leaned against the edge of the porcelain sink and reached out for her, trying to play off what I'd said.

She stiffened in my arms. "Me? This isn't like a line for each person you've ..." She covered her face. "You were so sure this would happen that you already ... oh, God."

It took a moment to understand why she would be embarrassed. I leaned back, but she wouldn't look at me. "Avery. What are you ...?" When the realization hit, I frowned. "Jesus, it isn't some kind of tally to show who I've slept with. I'd have to be one cocky son of a bitch to get a tattoo before I'd even slept with you."

She peeked at me through her fingers and then dropped them from her face. "Then why is that—" she pointed at my side "—because of me?"

It suddenly felt hard to breathe, and I stiffened when she touched the stripes again. The truth was weighing heavily on me. What would Avery think when she heard about my past? She had a right to know, at least partially, where I had come from. Now that I had opened my big fucking mouth about it, there was no turning back. Avery knew she was involved, I'd just fucking told her, and she would want to know. She deserved to know if she was going to chance being with me.

My mouth felt dry, and I swallowed back a couple decades of insecurity and anger. Kayla had died because of me, and it was my fault our family had fallen apart. My parents still hadn't forgiven me. How could I expect Avery to understand?

She reached out to my bare hips and pulled me toward her, looking up. "Talk to me," she said, quoting me from earlier in the evening.

I cleared my throat. "How much alcohol do you have?"

CHAPTER NINE

Avery

With my hair in knots and my insides wonderfully sore, I stretched in bed, the floor peppered with tossed undergarments. My apartment was familiar but unfamiliar. The sheets smelled like a sweet combination of my lotion, Josh's cologne, spilled cheap wine, and sex. I glimpsed at the clock, grateful it was my day off.

Josh was gone. I wasn't sure what time his shift had begun, but he had warned me before I asked him to stay that he wasn't so lucky.

I reached for his pillow that was once the spare, hugged it to my chest, and rolled onto my back, looking up at the ceiling. Every detail from the previous night replayed in my mind: the way his shoes sounded against my floor, the way his skin tasted, how his hands felt on the parts of me no one else had touched in quite a while. I remembered the glorious pressure of his fingertips digging into my skin, the filling sensation when he had slid inside me, his stomach gliding against mine with every thrust, his arms tensing, and the sound he had made when he came. My thighs tensed. I'd wanted the night to last forever, and I wanted to go back and do it all over again.

I let go of his pillow and rolled out of bed, trudging to the bathroom. The pipes rattled and whined when I turned the knob of the tiny shower. I paused, looking down into the trash can. A used condom. The soap dish had been moved. Droplets of water in the sink. Someone else had occupied the space of my apartment. It was strangely exhilarating.

I stepped under the water, for a moment mourning that I was washing away of any evidence that Josh had made himself at home against my skin. We had been tangled together for a night. We had gone from practically strangers to lovers in the span of a month—since the accident.

The water was hot, but I began to shiver. There was only one thing worse than Josh living up to his reputation. He had changed so much in such a short amount of time. I hadn't known him all that well before, but what I had known of him ... he had left all that behind. *Why me?* One of my instructors in nursing school had touched on the Florence Nightingale effect, where a caregiver develops romantic feelings for his or her patient.

I scrubbed my hair and skin, and then twisted the knob, standing in my shower, dripping wet and alone—again. I wasn't paranoid. This was all too good to be true, and at any moment, I would wake up. My head panged, and I made a mental note to find the ibuprofen.

I wrapped a white fluffy towel around me, feeling emptier as the elation from when I had first woken up faded. Josh was different because he wasn't himself. He had watched a woman he was casually flirting with get pounded by a tractor-trailer, and then he had held her until help arrived. That would be traumatic for anyone. The sad part was he didn't even know it was happening.

I jumped when three knocks shook the door. I tucked wet strands behind my ear and padded out of my bedroom and past the couch and coffee table. I peeked from the door, opening it just enough that the chain lock caught. Josh was standing on the other side with a sweet smile and two coffees. He was in a navy T-shirt with white insignia, navy cargo pants, and black lace-up boots.

"Hey," he said, his head dipping down. "Everything okay?"

"I'm, um ... What are you doing here? Aren't you supposed to be at work?"

He held up both hands. "I made breakfast. Sorry I had to leave so early. I should have brought my clothes, but you know ... didn't want to assume anything. Not that I did. I'm on the clock, but we just dropped off a patient at St. Ann's and I started missing you, and ..." As he rambled, he noticed the look on my face. His expression changed. "What's going on, Avery? Is everything all right?"

"I'm okay." I tried to smile, but it felt crooked.

"Let's talk." He scanned my body from chin to ankles, and then his eyes drifted back up, stopping on the water dripping from the ends of my hair. He leaned over to look past me, and then the muscles in his jaw ticked under his taut skin.

"I just have a headache. I'm really okay."

"Avery. Let me in."

I slid the lock until it released. Josh immediately pushed the door open, looking around. He passed me to walk into the bedroom, spent a few seconds in the bathroom, and then returned to the living room, tripping over the area rug beneath my couch.

"What are you looking for?" I asked.

He was breathing through his nose, slightly trembling, his eyes wild.

"You're angry?" I asked.

He looked away, his jaw tightening. Without thinking, I yanked the necklace he'd given me over my head and held it out to him. His mouth fell open, as if I'd slapped him in the face.

"Just wait a second, Avery. Let's take a second and think about this."

I arched my eyebrow, obstinate. The penny still dangled from the chain in my hand, just inches from his chest.

"Are you fucking kidding me? That's it?"

"Please," I said, unimpressed. "You can't get rid of me that easily." I pushed to my tiptoes and looped the necklace over his head before sinking back down on the heels of my feet, my hands on my hips. "Penny for your thoughts."

Lifting the small copper circle into his large palm, he stared at it for a moment before a ghost of a smile appeared, fading as quickly as it had arrived.

He sighed in defeat, but the fight had just begun.

"I thought maybe ..."

"What?"

"Someone else was here."

"What?" I shrieked. The only thing in the apartment that wasn't exactly the same when he'd left was me. I couldn't fathom why he'd even think such a thing. The dress he'd slipped off me hours before was still hanging halfway off the wooden coffee table, my bra was still in a small, lacy heap in the bedroom doorway, and my panties were still tangled somewhere in the sheets.

Josh huffed, trying to reign in his temper. "You answered the door with the chain locked and then left me standing in the hallway like I'm some stranger you don't want in your apartment ... You're acting all nervous and weird! What the hell was I supposed to think?" His voice rose as his frustration increased with each word.

"That I had someone in here the morning after we ... Are you *serious*?" My stomach turned. Someone had to have done this to him before. He was heavily guarded, and I had only scratched the surface of his armor. His eyes widened, as if he knew I'd seen too much.

"Whoa," he said, holding the coffees out in front of him. "Let's start over."

I crossed my arms across my middle.

"What's going on with you, Avery? Why are you acting so strange? Is it because of last night? Is it too weird now? Are you not sure? About ... *me*?"

"Stop. You're overreacting," I said, holding up my hands, palms out.

He looked at his watch and then sighed, a deep growl resonating from his chest. "I have to go. Please tell me what's wrong. I'm gonna go nuts all day worrying about it."

"Why?" I dropped my hands and groaned, exasperated.

He wrinkled his nose. "Huh?"

"*Why* would you worry about it?"

His face twisted, as if I had begun speaking a foreign language. "Avery, what the hell?"

"You're so different."

"So are you," he spat back. "You were fine last night. Now that we've ... you're trying to bail."

"I'm not trying to bail. But you ... I've dated people. You don't, you—"

"When?" he asked, his tone accusatory.

I frowned, insulted. "I've lived a long time before you came around, Josh Avery. You're not my first relationship, if that's what this even is."

"If that's what this *is*? What else would this be, Avery?"

"Well, the arrogance certainly hasn't changed."

He walked away with his fingers interlocked on top of his head. He let his hands fall to his thighs and then turned to face me. "You might have had boyfriends before me, but you haven't been this way with anyone else. I know it. You know it. Stop bullshitting me. What the fuck is wrong with you?"

"No one changes overnight, Josh. No one is one way their whole life and then changes for one person."

Disappointment darkened his face. "I haven't played games. I've put it all on the table, and now you're ... What are you *doing*, Avery? Is this the part where you try to push me away?"

"No," I said, tears burning my eyes. Pressure continued to build inside my chest. "Think about it. Why is this so easy for you? Why is this so different with me than with anyone else? You act so different around me. What do expect me to believe? You've had an epiphany?"

"Yes, a fucking epiphany! Tell me!" he yelled.

I swallowed, afraid if I said it out loud, the dream would be over. "Did this happen because of the accident? Because you saw me get hurt?"

"Yes," he said without hesitation.

Like a knee-jerk reaction, I sucked in a gasp, his confession feeling worse than the collision that had catapulted our relationship.

"Avery," he said, setting the cups on the coffee table. "If they're lucky, assholes like me have a moment where they wake up. Holding you after the accident ... that was mine. It's not because I feel sorry for you or I have some sort of God complex." He took a breath, trying to calm down. "I've been begging you for dates and I'm standing at your door with coffee because I'm different. I'm different because I want to be the man you think you see."

"You're not an asshole," I murmured.

"I was. We can agree this is a good change. I should have made a move a long time ago, Avery. I've wasted too much time already. Nearly losing you before I had you made me see that."

I chewed my lip, waiting for him to come to a different conclusion. It was all too real, too soon, and it terrified me that I was giving my heart to someone who knew how to break it.

"Avery ... baby ..." He looked at his watch, and what he saw made his jaw dance under his skin. "I have to leave for work."

I nodded. "It's okay. Really. I'm sorry I brought this up now."

"Tell me you're okay. Tell me *we're* okay."

I nodded again, and he walked over to me. He pulled me into his chest and I breathed him in, already feeling better. This wasn't a game or a challenge or post-traumatic stress. He cared about me. I just needed to believe I was worth caring about.

He kissed my temple. "Wait for me. I'll be back later. We'll talk more."

"I'm really okay. Just had a moment," I said, feeling foolish.

Josh knotted his fingers in my wet hair with one hand and tugged until I looked up at him. He sealed his mouth over mine, kissing me hard and forceful, keeping my bottom lip between his teeth as he pulled away, leaving his mark on my clean skin once again. "Eight hours," he said. He picked up his cup and slammed the door behind him, still amped from our argument and the kiss.

I went to the door, replaced the chain lock, and then backed up until the coffee table touched the backs of my bare calves.

"Holy shit," I breathed.

It was coming. I could feel it following me around my apartment, to JayWok, and sitting in the empty chair across from me while I ate my leftover chicken fried rice in the break room. With every bite, every sip of water, and every person who walked in and out, I was saturated. I was falling hard for Josh Avery, McPanties, the paramedic who couldn't be tamed.

"I love you, but you're fucking stupid. And yes, I mean Josh," Deb said, sitting across from me while licking grease off her fingers.

"He's not stupid," I snapped.

"You're right. He has good taste in women. Since last month. You know I would never insinuate that Carissa fucking Ashton tastes like anything but a cat fart dunked in leftovers from a yeast infection."

I swallowed back the bile that rose in my throat just from involuntarily imagining her description. "Deb, how are you friends with anyone who isn't a nurse? It's like I had to be able to keep it together while simultaneously cleaning up shit and holding a barf bag just to qualify."

She paused before taking another bite of her cheeseburger. "Didn't you?"

I rolled my eyes and threw a soy sauce packet at her face. "I'm outta here."

"Break's not over yet!" Deb called after me.

I walked out of the break room and down the hall, pressing the button to the elevator. It opened, and I stepped inside with a nervous new father and a brand new, empty car seat.

"Going home today?" I asked.

He beamed. "Yeah."

I looked down at the carrier. It was brown and cream. *No help at all.* "Boy or girl?"

He couldn't stop smiling. "Girl."

"Congratulations," I said.

The elevator doors opened to the maternity ward, and I waited for him to step out, then followed, stopping at one of the three large windows of the nursery. More than half the cribs were taken.

Georgia walked by in bright scrubs. Large pieces of golden-brown hair had fallen from her ponytail, and her eyes were red and tired.

"Full house?" I asked.

"Let me tell ya somethin'," she said in her thick Mississippi accent. "It's a full moon tonight. If you get bored in the ER, you come on up here and I'll show you busy."

I chuckled, and she winked, her scrubs swishing as she made her way to one of the delivery rooms.

"Cute, aren't they?" Dr. Rosenberg said from behind me. "I come up here a lot to center myself and recharge."

"I'm just trying to get away from Deb," I joked.

Dr. Rosenberg laughed. "I haven't seen you at Corner Hole lately. I guess you've been busy."

"I guess so," I said, staring through the glass with a smile. The babies were cute, but I was thinking of Josh. My face fell, and I looked at the doctor. "Since when are you a regular at Corner Hole?"

"Since I never see you anymore, I guess."

I pressed my lips together, but the edges of my mouth turned up anyway. "I know. I've been preoccupied."

"How is that going?" Dr. Rosenberg asked.

I didn't mean to, but I sighed. And then I gushed. And then I couldn't stop, even when I saw the doctor's expression change from polite to blank.

"That's great," he said. His tone was the one he used with Deb or the other nurses when they tried to chat with him. "I wish you all the happiness."

"You wish me *all the happiness*?" I said, disgust dripping from every word.

My reaction put a spark back in his eyes. "No, actually, I don't, but you haven't taken my advice thus far. I don't suspect you'll start now."

"What are you talking about? What advice?"

"That you should stay away from him. He's bad news, Avery. I know things are new and fun now, but ..." He looked around and then took my arm, gently guiding me around the corner. "Would you just listen to me? We were friends once."

"Were we?"

He seemed hurt. "I thought so."

He touched my face with his fingertips and I pulled away, glancing around. I startled when I saw Josh standing ten feet away, murder in his eyes.

I took a step back. "You knew he was there, didn't you?"

"Of course not," Dr. Rosenberg said. "Josh."

Josh nodded once, and the doctor excused himself, walking toward the elevators.

When Josh approached, I pointed to the empty spot where the doctor was standing. "That wasn't anything. He's being really weird, but I didn't ... that wasn't ..." While I fumbled for words, I noticed Josh's jaw twitching. "I know how it looks."

"How does it look?" Josh finally managed to say. His words were short. He was trying his best to keep from losing his temper.

"I can see that you're angry, but I'm at work. He's my boss."

Josh shoved his hands into his pockets and shrugged. "What the fuck does that even mean, Avery?"

I leaned in. "Keep your voice down!" I hissed. I started to walk past him, but he reached out, grabbing my arm.

I looked around to see if anyone noticed, and then back at him. "Let me go before someone sees."

"Are you still in love with him?"

My mouth fell open. "I was never *in love* with him. He's married. What kind of person do you think I am?"

Josh's brows pulled together. "C'mon, baby, open your eyes. He wants you."

I looked around. "So what if he does? Am I a robot? Just because the beautiful doctor all the nurses want is interested in me, I have to fall on my back with my legs spread? Give me a little more credit than that, Josh. Just because I fell for you doesn't mean I'm naïve."

Josh blinked, unsure whether to be flattered or insulted. "I don't know how to take that."

"Take it any way you want. My break's over."

"Let me walk you down."

"Dr. Rosenberg is likely down there. It's probably best you stay away from him," I said.

"Oh, he'd fucking love it if I stayed out of his way."

"Like it or not, I work with him. You're going to have to trust me."

"It's him I don't trust."

"Josh," I warned. "I love my job. If you can't be professional, stay away from Dr. Rosenberg. Don't ruin this."

He was clearly unconvinced, so I shouldered past him to the elevators.

"Avery," he called over his shoulder. He turned around, but the elevator doors were already closing.

CHAPTER TEN

Josh

I made my way to work, unable to ignore the stress and tension crawling through my muscles. What I needed was to hit the gym and empty my mind, but I didn't have time. I couldn't miss work, and any free time spent without Avery felt wasted, even if the late nights and early shifts would eventually make me crash and burn.

I'd scrubbed the back of the meat wagon after our last patient until my knuckles felt raw, but there was still a residual discontent rumbling just under the surface. The conversation we'd had about my sister still haunted me. Avery hadn't run away screaming, but I'd seen the pain in her eyes when I'd told her it was all my fault. I don't know why she'd stuck around after that. Maybe it was the alcohol. I worried that she would come to her senses any minute.

It was a relief that Avery hadn't insisted that I go into detail about each stripe tattooed on my ribs. If she had, I'd be even more of a fucking mess. Women usually just assumed the tattoos didn't have any meaning, so I'd never had to explain what it meant—not that I would tell them the truth anyway.

I was caught off guard that Avery not only asked, but cared enough to listen.

"Earth to Josh." Quinn waved his hand in front of my face and I slapped it away. He chuckled. "That girl has you sprung."

I shook my head as I rounded the back of the ambulance, stopping mid-step when I saw Doc Rose. He was checking his phone as he walked across the parking lot toward the ambulance bay doors, but when he recognized me, he dropped his phone into his pocket, staring right at me with a smug smile.

I nodded back to him, whispering a string of expletives under my breath.

"You really don't like that guy, do you? He still trying to put the moves on Avery?" Quinn asked, closing the back of the ambulance.

I wiped my hands on my pants, fantasizing about using the shears hanging from one of the loops in my cargos. Doc Rose was a cocky fucker now, but that fake smile would disappear if he was stabbed in the face. I shook the violent thought away. "Whoa."

"What?"

"Feeling stabby. Is this what it's like to be jealous?"

"Want to kill him?"

"Yeah."

"Yep. You're jealous. Is he bothering her?"

"She doesn't see it that way, not that she'd tell me if he were."

"Can't blame her there. Get your hand off your shears."

I pointed my whole hand in the doctor's general direction. "How does a guy like him, who has everything, just throw it all away? He's married, with kids. He has the whole American dream waiting for him at home."

"Pussy is a powerful thing, man. Look how it has you twisted."

"Don't talk about Avery like that," I warned.

Quinn held up his hands. "Who said it's the American dream to have kids? I don't want no little Quinns runnin' around here."

"No one does, brother," I agreed.

Quinn shot me a look, and then something in the parking lot caught his eye. "Speak of the Devil."

Avery was making her way across the lot, smiling brightly, a paper bag in her hand. My stomach growled as the red symbol on the side came into view, but my attention quickly returned to the skintight jeans she wore with a simple white tank top. I've never known another woman to look so fucking good with no effort.

"She's off today?" Quinn asked.

I kept my gaze on Avery. "Yeah."

"Did you know she would be here? Is that why you spent so much time cleaning out the back?"

"Maybe." I wiped the ridiculous grin off my face, crossing my arms and leaning against the fender of the ambulance, trying not to look too eager.

"I thought you could use some lunch," Avery said, stopping a few feet from me. She held out the bag from JayWok.

I walked toward her, looping my arms around her waist, lifting her feet from the ground and planting a kiss on her lips. She let hers part, granting me deeper access. I groaned, reluctant to pull away. Needing her had become worse, not better, and I wondered if it was normal to feel so desperate for her, a deep-seated worry that we didn't have much time left.

"Only if you join me," I replied.

Her smile widened, and she gave a quick nod to Quinn before returning her attention to me. "Of course. Let me go say hi to Deb, and then we can find some shade. It's too nice to eat inside, and we've only got a few weeks of summer left. Might as well enjoy it."

"Tell Deb I'd like to *eat out* too," Quinn interrupted. I recoiled watching him wink and then run his tongue over his lower lip. "She'll know what it means."

Avery made a gagging sound as she walked away.

I smacked him on the chest. "What the fuck is wrong with you?"

Quinn rubbed his chest, not looking the least bit apologetic. "What the fuck is wrong with you? You've lost your sense of humor. That girl has you wrapped around her little finger, man."

I watched Avery disappear behind the emergency room's sliding glass doors. I couldn't argue with Quinn. Avery scared the hell out of me, but I couldn't stay away from her, even if a part of me knew it wouldn't end well.

Before Avery, I'd made mistakes I was too ashamed to ever admit. I knew when I did, she wouldn't look at me the same way. Running my hand absentmindedly over my side, I pictured the large gray door that stood between my future and me only a few short years ago.

"Brooke!" I yelled, running into the lobby of the clinic.

Seeing Daniel pacing in front of a door, I knew exactly where she was.

Daniel took one look at me and shoved his shoulder against my chest, using all his strength to keep me back from the doorway. He was my closest friend, but if he didn't get out of my way, I was going to slam my fist into his jaw.

"You have to calm down, Josh," Daniel said. "You can't let her see you like this. She needs you to be strong for her."

I gripped his shirt at the collar. "What happened? I told her I would be back tomorrow. Why? I left for one fucking day!" I stared at the door, knowing I was already too late. My body shook, and I pushed against Daniel.

He put his hand against my chest and held me back. "Josh, stop. You're going to regret this."

I looked down and then glowered at him.

"You're my friend, Daniel, but if you don't take your hand off me, I'm going to break your fucking fingers."

Daniel sighed. "I can't. You know I can't. If you bust in there now, she'll hate you for it."

"You think I don't know what you did?" I said through my teeth. "What you're hoping you'll get out of this?"

I stepped back. I could have easily overpowered him, but I was so gutted I couldn't find it in me to follow through on my threats. Maybe what was really holding me back was what it would mean if I stopped her.

My face crumbled, and I rubbed the back of my neck. Maybe I was the selfish bastard Brooke had accused me of being.

"She needs me to be there for her," I said.

"If you had been, she wouldn't be here," Daniel spat out.

In one movement, I shoved him against the wall. He tried to push me off him, but I didn't budge.

A short, squat woman with chains hooked to her glasses touched me on the arm. "Sir, I'm going to have to ask you to leave if you can't calm down." Her slicked-back bun barely moved when she moved her head. Her matching blue scrubs had been ironed and starched, but the bags under her eyes told a long story of hard work and experience. She wasn't going to allow any nonsense, and even if she did, I couldn't make her day even harder. She was a nurse, just trying to do her job.

"Keep it down or you'll be sent outside," she said, her eyes focusing on my grip on Daniel. She would keep order, but I could see she was sympathetic to the guilt in my eyes. "Don't make me call security."

I released Daniel's shirt and shoved him one last time, walking several steps away, breathing hard.

"I should have left earlier," I said, pacing. "I wouldn't have hit traffic."

"It wouldn't have made a difference, Josh. She made her decision."

I thought back over the morning commute back to college after break. An accident on I-95 set me back a few hours. It was stupid, turning off my phone when she was two hours away, scared and pregnant.

"I didn't get her voicemail until this morning," I said.

Daniel stopped trying to pretend to comfort me. He was only there for one thing. He wanted to be the shoulder she cried on after she ended the only thing standing between them.

"We got in a fight," I said.

"I know."

"Of course you know," I snapped. "You just loved it, didn't you? Her crying to you about what a selfish jackass I am."

He didn't respond.

"I had to clear my head, Daniel. We don't even know each other, and we had a baby on the way."

Daniel barely listened, watching the door for signs of Brooke.

"I knew she was just scared. I knew she didn't mean it, but I'm scared, too," I said to no one. Daniel had turned his back to me. "I wasn't sure if I could handle this. I was terrified something bad was going to happen ... to her and the baby ... because of me. Because of my past. I'm a fucking tragedy magnet, you know that."

"Ironic, isn't it?" Daniel said, all pretenses vanished. "You ran because you were scared of something bad happening to them. Now Brooke is behind that door, doing something

she swore she couldn't do. You look away for a second, and someone dies. Just like Kayla."

"Fuck you," I said, sinking down on my haunches. I hung my head in my hands as I thought about the disastrous visit with my parents. I'd gone home to take a break from Brooke and the mess I'd created. Instead, Mom and Dad yelled at me for an entire evening. They'd said they didn't blame me for what had happened to Kayla, but I could see it in my mother's glassy eyes and smell it on her whiskey-laced breath. I'd managed to ruin everything for everyone who got close to me. I was fucking cursed.

"I just need to see her," I pleaded to the nurse.

She looked down at me, sad. "I'm sorry, I can't allow that. Family only." Her painful words were cut off by the door opening behind her.

I quickly pushed to my feet as Brooke came into view. Not so long ago, we had been strangers. The past two months had been a crash course of getting to know each other once she told me she was pregnant, and that the baby was mine.

Her eyes were red-rimmed and swollen, her platinum hair mussed. Her russet irises fell on me, and she wrapped her arms around her waist.

"It's done?" I asked, feeling the blood drain from my face.

Brooke nodded, a fresh sob racking her body. I wanted to wrap my arms around her, but it felt too familiar for two people who'd spent one drunken night together.

"I had to do it, Josh. I'm not ready to be a mom."

I nodded, linking my fingers behind my neck and blowing out a long breath. There was a lot I wanted to say. I couldn't understand how she could be so impulsive, why she didn't wait for me to call her back so we could discuss it, but I wasn't angry.

We had both been so scared, and now I wasn't sure how to feel. She'd made her choice, and neither of us could take it back.

I watched, helpless, as Brooke fell into Daniel's arms. Daniel's. He'd made sure it was him she ran to for comfort, and I stood there alone, feeling like I'd stepped into an intimate moment between them that I had no business interrupting. Perhaps I didn't. Daniel had told me after I'd slept with Brooke that he'd been in love with her since high school. When I told him the news about the baby, he had gone to her and promised to stick around, no matter what I decided.

Brooke's cries from the night before rang in my ears. She had said she didn't know me, didn't trust me, and she was at home worrying about the future while I was busy trying to deal with my own feelings about it all. She was right, and I couldn't blame her for saying it out loud.

Brooke's knees buckled, and Daniel held her, stroking her hair. He looked at me as if he felt I was intruding, too.

"Should I go?" I asked Brooke.

She turned to look at me, her cheek against Daniel's shoulder. "You're free, Josh," she said, sniffing. "We both are."

The sliding doors opened across the lot as the air whooshed, and Deb slipped outside, smiling brightly at Quinn.

I was gripping the JayWok bag so tightly in my fist, my knuckles hurt.

"You all right, man?" Quinn asked as he stood at the rear bumper of the ambulance.

"I'm good." I turned my attention back to Deb. "Where's Avery?"

"She's talking to Dr. Rosenberg."

My body moved toward the door of its own accord, but I stopped as the doors opened. Avery stepped out, laughing as she glanced back over her shoulder to Doc Rose, who followed closely behind. His palm was pressed against the small of her back as they walked, but she didn't seem to notice, or maybe she didn't mind.

When the doctor saw me, he smiled, laughing to himself as if he'd won. My blood boiled in my veins, and it took serious restraint not to take that first step, because after that, I knew I wouldn't stop. They separated, him heading toward his car and Avery in my direction.

"Hey," Avery whispered as she met me in the center of the lot. She pushed up on her toes to kiss me square on the lips.

I hoped she had done it on purpose, to show us all who was the friend and who was more. Her gesture helped my anger dissipate, and I looped my arm behind her back, lifting her from the ground, deepening our kiss.

Setting her back on the ground, I chuckled, watching her cheeks burn with embarrassment.

"What was that about?" she asked.

I shrugged, glancing over her shoulder at Doc Rose, who was yanking open his car door and slipping inside, clearly irritated. *Fucker*.

"What's that?" I asked, glancing down at the book she was clutching in her hand.

"Oh, it's just a book Rose was telling me about."

"Really?" I took it from her hand, flipping it over to read the back. *What kind of stupid shit is this?* "Looks good. Mind if I read it?"

"You read?" Her eyebrow cocked up as she eyed me suspiciously.

"What kind of uncultured swine do you take me for?"

"Does it have anything to do with the pissing contest you have going with the doc?"

"Hungry?" I asked, changing the subject.

She pulled her mouth to the side, likely deciding if she was going press me further. She nodded, her high ponytail bobbing behind her. "Starving."

"You are insatiable."

"Have I told you it turns me on when you use big words?" she asked.

"You should see the other big things I use," I said, handing her the white sack.

I groaned, stretching my back at the end of my long shift. I couldn't wait to see Avery, but I had a few errands to run. I glanced at the book that had been sticking out of my glove box for the past two weeks. It was about time I got it back to Doc Rose. That asshole had been doing everything he could to get closer to Avery. I could only ignore it for so long. When he had put his hands on her hips from behind, it had taken all I had not to kick his ass all over the emergency room.

I had somehow kept my cool. I couldn't afford to lose my job and lose Avery in the process. If Doc Rose wanted to play dirty, I couldn't let him play alone.

I turned up the radio, drumming my fingers against the steering wheel as I headed up I-95 North toward Alapocas.

I didn't have much of a plan. My only goal was to remind the doc that he had just as much to lose as I did, whether he realized it or not. He had stopped pursuing her weeks ago and had begun to enjoy the arguments his flirtations would spawn. I'd dealt with his better-than type my whole life, but I'd be damned if I'd let him destroy what I had with Avery.

I parked along the curb of Doc Rose's house, killing the engine as I looked over the brick shaker-style home that I'd seen so many times dotting the Pennsylvania countryside. I'd pictured Rose in one of those Victorian-style homes that overran the squares in Gettysburg, but I was surprised to see that his home was much more modest.

I watched a light in the upstairs flick on, illuminating a silhouette before turning off. The entire downstairs seemed to be lit like they were having a party. Part of me hoped they were so I could out his slimy ass in front of all their uppity friends, too.

"Your electric bill must be fucking outstanding," I grumbled to myself as I opened my car door and made my way up the extra-wide sidewalk leading to a small, sloped entranceway.

I knocked, glancing around. As the sun sank below the buildings, the neighborhood was cloaked in darkness, making my visit feel even more ominous.

The door opened to reveal a woman, smiling with curiosity in her eyes and wrapping her thin, Robin's-egg-blue sweater across her torso.

"Can I help you?" she asked as the sound of something electronic caught my attention behind her. I glanced down at the young teenage girl, who rode up behind her in a red electric wheelchair. The woman shifted her body to block my view.

"Are you lost?" she asked.

I swallowed hard, regretting coming to Rose's home.

"Is it the pizza?" Rose's deep voice called from behind his wife as he stepped forward, rifling through his wallet and pulling out cash. When he finally glanced up, the tiredness in his eyes was immediately replaced with alarm.

The moment I saw the fear in his eyes, my regret melted away. This motherfucker was guilty.

"Josh." He tried to hide the surprise in his voice by clearing his throat. He clasped his hand down on his wife's shoulder.

"I got this, hon. Josh is a colleague." He pressed his lips to the top of her head as she slipped by him. The daughter followed her mom further into the house while Doc Rose closed the door behind him.

He looked down at the book in my hand, nodding slightly.

"I don't know what Avery has said to you, but I'm sure she has the wrong idea."

I swallowed back the apology and the guilt I'd felt for showing up at his home. "What does she think is going on, Doc?" I asked, gripping the book tightly to keep from punching him in his smug face.

"Avery is a nice girl. She's sweet and young, and she looks at me like I'm somebody special, not just the guy who plays nursemaid at home."

"You want *pity* now? Is that it? Man the fuck up. Whether you see it or not, you have a life most have only dreamed of."

He scoffed, shaking his head. I knew guys like him didn't expect to struggle, but no matter where we came from, life was cruel. I knew that firsthand. Bad things happened to good people, and sometimes, God liked to shine his magnifying glass down on the biggest ant just to watch it squirm.

"Sometimes it's hard to see the silver lining," he said.

"You have a wife, children, a home, and a six-figure salary. What more could you possibly want?" I tried to keep from raising my voice. His jaw tightened, and I widened my shoulders at the silent exchange between us. "Avery is off the table."

He smirked. "Is that a threat, Josh?"

"No. You won't be a very good doctor if you have two broken hands." I slapped the book against his chest. "That's a threat." I held his gaze for a moment longer before hurrying down his sidewalk and into my car. I needed to see Avery or I was going to lose my mind.

CHAPTER ELEVEN

Avery

Just as I stepped out onto the sidewalk, a golden leaf drifted from the maple tree that stood in front of my building, and rested on my sneaker. I pulled my scrub jacket tighter around me, looking for Josh's car. He'd just dropped me off from work, and then said he'd be right back, but he'd been gone for half an hour, and the sun was beginning to set.

Glowing Jack-O-Lanterns flickered on our stoop, and plastic ghosts hung from the trees lining our street. Night clouds were beginning to build in the west, making the breeze feel colder. Halloween was approaching, one of my favorite seasons, but fall felt wrong this year. I couldn't quite put my finger on it, but even with the chill in the air and the spooky decorations, I felt time slipping away from me.

An older car slowed to a stop in front of me and honked. The lime green practically glowed against the thick black stripe down the side. The car looked angry, and strong, and bright enough that no one would accidentally run into me again.

Josh killed the motor and then jumped out, grinning from ear to ear. "She runs!" he said. He patted the black hood with the palm of his hand before jogging to where I stood on the sidewalk. He squeezed me to his side, staring at the beast of a car like a proud parent.

"It's great," I said.

He turned to me, his eyebrows pulling together. The adorable double lines between them made me a little giddy. We were at that phase where every little thing he did was magical, and for the most part, he could do no wrong, but now he was looking at me like I'd just eaten his last favorite cookie.

"Great? She's yours, Avery. I've been working my ass off to get her ready for you."

"Mine?" I said in disbelief.

"I do not appreciate your dubious tone," he said, still frowning.

I reached up to smooth out the lines I loved. "You showed me an avocado-green beater. This is a shiny, um ... what is it?"

"This, my adorably clueless lady, is a 1970 Dodge Challenger in Sublime Green. A nice step up from the baby-shit color of your last car that was left smeared on the highway, I may add. She just needs a name."

"This is ... this is too much."

He placed his hands on my cheeks and kissed my forehead. "Sweetheart, for the bargain price of three ninety-nine and free labor your rather dashing, brilliant mechanic boyfriend gifted to you, this shiny Dodge fucking Challenger is yours."

I turned toward the Challenger in disbelief. "Stop. This isn't funny."

"I told you that you'd have wheels by your birthday, didn't I?"

"But ... my birthday isn't until next week," I said, still lost in utter shock and awe. I'd been a little down about the approach of my mid-twenties, but Josh standing in front of me, giving me the best gift I'd ever been given, trumped the pang of turning twenty-five.

He placed a cold set of keys in my palm. My jaw unhinged, my mouth hung open.

"Oh my God," I said, still staring. I blinked and then threw my arms around him. "Oh my God! I have a car?" I asked, leaning back to look him in the eyes. He nodded and I hugged him again. "I have a car! I'll pay you back. Every penny." I grabbed my penny necklace. "I love it! I *love* it!"

"You love the car? I'm getting kinda jealous," he said, his sweet grin wrinkling his five o'clock shadow.

I looked into both of his eyes, one after the other, back and forth, just like the girls in the movies. I wasn't sure which one I should tell the truth to. I wished I could look into both of them at the same time. "Don't be jealous. I've loved you longer than the car."

Josh laughed once, waiting for me to admit I was joking. The longer he didn't respond, the more nervous I got.

He closed one eye, turning his head to hear me from one ear. "You love me?"

I cringed, not sure what the right answer would be. "Yes?"

He pulled in a deep breath and then let it all out at once with a laugh. He tightened his arms around me and he buried his face in the crook of my neck. His voice was muffled when he said, "I'm just going to hold you for a minute. This is, um ... this is more new stuff for me."

"No pressure. You don't have to say it back," I said.

His head popped up. "Say it *back*?"

"I mean ..." I shook my head, feeling closer to vomiting every second. "You know what I mean."

Josh kissed me once, and then again, a tiny, slow kiss that meant something. "I've been saying it this whole time, Avery. You just haven't been listening."

I looked up at him, unable to stop the ridiculous grin spreading across my face. It was so much easier to fall for someone without pretenses, without worrying about judgment or rejection.

"Want to take her for a spin?" he asked, holding a set of keys in front of my face.

I took them, noticing two keys on the chain. A bigger, silver one, and a smaller one, older and brass in color. "Is this little one the spare?"

Josh scratched the back of his head the way he did when he was nervous. "I, uh ... thought you may want to let yourself in to my place whenever you want. I know Dax would love having you around more often, and a key ring with one key looked kind of stupid."

"You're giving me a key to your apartment?" I asked.

He shifted nervously. "Well ... yeah."

"Because your dog likes me and so my key ring doesn't look stupid," I deadpanned.

"No," he said, holding his hands over mine. "Because I want you to have it. It feels ... I dunno, like the next step. And that's where I was hoping we were headed."

"To the next step?"

He let go of me and shook his head. "Now *that* sounds stupid. This isn't going the way I'd hoped."

I held up the key ring, watching the sun reflect off the metal. "This is the best present anyone has ever given me."

He beamed. "I'm glad you think so. I wasn't sure I could pull it off at first, but I kept at it." He stood tall. "There's not much I can't fix."

I pulled Josh's shirt into my fists. He was wearing his light-blue short-sleeved button-up dress blues with a white long-sleeved thermal underneath. I was aware of how strange it was that something as simple as a thermal shirt could turn me on, but I pulled him toward my building.

A mischievous grin crept across his face. "Baby ... we've gotta meet Quinn and Deb in half an hour."

"Yep," I said, walking backward. I stepped up one stair, and then the next, continuing back until I reached the top of the stoop. I reached back, opening the door, but he held on to the doorjamb.

"Avery," he said softly, but my name was cut off when I covered his mouth with mine.

I yanked him through the entrance and up the flight of stairs to the second floor. I had already unbuttoned his shirt and was pulling up his thermal when my back slammed against my door.

Josh smiled against my mouth, pulling my keys from my hand and reaching behind me to unlock the door. He lifted me up, and I hooked my ankles at his backside as he carried me across the threshold. With a slam, he kicked the door shut, and then we were on the floor, frantically tearing at each other's clothes.

My skin burned as he yanked the denim down my legs, rough and careless. That is what I loved most about Josh: he didn't hold back. Everything he felt was raw, and passion was no exception. I gripped my scrub top and, in one motion, slipped it over my head. Getting lost with him had become my favorite thing. Josh wasted no time shoving my tank top up my stomach and over my chest, palming my right breast in his cold hand. My fingers trembled, fumbling to find the button of his jeans. Once the small piece of metal was in my hand, I worked frantically to free him from the confines of the fabric.

He backed away, his hand covering mine.

"Slow down, baby." He pressed his lips to my jaw, working

his way down my neck. I groaned in frustration as he chuckled against my skin.

"What are you? A sadist?" I asked, only half teasing.

He looked up with an innocent smile, the dimple in his cheek deepening. He stretched his neck to place a soft kiss on the tip of my nose.

"Avery," he whispered against my cheek, pulling on the drawstring of my scrub pants. "I want to do something with you I've never done."

I swallowed, imagining painful, wicked things that weren't at all comfortable. "Like what?"

He frowned, pushing up onto his hands to hover above me. "Do we really have to discuss it first?"

"Yes," I said without hesitation. "I'm a little nervous. There's not a lot you haven't done."

He looked away, brushing his chin against his shoulder. After a few moments of thought, he looked down at me. "I want to take my time. I want to look into your eyes and make love to you."

"That's sweet," I said, sincere. I touched his face. "Can we try that later?"

He made a face, clearly unhappy.

I reached down into his jeans, cupping his warm skin in my palm.

He held his breath.

"I need you inside me. We can take our time later when my thighs aren't screaming to be wrapped around you."

"Avery," he protested, his breathing labored.

I gripped his girth and gently squeezed. "Please."

His lips curved up into a wicked grin before he lifted his weight from my body. His thick fingers curled around my hips as he gripped my flesh so tightly I knew I would find purple marks that would last for days. With one swift movement, he flipped me onto my stomach, my knees sturdy on the thick gray rug, my palms slapping flat on the wooden floor.

Just outside the frosted windows of my apartment, the leaves had long changed and covered the ground. Inside my apartment felt like the height of summer. Beads of sweat formed along my hairline, and a thin sheen of sweat formed between my palms and the floor.

I listened to the teeth of his zipper slowly open behind me before he slipped his fingertips under the edge of my panties, twisting and tugging until the fabric bit into my flesh and gave way, leaving me exposed to him. He grabbed my hips again and pulled me back until I was completely on the rug. With his other hand, he guided my torso lower, directing me to rest my cheek against the soft carpet.

His warm body covered mine, his lips grazing my back as his tip teased my entrance.

My fingers knotted in the fabric of the rug, bracing for him. I bit my lip hard, trying not to beg.

He leaned forward, his torso covering my back. I tensed, hoping at any moment he would slide inside me. Instead, his lips ghosted along the shell of my ear.

My breathing became ragged the more desperate I grew for his touch. My insides ached, and just when I thought I couldn't stand it any longer, I backed into him. He moved away just enough to keep from me what I wanted. I groaned in frustration. "Jesus, Josh, *please*."

"This how you want it, baby?" His breath tickled my ear, causing me to shiver beneath his tight grip.

"Yes," I moaned, once again pushing back against him.

"Then tell me."

"I want you."

"Just me?"

"Of course just you," I said, exasperated.

He kissed my cheek, amused. "Say it again, Avery. Tell me you love me."

I looked over my shoulder. Josh brushed my hair away from my face and across my back. He kissed my bare shoulder, waiting patiently. He wanted to look into my eyes, in this vulnerable position, and watch me speak the words he needed to hear. And I would, because there was no doubt in my mind. "I love you, Josh."

He gripped my hips and thrust once into my slick entrance until he was completely inside me. I cried out, waiting for him to pull back and rock into me again.

He didn't move. Instead, he ran his palm over my backside, pulling back on my hip with his other hand, keeping himself submerged, savoring the moment.

After a few seconds, he began moving against me, slow and controlled.

"I love the way we fit together." He pressed his lips between my shoulder blades as he rocked his hips. "I love how your body moves in sync with mine." He pulled back again, this time almost out of me entirely before slowly rocking forward. I whimpered, arching my back. He ran the tip of his tongue just under my ear as he rolled his hips a little faster this time. "I love those sexy fucking sounds you make when you're turned on." His voice was strained. I wasn't the only one feeling tortured. His breath hitched and he groaned. He was at his limit.

"What else?" I panted, rocking at a steady rhythm with him.

"You, Avery," he breathed. "I love you ... so fucking much." He pulled out and flipped me onto my back, but before I could protest, he was inside me again, this time cupping my jaw and staring into my eyes while he came. He leaned down, pressing his lips hard against mine, kissing me deeply, as if he didn't know what else to do while the moment consumed him.

Once he stopped trembling, he leaned back, a tired grin on his face. He kissed me once more and then began rocking against me, still looking into my eyes. He reached down with one hand and hitched my knee to his hip, and then he tensed, sinking himself deeper inside me. He didn't pull back, instead moving his hips in small, slow circles, making my sensitive parts beg for more.

My eyes involuntarily rolled back and I sighed. "You feel so good," I whispered. At that rate, it would take me a long time to finish, but I could feel something boiling deep inside me, building slowly, something I wasn't sure I could handle.

Josh kissed and licked my neck, tasting my mouth, using a free hand to caress my face and hair. I hooked my ankles at the small of his back, allowing him even deeper, and he moaned. "Fuck, I think I'm going to come again."

Those words sent me over the edge, and I bucked against him, reaching around to press him deeper inside me, faster, harder. I cried out, and so did he, climaxing at the same time.

When the moment passed, his eyebrows shot up. "Holy shit," he said, panting. "That's definitely a first for me."

I covered my face, feeling overwhelmed and emotional. We were just having the best sex of my life, and now I was crying. It was humiliating, yet I couldn't stop.

"Avery?"

I shook my head, feeling hot tears fall down my temples.

"Baby." He pulled my hands away. "What's wrong?"

"Nothing. Please ignore me. I feel so stupid."

He took my hand and kissed my knuckles. "Tell me."

"Have you ever been so happy you don't know whether to laugh or cry?"

He shook his head. "Have you ever had something so amazing, you were terrified to lose it?"

I nodded, sniffing. He said exactly what I was feeling, even if I couldn't explain it myself.

"I'm not going anywhere," he said, using his thumb to wipe my tears.

My mind flashed back to the crash, feeling his hand in mine. "You've said that before … after the accident."

Josh thought for a moment and then breathed out a small laugh. "See? I meant it."

"Even if you didn't know it at the time."

"I meant it then." He bent down to kiss my lips. "And I mean it now."

I smiled. "Wouldn't be the first time someone promised to stick around. Sometimes you have to let go, whether you want to or not."

"Not me." He gestured toward the frame on my nightstand. "Why don't you ever talk about them? Why don't they call?"

I thought carefully about my answer. Giving away that part of me was a bigger step than key rings or cars. "My dad was driving my mom and me to dinner after high school graduation. We were laughing, making plans. All I remember after that was flashing lights."

His eyebrows turned in, and he swallowed. "How bad were you hurt?"

"Concussion. I was unconscious for twenty or so minutes." The news bothered him. I touched his face. "What?"

He shook his head. "The thought of you being hurt and alone in the car with your … your parents."

I looked away. "They were ejected. Mom died instantly. Dad went quickly. I didn't see them until the firefighters cut me out of the car."

"I won't say you were lucky, but ..."

"Good. Don't. I hate it when people say that."

He kissed my forehead. "Okay. Then I'll say *I'm* lucky. You survived. Twice. And now you're here."

I bit my lip. "You don't have to keep saying all of these perfect things. All you have to do is stay."

He scanned my face, staring down at me like he wanted to pick up every broken piece anyone had ever left behind. "I'll do both."

"Happy birthday to you," Deb sang, handing me a cupcake with pink icing.

I sniffed. "Strawberry shortcake?"

"You know it." She winked.

"Thank you, Deb."

I stopped in the center of the hallway, mid-step, closing my eyes tight. "Damn it."

"What?" Deb said, frozen.

"I'm either going to have to wear a pad or start bringing a change of panties."

"Was that Josh's present to you?" Her nose wrinkled. "Maybe you should stop being a cum dumpster."

"Actually, it was breakfast in bed, a scarf, and a heart key ring, and four months ago, you were begging me for details!" I said, offended.

"Four months ago, I wasn't getting laid. I have my own dirty sexcapades to get me through the day now, thank you very much."

I pointed at her. "You and Quinn? Since when?"

"Since I fucked him that one time."

"That one time," I deadpanned.

"Do you feel that?" she asked.

"Feel what?"

"The jealousy you're feeling for my amazing and very regular sex life. No, it's okay. Keep at it. It feels nice."

"I'm, um … going to the fourth floor."

Deb shot me a look of disgust. "For someone who hates babies, you sure like hanging out in the maternity ward."

"I don't hate them. The newborns are actually kind of calming. I make up stories about what kind of lives they'll lead and what they'll do when they grow up."

"You're freakin' weird," she said, and then headed for the waiting room.

I stopped at the elevator and pressed the up button. Dr. Rosenberg was already inside, holding a tall Yeti mug full of coffee. Steam puffed from the spout, and he waved it away with the thin stack of papers in his other hand. He was immediately uncomfortable, and he stepped aside, giving me plenty of room.

"Doctor," I said.

He nodded, pretending to look over the papers in his hands.

"Everything okay?" I asked.

"Yes, of course," he said, still staring at the papers. He wasn't reading them; they were upside down.

"Did I do something to upset you?" I asked. My mind went over every possible scenario. Maybe he was angry I was still seeing Josh, or maybe I had pissed him off during that morning's code. I couldn't think of anything.

"Reid," I said quietly.

He looked at me, and the elevator dinged. The doors opened to the maternity ward.

Dr. Rosenberg stepped out into the hall, stopping at the line of windows. The nursery only had a few newborns, flailing their arms or sleeping.

"I need to tell you something, but I'm not sure I should," Dr. Rosenberg said.

"Is it personal?" I asked.

"Yes. It's about Josh."

I sighed. "Doctor—"

"He came to my home, Avery. He told me to stay away from you."

My head snapped in his direction, but he continued to stare at the babies without expression, as if he'd just told me it may rain.

"You're lying." I didn't bother to hide the bite in my tone. I'd become fiercely protective when it came to Josh.

"You can ask my wife. And my daughter. They answered the door."

I blinked and then looked through the glass, blank-faced and feeling foolish. So many emotions swirled inside me I couldn't sift through them. A lump formed in my throat. "I'm so sorry," I managed to say.

"I should stay away from you, but because I care about you, I'm going to say this one last time, Avery. Josh has become dangerous. He's unpredictable, possessive, and emotionally immature. That can be a scary combination if you let this continue. Do you understand what I'm saying?"

I nodded, unable to look him in the eyes. My cheeks flushed. "He's not like that with me. He—"

"They never are until they are. You know as well as I do that it's a process. We see it every day in the ER. You think those women get punched and kicked on their first date? You think their husbands separate them from the people who care about them right off the bat? You know how this works, Avery. You're smarter than this.

"What I'm most worried about is that I can't help you anymore. I have a family to care for, and Josh has made it impossible for me to continue our friendship." He turned to me, sadness in his eyes. "I wish you the best. I really do. Good luck."

I wanted to tell him he was wrong about everything, but what he said made sense. I couldn't argue when part of me worried his assessment of Josh was true. "Th-thank you," I said. I watched him walk away like it was nothing. Like he hadn't just ripped my heart from my chest.

CHAPTER TWELVE

Josh

Avery's eyes were wide and full of fire as she slammed my apartment door behind her and slapped her key onto the countertop while I worked to prepare her the meatloaf she'd requested for her birthday, using Quinn's mom's recipe.

I glanced over at the cake I'd made and used a clean dish towel to cover the sloppy icing. It wasn't great, but stores didn't sell strawberry shortcake birthday cakes, so I'd had to do some research online.

"Bad day, baby?" I asked, tossing my oven mitt on the counter. I leaned against the peeling Formica, folding my arms over my chest.

"Depends. Do you consider being humiliated a good thing, Josh?"

I fidgeted to stall, trying to decide how to answer. Her question sounded dangerously close to a trap. "Um ... no?"

"I guess you didn't think that over when you went to Doc Rose's house."

"Fuck." I rubbed my palm along my taut jaw ... *I'm going to beat that prick's ass.*

"We're lying to each other now?"

"I didn't lie."

"You deliberately kept the truth from me. Omission is lying."

"I definitely didn't want you to find out today." I wiped my hand on a dish towel and reached for her. "It's not as bad as it sounds. I dropped off his book and we had a little chat. That's it. I didn't realize that the man was such a pussy he'd run and tell you. Especially not on your fucking birthday."

She folded her arms over her chest, and I braced for the inevitable fight, but nothing happened. She just stared at me with disappointment in her eyes.

"Look ..." I pushed from the counter and stepped in front of her. "If it makes you feel better, I'll talk to him."

"You've already talked to him. You mean you'll apologize."

I clenched my jaw, biting back the comments that came to mind. "No."

"*No?*" She glared at me, yanking her hands from mine.

"I won't apologize for fighting for what we have."

"If you already have it, you don't have to fight for it!" she seethed. "We've already talked about this, Josh. Jesus!"

I wasn't going to back down for something so ridiculous. I had been protecting what we had by making sure Doc Rose knew I wouldn't allow him to destroy it. She stomped into the living and I followed.

"Avery, I'm sorry if you were embarrassed. You're right. I should have told you. But he crossed a line. I probably did him a favor. If he keeps it up, he's going to lose his family."

She turned, her eyes glassed over and the corners of her lips tugged down. She sniffed. "Damn you. I defended you, and he was right."

"What?"

"We're not kids anymore, Josh. You can't threaten to beat someone up for eyeing your toy."

His face twisted in disgust. "You're not a fucking toy, Avery. I've never treated you like that. And he wasn't just eyeing you, not that it makes any of his bullshit okay. He has a family. You didn't see him smirking at me every time he was around you. He thought it was a game. You're not a game to me. You're my family. He may take his for granted, but I sure as fuck *don't*."

Avery's bottom lip quivered. "I don't need this."

"You don't need me." I said the words without emotion, trying to stay calm, but anger surged through me. "What the *fuck*, Avery? You know what? That's fine. I need you enough for the both of us."

"That's the problem," she blurted. "You're being irrational. You don't think things through. This is still new, you and me, and it's happening really fast. We need to step back for a second."

Slipping the penny over her head, she gritted her teeth and then shoved it at me.

I felt broken, like the moment had come when I'd finally lose everything. "For my thoughts?"

"No. I don't even want to know what you were thinking." She set the necklace down on the coffee table.

I stared at the necklace like she'd put a poisonous snake on my table. "Avery," I said, swallowing down the sudden panic. "You can't ... you can't just tell me you love me and then bail at the first sign of trouble."

She hesitated, mulling over what I'd said. I relaxed a tiny bit before she shook her head. "You wanted a girl like me, didn't you?" she said, wiping her cheek with her wrist. "Sensible, selective, and worthy? This is what girls like me do, Josh. We pay attention to the red flags, and you are a giant fucking red flag." She turned on her heels, slamming the door behind her.

"Fuck," I growled. I pushed up on the edge of the coffee table, flipping it onto its side before collapsing back onto the couch and burying my face in my hands.

I'd never let anyone in like I had Avery, and now I'd let her down. I knew going to Doc Rose's had been a dick move, and that was exactly why I hadn't told her what I'd done. But that didn't make it okay for her to just walk out on me. That wasn't what love was about. At least, that's what I thought.

I picked up the table and her necklace. I decided to try to distract myself with housework, but I kept running across things that reminded me of Avery. One of my pillows smelled like her shampoo, her razor was in the shower, her toothbrush in the holder, even the dish soap, which I changed because she preferred the green kind over the blue. I scrubbed harder and moved faster, but nothing worked. I kept thinking about the hurt in her eyes before she walked out, and guilt consumed me.

My apartment was cleaner than it had ever been, but it had never felt lonelier. Dax was sniffing at my feet, sensing something was wrong. I dug my phone from my pocket as I pushed to my feet and began pacing the floor, careful not to trip over Dax, who was anxious to get my attention. I hovered my finger over the screen, trying to decide who to call. If I called Avery and she didn't answer, I knew I just may lose my fucking mind.

I dialed Quinn's number instead. Being alone with my thoughts was never a good idea.

He answered after three rings.

"I fucked up, man." I ran my hand over my messy hair and continued to pace.

He groaned, and I could tell I'd woken him. "What did ya do now, dumb fuck?" he asked during a drawn-out yawn.

"She left me. Avery fucking *left* me."

"What?" he yelled. I could hear a female's voice grumbling in the background.

"That Deb?"

After a scuffle, Deb's voice was crystal clear on the other end of the line. "It better be Deb or your friend here would be two apples short of a picnic if you smell what I'm stepping in."

I closed my eyes, keeping my voice low and even. "Please put Quinn back on the phone."

With an exasperated sigh, there was some muffled noise before Quinn was back on the line.

"I went to the doc's house, Quinn."

Quinn chuckled. "You did what? Because if I heard you right, that was idiotic, brother, even for you."

"I know," I said, rubbing the back of my neck, pacing while I spoke. "But he's married. His fucking wife answered the door."

"Whoa, Josh. You need to think about this. Doc Rose's family is none of your business. I love you, man, but you crossed the line."

"He crossed the fucking line!" I snapped.

"Josh," Quinn said, keeping his voice calm. "You have to trust Avery to handle it. You can't control everything."

"I know," I said. My lungs weren't getting enough oxygen, and I sat, struggling to breathe as Dax pawed at my leg.

"It's going to be okay," Quinn promised. "She's mad now, but she'll forgive you. Deb is nodding her head. She agrees with me. She loves you."

"Yeah?" I said. I covered my face, unsure whether he was placating me or being sincere.

"Yeah, man. Get some rest. It'll be better tomorrow."

We hung up, and I trudged to the bedroom, falling onto the mattress fully dressed. The coils squeaked, and I groaned. Something else to remind me of Avery: her sighs when we were naked about where I was lying now. I stared at the ceiling, praying to fall asleep, and then glanced through the doorway at the hutch in the living room. I promised myself never to drink for any other purpose than entertainment, but getting just drunk enough to sleep was very fucking tempting.

I sat up and looked at the clock. Both hands were on the eleven. I looked at the hutch again and then pulled out my phone, dialing Avery's number. It rang several times before her voicemail picked up. "Please call me back. I don't wanna fight, I just want to ... I'd like to at least apologize. You can do whatever you want with it."

I hung up and looked at my watch for the dozenth time since she'd left. She wasn't at work. There were very few places she could be at that time of night.

I grabbed my wallet and headed down to Corner Hole. She wasn't going to call me back, and I couldn't sit around and wait. After she heard what I had to say, I would give her some space, if that's what she wanted, but I couldn't walk away from us.

I shoved my hands deep into my jeans pockets to protect them from the crisp air, thankful for the oversize Adidas hoodie Avery loved to claim as hers on cold nights.

I hurried down the block to my car and drove straight to the bar. The door opened and closed, letting in the cold night air. The radiator rattled, struggling to keep up. I scanned the crowd, looking for a head full of long, honey-blonde hair, recalling the first night I'd seen her there. After several minutes and no sign of her, I sat at the edge of the bar and ordered a double Jack Daniels.

"You look sad," Ginger said. "You sure?"

I hesitated and then waved her over. "It's cold as fuck in here. Keep them coming." The bar wasn't that busy, but at least I was around other people. The last thing I wanted was to be alone.

I drank my shots, thanking Ginger for her generous hand as she poured. She leaned forward, pressing her ample breasts against the bar as she asked me what was wrong. I averted my gaze, assuring her everything was just the way it was supposed to be. The luck of my shiny penny had worn off. I pressed my palm against my chest, feeling the cold of the metal against my skin, keeping her close to my heart.

I ordered another round for myself and retrieved my phone from my pocket, dialing Avery's number again.

I drank down one shot while I listened to her chipper voicemail greeting.

You've reached Avery Jacobs. Please leave your name, number, and a brief message, and I'll get back to you.

After the beep, I began to ramble. "Baby, I know you're mad at me. I deserve it, okay? I deserve for you to yell at me and be pissed, and even for you to throw your necklace at me, but I don't deserve to get dumped. I'm a fuckup, but I can fix this. It's what I do." I rubbed the heel of my hand against my eye before tipping the next shot glass to my lips.

"Don't be so hard on yourself, sweetheart," Ginger said as she shook her head and refilled my glasses.

"Bending over like that won't get you a bigger tip," I joked, my words sounding like my tongue was swollen against the roof of my mouth. I nodded a thanks to her and picked up another one and a half ounces of Jack, draining the contents down my throat. My heart sank as the liquor began to weigh heavily in my veins, slowing my entire thought process. "I love you, Avery. I don't think you understand what it means when I say that to you, but I do." I clicked to end the call, knowing that as the alcohol slowly took hold I would probably only upset her more.

I drank a third shot and peeled off my sweatshirt, feeling overheated in the small crowd. I tossed it on the bar, and Ginger rolled her eyes as she took it and hung it on a hook behind her.

"What did you do to that poor girl?" she asked as she set a tall glass filled with water in front of me.

"What's with this shit?" I asked as I pushed it away in disgust, ignoring her question.

"You need to slow it down. There's no way in hell I'm carrying you out of here."

"Just throw me away with the trash," I mumbled, feeling sorry for myself. I could have just as easily defaulted to anger, but I was the only one to blame for my situation.

Ginger shook her head, filling another shot glass. She held out her hand. "Keys."

"What?" I said, wrinkling my nose.

"Keys," she said, this time more firm. I dug into my pocket and pulled out thirteen cents, a piece of lint, and my car keys. She took them, and I lifted the tiny glass in thanks before tipping it back.

The night crawled along minute by painful minute with no sign of my girlfriend. I was set to wander out in the freezing cold just after midnight when a smug Doc Rose walked in.

I watched him chat up a few other men who were also stupidly overdressed for a hole-in-the-wall bar. They must have been doctors, too. He waved to them and then sat on a stool at the opposite end of the bar, checking his watch, as if he were waiting for someone.

Part of me hoped it was Avery he was waiting for; the other hoped to God it wasn't, worried what I'd do if it was.

"You okay?" Ginger asked.

"If Avery walks in and sits next to that puke," I said, holding myself up by the elbow. "Get me out of here before I kill him."

"You think he's here for her?" she asked, staring at Doc Rose.

"I've got all night, so I guess we'll find out. Pour me another one."

"Josh—"

"I said pour me another one."

She shook her head, placing an empty glass in front of me.

CHAPTER THIRTEEN

Avery

I spent the evening drowning in guilt and then being mad about it. I shouldn't feel bad. I was right. He shouldn't have confronted Dr. Rosenberg. I'm an adult. I could have handled it! *What the hell was he thinking?*

But I hadn't handled it. Josh had told me a dozen times my friendship with the doctor bothered him. I should have addressed it. But Josh had made his choice. This was my career he was messing with. How could I look Dr. Rosenberg in the eyes and tell him I'm still with the crazy guy who threatened him over nothing?

I washed the three dishes in my sink and then went to JayWok. After looking at the menu, I decided I wasn't hungry and walked back, stomped up the stairs, and slammed my door behind me. I crossed my arms in a huff, wishing I didn't have the day off.

The look in his eyes fractured my heart. Being alone in my apartment, looking at my former spare pillow that was supposed to belong to Josh, I was an emotional mess.

My phone rang, and I picked it up, unable to answer it fast enough.

"Deb?" I said, my eyes instantly filling with tears.

"The hell, Avery?"

I sighed. Josh must have already called Quinn.

"I could have handled the situation better," I admitted. "I could have discussed it with him instead of acting like a spoiled soap opera wife. I mean ... good *God*, handing back the necklace and stomping out? I am supposed to be the reasonable one, and he kept saying practical things like *we love each other* and I couldn't *just end things*. He was right, but he was fucking wrong!"

"Yep."

I paused, surprised. "Yep? That's all you have to say?"

"Avery, keep venting. You're not done."

My bottom lip trembled. "I shouldn't have handed him back the necklace. That was overdramatic. That was cruel."

"Uh-huh."

"Uh-huh I'm cruel, or uh-huh you're acknowledging that you're listening?"

"The latter."

"So, I screwed up. But a jealous toddler tantrum?" I said, pacing. "We are too old for that. He confronted Dr. Rosenberg! That was fucking insane!" I tripped over the edge of the rug and then kicked at the rolled up corner. "I went there thinking we were going to make a mutual decision to take a step back and slow things down, but the next thing I know, I'm breaking up with him! I broke up with him, but I still love him. What do I do?"

"Um ... get back with him? He still loves you," she said, sounding bored. "He sounded like he was a fucking mess when he called Quinn. All you have to do is forgive him and he'll learn his lesson and you can keep being gloriously happy."

I stuttered. "Is it that easy? I mean ... people just do that?"

"Yep."

I thought for a moment, looking around the room at my

empty walls and pillow-less couch and curtain-less windows. Josh's pillow was my favorite thing in the apartment. There was a reason for it. I'd made my point—albeit rather dramatically. Couples fought and made up all the time. We could, too. Maybe.

"He made his bed," Deb said. "You should lay in it."

I raked my hair back, flustered. "Would you date a guy like Josh? Who did what he did?"

"Fell in love with a girl and freaked the first time someone threatened to steal her? Oh yeah."

"Deb," Quinn said, sounding sleepy in the background.

"You okay?" Deb asked. "Say the word, and I'll be over. Quinn snores, anyway."

"No," I said, sniffing. I looked out the window at the green beast parallel parked in the street in front of my building. "I'm going to find him."

We hung up, and I put on my navy-blue puffy coat and boots. I grabbed the keys with the heart key ring Josh had bought for me and a scarf, wrapping it around my neck while I jogged down the stairs.

I passed my car and shoved my hands in my pockets, watching my breath puff out in front of me while I walked the three blocks to Josh's building. His car wasn't there, but I buzzed him anyway and waited. He didn't answer.

I waited on the porch until my teeth began to chatter, and then started down the steps.

"Hey, Avery," Cinda said, passing by. "Did you lose your key?"

I cringed. "Gave it back."

"Oh," she said, glancing back to his empty parking space. "I don't think he's home."

"Do you know where he went? You don't have to tell me."

"I know Josh, and if you gave back your key, I'm sure he's

not happy about it. He probably said something stupid, am I right?"

I shrugged. "We both said something stupid."

She smiled. "I bet he'd want me to tell you where he is." She pulled her mouth to the side. "But I don't know. I'm sorry. You can come in and wait at my place until he gets home."

"That's okay. Thanks, Cinda."

I trotted down the stairs, running all the way to my parking spot.

The Dodge growled to life when I twisted the ignition, and I pulled away from the curb, turning toward St. Ann's. Corner Hole was just a half-mile from the hospital, and that was the only place I could think Josh would be if he wasn't home or at Quinn's.

The Dodge grumbled before I killed the ignition and lights. There were only a few cars left in parking lot, including Josh's. I was suddenly nervous.

What are you doing, Avery?

I looked forward and pulled on the lever. I loved him, and we were going to have to weather some bullshit. We all had garbage to pack away. I couldn't expect Josh to do a one-eighty and maintain perfection at all times to boot. That wasn't fair.

Gravel crunched under my boots as I walked toward the brick veneer of Corner Hole. A fluffy white flake fell on my nose, and I looked up, seeing a million matching pieces of frozen sky pouring from the black above. I closed my eyes and smiled, hoping Josh would come outside with me so we could share our first real snowfall together.

I pulled open the door and walked in, smelling stale beer and cigarette smoke. The golden glow of the jukebox in the corner was the main source of light besides the lights strung above the bar. I smiled, thinking of the night Josh had made me stop hating Christmas.

Only a few men were sitting at the bar, none of them Josh. I sat on the middle stool, watching a new bartender washing a glass with a white cloth. He walked over to me, his pecs flexing under his tight black V-neck. His eyebrows were perfectly manicured, so when he leaned over, pretending to flirt, I didn't take him seriously.

"You're new," I said.

"Yes."

"Avery."

He smiled. "Oh, *you're* Avery. Happy birthday."

I narrowed my eyes at him. "Thanks."

"Jesse," he said.

I placed a twenty-dollar bill flat on the counter. "Here's your tip. I just want a Diet Coke."

"Keep 'em coming?" he said with a smirk.

"Just the Coke, please. Oh, and ..." My words trailed off when I noticed my favorite soft hoodie hanging from a hook behind the bar. At first, I sat up taller and looked around with a ridiculous smile, but it disappeared when I saw Michaels stumble out of the men's bathroom, her lipstick smeared, her hair disheveled, tugging at her slutty skirt. She glanced around, wiping the sides of her mouth with the back of her hand.

I focused on the hoodie and then Michaels as my stomach twisted. "He wouldn't," I mumbled under my breath. The door opened again, and I froze. "Oh, fuck." My mouth fell open. Relief and then disgust washed over me in waves.

Dr. Rosenberg tried to seem nonchalant as he made his way across the bar, his cheeks flushed and his fly down.

"Avery," he said, stumbling to a stop. He smelled like whiskey and bad choices. "I didn't think you came here anymore."

"Looking for Josh." I leaned away from him a tiny bit,

unable to hide my revulsion. I looked away, hoping Josh would walk in at any moment and save me. He had been right about Dr. Rosenberg all along. Just because the doctor had a family didn't automatically make him a good man. Josh didn't try to hide his conquests, and the whole of St. Ann's thought he was a player, an asshole. The real snake was the beautiful doctor with the wedding ring and the house in Alapocas.

"Avery?"

"What?" I snapped.

Dr. Rosenberg had the gall to act surprised. "Is something wrong?"

I looked down at his open fly, and then away. "No."

"If you're looking for Josh, he's upstairs."

"Upstairs?"

"With Ginger. He's drunk." He eyed the lights hanging from the ceiling. "Drunk doesn't adequately describe his state, actually. I tried to warn you about him."

"Why would he be upstairs with Ginger?" He was a liar, and liars lie. I had already made one mistake by believing him. I wasn't about to fall for it again.

He shrugged. "She lives above the bar."

"*Ugh.* You would know. Zip up your pants and go home to your wife."

Dr. Rosenberg stiffened and then looked down, quickly pulling up his zipper and then making a beeline for the door.

Jesse used his soda gun to fill my glass, pretending he hadn't overheard our conversation.

"Where's Ginger?" I asked.

"Upstairs," Jesse said.

I nodded, wondering if I really wanted to ask my next question. "Is she alone?"

"Tell her, Jessepoo," Michaels said, crawling onto the stool next to me.

I recoiled and then groaned in frustration. "For fuck's sake, can this day get any worse?"

"Josh is up there. I was trying to take him home, but he wasn't having it," she said with no shame, slurring her words.

I snarled my lip, leaning back so she couldn't breathe in my face.

"Ask him," Michaels said, her drunken eyes slowly looking to the bartender.

Jesse shook his head. "Don't put me in the middle. I need this job."

I placed both palms on the bar, pressing my lips together in a hard line. "Jesse. You would want to know if you were me, wouldn't you?"

Jesse looked up at me from under his long lashes and then shrugged one shoulder in concession.

"Is he up there with her?" I demanded.

Jesse wiped the counter with a rag in a large circle, trying to keep the guilty look off his face. That was all the answer I needed to know. I nodded once and then stood, my knees feeling like they may buckle under the weight of his silent confession.

"Don't take it personal, honey," Michaels said. "If it makes you feel better, he wasn't interested in anyone until he could barely walk."

Jesse reached across the bar. "He wasn't interested in anyone at all. He asked for you at least a dozen times the first twenty minutes of my shift. I think he's probably up there passed out. No man can get it up when he's that wasted. If he's not unconscious, he's vomiting. Either way, he's not doing what you think he's doing."

My head fell. "So, what? I go home and hope he's not fucking her brains out?"

"If I were you," Michaels said, swaying on her stool.

"Careful," Jess said, pointing at her.

She waved him away. "If I were you, I'd go up there. But it's the hair," she said, pointing at the orange frizz piled on her head. "We do crazy shit like that."

"If I were you, I'd close my legs for five minutes and invest in a decent bra," I mumbled under my breath.

I left poor Jesse with Michaels and then passed the bar, pulling on a wide brown door.

"That's storage," Jesse said. He gestured to a gray door in the back next to the jukebox, painted to blend in with the wall. "That's hers. Knock, please, and don't cause a scene."

"Thanks, Jesse."

"Don't thank me yet," he said, pouring another drink for Michaels.

My feet moved slowly. Every step grew more difficult the closer I came to Ginger's door. I opened it between songs, making the creaking of the hinges seem amplified. Before me were twenty or so dusty stairs, at the top another door. I climbed quietly, although I wasn't sure why. If he was mid-thrust, I certainly didn't want to catch them in the act. My stomach roiled at the thought of someone else beneath him.

When I reached the door, I knocked—quietly at first—and then again. I used the side of my hand to knock the third time, and then I could hear rustling around.

"Ginger," I heard Josh groan. "Ginger! There's someone at your fucking door!"

I swallowed against the lump in my throat, already feeling tears well in my eyes. I knocked again, and then Josh's feet stomped across the room. The door swung open, and he blanched.

"Avery," he said, his bloodshot eyes wide. He was in a T-shirt and boxer briefs, as if he'd made himself right at home.

"I just, um ..." My words caught in my throat. "Wanted to see for myself."

I turned, but before I took the first step, Josh grabbed the hood of my coat and tugged me backward. "Wait!"

I flipped around, slapping his hand away. Before he could speak, I held up my hands. "Just! I don't want to cause a scene. I know. This," I said, gesturing to his underwear, "is your thing, and we just broke up. You running to fuck something to feel better isn't surprising."

"Ouch," he said, struggling to focus. His eyes were rimmed with red, his face blotchy. "I guess I can see why you'd assume that, but you really think I'd do that on your birthday? C'mon, Avery, give me a little bit of credit."

I nodded once. "Sorry," I said, and then began to turn for the stairs.

"Avery?" he said. I stopped. "Did you see my car outside?"

"Yeah."

"Did you come in here looking for me?"

I hesitated, but it was better when we didn't pretend. "Yes."

His voice was low and controlled. He was being careful. "I didn't sleep with Ginger. She just brought me upstairs to sleep off the whiskey. I came here looking for you, too. That should tell us something, right?"

"Who is it?" Ginger asked, poking her wet hair and bare shoulders out of the bathroom, a thin yellow towel wrapped around her.

I looked at her, and then to Josh, devastation settling heavily in my chest.

He held out his hands, shaking his head, desperation in his eyes. "Baby ..."

A half-smile quivered on my face. I began to speak, but there was nothing left to say, so I simply turned around and jogged down the stairs, running across the bar. My keys jingled as I readied them to unlock the car, and while I fumbled for the right key at my door, Josh yelped.

"Ow! Fuck!" He hopped on one bare foot, holding the other, still in his T-shirt and boxer briefs.

I finally found the key and twisted the lock, opening the door.

"Avery!" Josh barked. "Fucking wait!"

A handful of people in the parking lot turned toward the scene he was making. I cowered under their curious eyes.

Josh pointed at me as he limped over the rocks. "Don't you open that fucking door, Jacobs!"

I stood tall, exasperated. "Why not? We're obviously not good for each other, Josh. What the hell were we thinking?"

He carefully navigated the gravel under his tender feet, breathing hard when he finally made it to the Dodge. He pushed on the hood to support some of his weight, his breaths puffing out in quick, transparent clouds.

"That I love you," he panted. "I love you, and I wouldn't do that." He pointed up toward Ginger's upstairs apartment. "It *never* crossed my mind. All I think about is you. Do you hear me, Avery? There is no one else. There will never be anyone else. You can shove that necklace down my throat and laugh while I choke on it, and I still wouldn't run out to fuck someone else. The only thing that will make me feel better ..." He panted, his face tinged with a pale shade of green. "... is you."

He shook his head, grabbing his knees as he tried to catch his breath, and then he heaved, expelling everything in his stomach.

"Jesus," I said, watching the liquor and whatever else splatter on the ground.

He heaved again, and I awkwardly patted his back.

A creaky, dirty yellow cab pulled into the parking lot, the tires crunching against the gravel. The window rolled down and I smiled, surprised.

"Mel!"

"I thought you might need another ride."

"I'm sober. I'm giving him the ride."

Josh glanced up to see the wrinkled veteran staring down at him with a frown and then heaved again. "You're taking me home?" Josh asked.

I reached into my pocket, giving Mel the money I owed him. Mel narrowed his eyes. "What's that?" he rasped.

"The money I owe you. I'm sorry it's taken me this long."

He waved me away, unimpressed.

"Please," I said, holding out the bill.

He snatched it out of my hand. "You sure you don't need a ride? You might need a chaperone with this one."

Ginger ran out in a robe and fuzzy boots, carrying his pants, hoodie, and wallet. "We didn't do anything!" she yelled across the parking lot. "Don't leave!" When she reached us, she noticed the puddle of vomit on the ground and made a face, holding the backs of her fingers to her nose. "Oh, gross. I'm so sorry. I knew better than to let him drink that much."

Josh made another hurling sound and more liquid came up.

"How much did he drink?" I asked, helping to steady him.

"I'd have to look at his tab. Pretty sure he spent his whole paycheck."

"Pussy," Mel grumbled, lifting up his hat and then pulling it back down. He pulled his shifter down. "You still got my card, sweetheart?"

"Still got it," I said with a smile.

Mel pulled away and Josh vomited again, this time leaning

so far over he almost fell face-first into the puddle below.

"Damn it, Josh," I scolded him, rubbing my palm against the tensed muscles of his back.

His arm shot out and he held my leg, spitting and groaning.

"Avery," Ginger said. I looked up at her. "We didn't. I couldn't let him drive. I did pull off his jeans because he'd spilled a shot on them and they stunk and I didn't want it on my sheets. But if you go upstairs and look, you'll see that I'd made me a pallet on the couch."

I looked at Josh, unconvinced.

"I know how he feels about you," Ginger said. "I wouldn't do that to him."

"And," Josh said, still bent over.

Ginger smiled and rolled her eyes, handing me his things. "*And* Michaels tried to persuade him several times that she was ready if he was willing, and he made it clear he was only going home with *you*."

"You're a good boy after all," I said, running my hand over his back in a small circle.

He swallowed. "Yes, but if you keep doing that, I'm going to puke again."

"Sorry," I said, grabbing his arm and reaching around his back to guide him.

"Where are we going?" Josh asked.

"I'm taking you home," I said, walking him to the passenger side of my car.

Ginger winked at me before walking back to the bar.

"Ginger," I called after her. She stopped, her hand on the door as she turned around. "Thanks for taking care of him."

Her smile grew, and she nodded before disappearing inside the bar. I slid into the driver side, looking to my right. Josh had already leaned his seat back, his arm thrown over his eyes.

I leaned over, covering him with his hoodie.

He peeked at me with one eye. "I wish I didn't feel like shit. I so want to hold you right now."

"Shower and toothpaste first, then I'll think about it," I said, pulling the gear into drive.

Josh reached over, feeling blindly until he found my hand and then squeezed. "Thank God," he whispered, pure relief in his voice. "Thank God."

CHAPTER FOURTEEN

Josh

It had been seven weeks and four days since I thought I was going to lose the one person in the world who saw me—the *real* me.

That moment was enough to make me realize I should definitely never take eight shots of hard liquor on an empty stomach, but more importantly, that I wanted to spend the rest of my life with this girl.

I wanted to prove I was serious and committed to her, but I knew it would take more than a penny, even though since the second she'd put it back on, she'd cherished that necklace as if it were one of the queen's jewels.

"I can't believe you're going to propose, man." Quinn glanced over at me from the driver seat of the ambulance with a grin on his face.

"Like you haven't thought about it," I shot back. The wagon rocked back and forth after Quinn hit a pothole too fast, and I reached for the overhead handle.

"What Deb and I have is different."

"Judging by that weird fucking swing she had you put in your bedroom, I'd have to agree with you."

We laughed, but it did little to settle my nerves as the

diamond ring I'd picked out for Avery burned a hole in my pocket.

I'd never pictured myself settling down with anyone, but now it felt like the world would crash and burn around me if she didn't say yes. *Why was I so scared?*

Quinn's expression turned serious. "Can I ask you something? Something you may not like?"

I frowned. "Sure."

"What's your hurry, brother? It's been what … six months?"

"I don't know. It's like an itch in a place I can't quite reach. It's this vague worry in the back of my head. It's always there."

"Like what?" Quinn asked, his nose wrinkling.

"That if I don't nail this down, she's going to disappear. Sometimes, when I'm lying in bed with her, I feel like she's there, but she's not. Like it's literally too good to be true."

"That's just your insecurities talking, man. Avery is in love with you. She sees how much you've changed. She knows you think this is something special."

I shook my head. "That's not it, Quinn. I know she loves me. I'm not worried about her."

"Then what?"

I shook my head. "I don't know. Like something's just on the edge, waiting to fuck things up. Something out of my control."

"You can quit worrying, Josh. We control nothing."

I grimaced. "You're not making me feel any better."

Quinn took one hand off the wheel and slapped my shoulder. "You'll be fine. She's going to say yes and you'll live happily ever after."

"Hey," I said, pulling his hand off me. "Keep your hand on the wheel."

He sighed and shook his head. "It's already started."

"What do you mean?"

"I'm your first partner, so I get why you don't see it. See, the guys start out here, and they inevitably find a serious girlfriend, because—" he popped his collar "—the uniform gets 'em wet."

I rolled my eyes.

"Then the worry starts. They quit running toward the burning cars, they start wearing their seat belt, they start saying pussy things like 'Keep your eyes on the road, Quinn,'" he said, lowering his voice. "Like before you got engaged or had a kid you didn't have anything to live for."

"I didn't."

"*Psh*. Pussy."

I smiled, never so grateful for an insult.

My shift ended, and I hurried over to Benched for a workout. Lifting always helped clear my head, but even after an hour and sweat pouring from my body, my head was still consumed by thoughts of Avery. It had been that way for weeks, which was why I bought the ring. Nerve-racked or not, I had to make it official, had to make her mine. I just needed it to be perfect.

With my thoughts overrun by planning for our future, I hurried back to my apartment to prepare dinner, knowing Avery would be too tired to cook when she finished her shift.

I'd picked up a few groceries the day before. Now that Avery had been spending more nights at my place, I tried to keep more in the fridge. Unfortunately, I lacked any real cooking skills, so I was attempting to make spaghetti, which didn't look like it could be that hard.

I was just dishing the noodles onto plates when Avery walked in the door with a groan. Her ponytail had slid down to the nape of her neck, and dark circles shadowed the underneath of her eyes, but she still looked beautiful in her peach scrubs.

"That shift was never-ending," she huffed as she kicked off her sneakers. She padded her way to the kitchen, rising up on her toes to kiss my cheek.

"I hope you worked up an appetite."

"*Mmm* ... what's that smell?"

"That's not very nice. Dax can't help his ... aroma."

Avery laughed, shaking her head. "I thought you couldn't cook?"

"I figured it was time I learned." I grabbed both of our paper plates and carried them into the living room, placing them on the coffee table. "We need to get a real table."

Avery looked at me sideways with an amused smirk before she picked up her fork and began to spin the noodles. "A table? You don't even have real plates."

"Neither do you." I elbowed her lightly, taking a bite of my food. *Damn, I'm not a bad cook after all.* "Maybe we can buy a set at The Kitchen Store this weekend."

"Plates?"

"Why not? Normal people have dishes. They also have this really cool silverware made out of metal."

"Yeah." She breathed out a laugh. "But those people live together, Josh."

"You're right. We can move your stuff in this weekend. I can get Quinn to help. We can get dishes and a table next weekend. And a strainer. You don't even want to know what I had to do to strain the noodles," I said, hoping to God she didn't freak out.

Avery dropped her fork, her mouth gaping open. "Seriously?"

"I mean, I'd have to ask him first, but he wouldn't mind helping out if he doesn't have plans with Deb."

"So, you're going to ask Quinn. How about asking me first?"

My heart felt like it seized. I slowly turned to her, swallowing hard. "Avery," I began, nervous as hell. "Move in with me."

She placed her small hands on either side of my face. "On one condition."

"Name it."

"My apartment is at least ten years younger. How about you move in with me?"

"Yeah," I said without hesitation.

"Maybe we should think about this for a week or so. We shouldn't make a decision like this without really thinking it over."

"Avery, I've thought about it. A lot."

"You have?"

"You haven't?" I asked, feeling nervous all over again.

"It's a big step."

"I know this is what I want. I don't wanna waste any more time."

"Living together can really be hard on a relationship."

"I'm starting to wonder if it's you who isn't sure about us."

"It's not *us* I'm unsure of. It's the living together, family … the entire idea just makes me nervous. I don't have a lot of good experience with family."

"You have me," I said, feeling hurt. Avery was all the family I'd ever needed, and as far as I was concerned, we already were. "We can make family a good memory for us, Avery. I thought that's what we've been doing."

Her shoulders sank. This was so unlike Avery that I wasn't sure what to do. I had known from the beginning a relationship with me scared her, but after everything, I'd thought we were past that.

I lifted her chin with my finger, forcing her to look me in the eye. "What can I do?

"What do you mean?"

"I'm not giving up, so tell me what I need to do to make you okay with this."

"There's so much we don't know about each other. I haven't even met your parents."

I visibly cringed. I wasn't expecting that at all. "Avery, that's not a good idea."

"Are you ashamed of me?" she asked.

"What? No, hell no," I said.

"Then why?"

"It's hard to explain," I said.

"Something I'd have to see for myself?" she asked.

I closed my eyes. "You don't know what you're asking."

"How are we supposed to live together if you don't trust me to love you? I'm not going to judge you because of your parents, Josh. I know you don't judge me because of mine."

My eyebrows pulled in. "Your parents died, Avery. How could I judge you for that?"

"Because I lived, and they didn't."

I blinked then shook my head. "Don't say that. It was an accident."

"So was ours, but it's still my fault. Don't think I don't remember pulling out on a red light."

"Stop," I said, watching her eyes gloss over. "I don't want you to blame yourself for either. What good would it have done if you'd died with your parents? They wouldn't have wanted that, Avery."

"I know," she said, picking at her nails. "But I thought you'd understand."

"Understand what?"

"Feeling guilty. We were both kids."

I stood. "Oh, no. You can't compare the two. And this isn't about me."

She reached for me, but missed.

"Don't do that."

"Do what?"

"Bring up my sister to avoid talking about your parents." I felt my cheeks warm, and I began to pace. It was a strange feeling, wanting to hold her and walk out at the same time.

She shook her head. "That's not what I'm doing."

"You sure?"

She blinked, looking around the room, as if the answer were in the corners. "I would be a horrible person if I were."

"You've been doing it your whole life, Avery. I know exactly how it is. I don't blame you, but you have to stop."

"I'm sorry," she said, her voice breaking.

"You don't like talking about them. You've barely said a word about them, but you can talk to me."

"What else should I say?"

"That you miss them. How it affects your life now. How it affects us."

She lifted her hands and let them slap against her thighs. "I miss them. Being forced to let them go made it impossible to hold on to anything. I could let go of Deb, my job. I could let go of you—right now, if I wanted—and not bat an eye." She covered her mouth, shocked at her own admission.

A shot of adrenaline rushed through me. "Avery ..." My teeth clenched. "Do you love me?"

"Yes," she said without hesitation.

Every one of my muscles relaxed, and then I pointed at her phone. "Call work. You'll need a four-day weekend."

Her hands slowly lowered from her face. "Why?"

"I'm taking you to Savannah to meet my parents."

Avery was fidgeting with her yellow skirt that hung just below her knees. She was nervous about meeting my mother, and the icy road conditions did little to calm her fears.

Thankfully, we were heading south, where ice and snow wouldn't be an issue.

"Are you sure this is okay?" she asked for the tenth time as I pulled off the highway, into a gas station.

"Yes."

I could feel her watching me as I put the car into park next to a pump.

"You've barely said anything in the last hour," she said.

"Sorry. I've been thinking."

"About what?"

I sighed loudly, rolling my neck from side to side, needing to stretch my stiff muscles. "A lot of stuff, baby. Do you mind getting us snacks?"

She thought for a moment before she smiled and shook her head, causing her messy bun to bob back and forth.

I handed her a twenty from my wallet. "Could you grab me a vanilla Frappuccino while you're at it?"

Avery took the bill from my fingers and pushed open her door. She walked across the lot, giving me a reprieve from her line of questioning. A couple of guys noticed her tiny skirt that was barely visible beneath my Adidas hoodie, and I bristled.

I got out of the car and began pumping gas while watching Avery through the large glass window of the gas station. She hated road trips, but she was excited to drive down with me to meet my family. I struggled to create a better memory for her, knowing what waited for us in Richmond Hill. I was dreading having to see my mother again. Last time I had been home, she was falling down and incoherent for the majority of my visit. But, if enduring her for a few days would make Avery happy, then I would gladly suffer through her presence.

While I waited for my tank to fill, I pulled out my cell phone and called my mom. After several rings, she answered, uncertainty in her tone.

"Hello?"

I squinted one eye, already regretting the call.

"Hello?" she said again.

"I'm coming home for the weekend," I blurted out.

"Josh? This weekend? You could have let me know a few days ago. The house is a mess." I rolled my eyes, pinching the bridge of my nose. My mother hadn't cleaned her own home in years. She paid someone to come do it every few weeks.

"I'm not worried about the house. I'm bringing a friend." I glanced up at the window to see Avery standing at the cash register, waiting to pay. "Is that going to be a problem?"

She was silent for a moment before responding.

"Of course not. Your friends are always welcome here."

I mumbled a good-bye before disconnecting the call.

Avery returned, smiling brightly with her hands loaded with candy. "I thought you said it would be warm when we hit South Carolina?"

"I said it would be warmer. I told you not to wear a dress."

She narrowed her eyes as she handed me my drink and made her way to her side of the car, slipping inside.

I hung the gas nozzle back on the pump and pressed the heels of my hands against the top of the car. I needed a second to get my head right before climbing into the car next to the girl I was trying to marry.

"I just wanted to look good for your parents."

Rubbing my palm against my stubbled jaw, I spoke without looking at her. "I know, baby. I'm just ... a little stressed."

"If you don't want me to meet your parents—"

"It's not that, Avery. It's my mom. She's going to make this weekend hell."

"I can handle one weekend." She touched my leg. "Nothing she can do will ever change the way I feel about you. You know that, right?"

I recoiled from Avery's sympathetic frown. Her feeling sorry for me was the last thing I wanted. I didn't want her settling for the pathetic paramedic with a sad story instead of choosing Italian leather and a house in Alapocas. Even if she didn't want to admit it, that fantasy sparkled in her eyes every time she looked at Doc Rose.

"Josh," she prompted.

"I may have ... downplayed Mom's drinking problem. Last time I saw her, she could barely function."

"Oh ..." She fell silent.

"It's okay, Avery. You didn't know. I didn't tell you how bad it was. I haven't told anyone," I said, sighing.

"Josh—"

"It's not a big deal, Avery. I should have told you. It's just a tough topic."

"But it is ... a big deal," she said. "If you want to talk more about it, you can trust me." She blinked her big green eyes, hopeful.

From the beginning, my past had been off limits. To Avery, talking things out made everything better. "Trust has nothing to do with it. I just don't want to keep reliving it."

She opened her mouth to speak, but saw me readjusting my grip on the steering wheel. I started the car and headed to the on-ramp of I-95.

"I'm sorry. I didn't mean to push."

"I know you want to help, baby, but there isn't much to say."

"You're stressed. I just thought that maybe talking about your mom would make you less worried about seeing her."

Stepping on the gas, I hurried to get up to speed with the other drivers. I drifted in and out of the passing lane as my memory was assaulted by visions of my childhood.

"She never recovered from losing Kayla. Their marriage suffered because of it. Nothing was the same after that. It was bad, and then it got worse. A lot worse. She turned to vodka, and he turned to other women."

Avery's fingers pressed into my leg. "That's awful."

I tossed those words around in my mind. *Awful. Was it?* She had checked out of our lives years ago. Not only had she withdrawn from me when we lost Kayla, but she had completely ignored my father. He was hurting too, and she had forced him to grieve alone. I didn't blame him for seeking companionship from other women. He had suffered as much as she had, but he had been forgotten.

"He never blamed me. Not once."

"Because you were a little boy, Josh."

"They should have gotten a divorce a lot sooner than they did," I said, picking at the steering wheel.

"Maybe they were afraid to lose anyone else."

I glanced over at her, seeing a familiar, old hurt in her eyes. "Dad was finally able to make peace with the fact that his family could never be the same. That's when he bought our first Mopar, a sixty-eight Dart GTS in Rallye Red with a 383 Magnum. We worked on it together every free moment we had. She was beautiful. When she was finished, Dad sold it and bought a sixty-nine Frost Green Road Runner with a big-block. We found comfort in restoring old cars. It was cheap therapy. I don't know what I would have done without my dad."

"Do you have to see your mom every time you visit your dad?"

"No, I guess not, but I feel like I should. She makes it harder than it has to be. She blames me, with every drink, every glare, every breath. Probably why I don't come home as often as Dad would like."

Avery covered her mouth and shook her head. "I am an asshole. I should have talked to you more before insisting we come here."

I offered a small grin. "You were right, though. You need to know what you're dealing with before you shack up with me."

"That's not why," she said, shaking her head. "I just thought maybe ... if I met them, somehow things would get better. That's stupid, I know." She became more flustered with every word.

I looked over at her, her cheeks pink, her eyes glossed over. I was complaining about having parents when she didn't have any.

"Jesus, Avery. *I'm* the asshole." I took her hand in mine, pulling it to my lips and pressing a kiss to her fingers.

"No, I get it."

"You ... you wanna ..."

"Talk about it?" she asked with a knowing look. She raised an eyebrow. Damn it if she wasn't rubbing off on me.

I shook my head and squeezed her hand. "I'm just nervous. You know that, right? I'm honestly not purposefully being a dick to you. If I didn't think it was important, I wouldn't be so worried."

"You're supposed to be trusting me," she said, squeezing back.

I glanced over at her and then let my shoulders relax. "Okay. Let's do this."

She beamed, and I pressed my foot on the gas.

"I wasn't sure you were really coming," Mom said as we stepped inside the living room. I could tell she was as nervous as I was, and the smell of bourbon wafting in the air around her didn't escape me.

The paint, carpet, and furniture still looked the way it had when I lived there.

"Mom, this is Avery. Avery, this is my mother, Mary."

Mom grinned, pulling Avery in for a tight hug. "You are a pretty little thing," she said as she pulled back, looking her over.

I could tell Mom was shocked that the *friend* I had brought home was female. I could have told her I was seeing someone, but I hadn't called her since the accident.

"Pleasure to meet you." Avery's voice shook, but she kept a smile on her face. It occurred to me why she was nervous. She wasn't judging me, or even my parents. She wanted this to be perfect because she loved me. Guilt panged in my gut from what a jerk I had been for most of the trip.

"I expected you earlier," Mom said as she made her way toward the kitchen. I slid my fingers in Avery's and gave her hand a gentle squeeze as we followed. Mom's back was to us, but I could tell by the sound of glass clinking she was refreshing her drink.

"You didn't know I was coming until a few hours ago."

"It's my fault. I made him stop at least a dozen times," Avery said.

Mom smiled at Avery, but once she glanced in my direction, her lips pressed into a hard line.

"Well, at least you made it." She shook her head in disapproval as she picked up a tea towel, folded it, and dropped it back on the table.

"Did we miss dinner?" I asked, rubbing my thumb over the back of Avery's hand.

Mom laughed. "You know I don't cook."

"I'll order something, then. We haven't eaten. You have a menu for Wok n Roll?"

Mom pulled open a kitchen drawer, sifting through a few menus before holding one out to me. Avery's eyes lit up at the thought of Japanese food.

"They don't deliver anymore. You'll have to pick it up," Mom spoke as she swirled the amber liquid in her glass.

"No problem."

"Are you hungry?" Avery asked, her voice almost shrill.

"Whatever," Mom said, waving us away. "Just something, I'm not picky."

I pulled Avery from the house, unable to walk fast enough. Once we sat in the car, Avery touched my knee.

"You okay?"

I nodded, pulling back my cheeks to form some sort of a smile.

"You don't have to pretend for me. It's okay. We can leave if you want."

I looked down. "If you're looking to marry into a new family, mine isn't it, Avery. I shouldn't try to cheat you out of that."

"You're my family, remember? And I'm yours."

I kissed her knuckles and started the engine, pulling out of the drive and onto the road. "We should stop by Dad's."

"Is he close?" Avery asked.

I breathed out a laugh. "Just down the road."

She smiled, and I made a detour to my father's home. I hadn't let him know I was coming. Part of me had been afraid that after Avery met my mom, she'd want to go home.

When I pulled off the main road onto the dirt path leading to his trailer, I felt like I had been gone too long. I grabbed Avery's hand and squeezed.

"You look happy," she observed with a surprised grin. "Thinking about dinner?"

I parked my car next to my dad's flat-black Impala and turned off the engine. "But you're getting ready to meet the best damn cook this side of the Mason-Dixon."

My father stepped out onto his porch as we exited the vehicle, his grin widening as he recognized who had come to see him.

"My boy," he called out proudly as he hurried toward me with open arms. I grunted as he pulled me in for a bear hug that knocked the air from my lungs.

"And who is this?" he asked as he pulled back from our embrace.

"Dad, this is Avery. Avery, this is Silas, my father."

"Wow," she said. "The resemblance is incredible."

"Your name is Avery?" Dad asked, fighting a laugh. "You've got to be shittin' me."

"God has a sense of humor," I said.

"He sure does. That's how you got this ugly mug," he shot back, winking at Avery.

The worry in her eyes had all but disappeared, and she seemed more like the girl I'd fallen in love with.

"We don't look that much alike," I said. "My hair isn't gray." I laughed as my father hit me lightly on the chest with the back of his hand.

"Watch it, boy. I can still kick your ass," my father warned.

He grabbed Avery in a playful hug, lifting her from the ground as she squealed.

"You wish, old man."

With Avery's feet firmly planted back on the grass, we fell silent as he took us in.

"It's been too long, Josh."

"I know." I nodded in agreement as I looked over his old Impala.

"But I see you've been taking care of Mabeline." He nodded his chin toward my car. "I must have taught you somethin' right."

"Avery, if he's half as good to you as he is to that car, you're one lucky lady."

She looped her arm in mine and snuggled against my side, and I felt a little taller, seeing her so happy, and maybe even a little relieved to be around my dad.

"He's a good man. He works hard. I'm very lucky. You should be very proud."

"I am." Dad's smile wrinkled the skin around his eyes. "Did Josh ever tell you about the time he grabbed the neighbor's horse fence and pissed himself?"

"We gotta get back to Mom's," I said, rubbing my hand roughly over my hair.

Avery struggled to keep a straight face.

"You'll be back before you leave?" His question was more of a warning. I nodded, letting him pull me in for another hug.

Avery spoke up as he released me and embraced her. "I will make sure of it."

"All right, old man. That's enough. Let my girl go."

Dad stepped back as he looked us over, nodding approvingly. "You did good, son. You did real good."

"Thanks, Dad, but I already knew that," I said with a grin. I hooked my arm around Avery's shoulders and walked with her back to the car.

After stuffing ourselves with sashimi, teriyaki chicken, and chicken fried rice around Mother's kitchen table, Avery went into my old bedroom to take a quick shower.

Mom was stumbling around the kitchen while Avery dressed for bed. Avery groaned from the bathroom, and I knocked on the door.

"Everything okay?"

"Fine!" she said with the chipper voice she only seemed to have around my mom.

I joined Mom in the kitchen, watching her pour herself another drink.

"Hey. Why don't you ease up since Avery's here," I chided.

"Mind your business," she grumbled.

Avery appeared, forcing a smile. She waved me away when she saw the concern on my face.

"You look a little green, young lady," Mother said, talking with her glass of bourbon.

"Fine," Avery said, sitting at the table. "I feel fine."

"Well, you don't look it," Mom snapped.

"Jesus Christ, Mom. C'mon."

Avery shook her head, silently asking me to stand down.

"How was the drive down?" Mom asked. "Besides the constant bathroom breaks, of course," she said, eyeing me.

"Fine," Avery said, pressing her lips together. A thin sheen of sweat formed on her skin. She swallowed.

"Baby," I said, reaching across the table.

"I'm f—" Before she could finish, Avery covered her mouth and ran down the hall to my room. Sounds of her heaving traveled to the kitchen, and Mom shot me a smug look.

I chased after my girlfriend, stopping in the bathroom doorway. The mirror was still fogged from her shower.

"Go away, please," she whimpered, spitting into the toilet. "Oh, God ..." She heaved again.

"You were feeling fine earlier. Maybe it was the candy?"

"Food poisoning. Has to be the Japanese," she said before hurling again. "I'm dying. I'm going to die."

"I'll get you a cool rag."

"Thank you. Then please leave. I don't want you to see this. It's going to get ugly really fast."

I rubbed her back, knowing exactly what she meant. I wouldn't want her to see me like that, either.

I fetched her a cold rag and then shut the door behind me. "I'm going to check on you in ten minutes," I said through the door.

"Please don't."

I pulled back my old gray and black comforter, and then placed a garbage can on the floor. Mother was still in the kitchen, watching me search through the cabinets for a clean glass.

"For fuck's sake, Mom. Glasses."

"Watch your language," she said. "Water bottles in the fridge."

"You have something to say?" I asked, grabbing two bottles of Aquafina.

"I didn't say anything."

I spun around to see her struggling to light her cigarette from a match, her eyes nearly closed.

I sat the bottles on the counter and took the matches from

her. She watched me with a frown and heavy eyes as I effortlessly tore one away from the matchbook and lit it for her.

Leaning toward the flame, she puffed and then exhaled, enveloping her face in a cloud of smoke before inhaling and choking out a cough.

"I know something is on your mind. Spit it out."

"She's sick, huh?" Mother blew out a cloud of smoke and I waved it away.

"She'll be fine by morning. It's been a long trip. The cigarette smoke isn't going to help, if you're wondering."

"I wasn't," she said, blowing out another puff. "So, this is why you're really here? You got another girl knocked up and now you want my help." Still the mother I remembered. After Kayla had drowned, she didn't enjoy life sober.

I laughed once. "You can't be serious. How could you help anyone in this shape?"

"I'm not pregnant." Avery's voice was quiet.

I spun around to see her leaning against the kitchen wall in one of my T-shirts and basketball shorts, her chin beginning to quiver.

"Avery," I breathed. I grabbed the bottles of water and walked toward her. When I reached out for her, she held up her hand to keep me back.

She took a water from my hand. "I feel better. I'm going to bed."

"I'll come with you," I said.

I glared over my shoulder at my mother, hoping it would be the last time I'd have to look at her.

Following Avery to my room, I twisted the lock on the knob while I watched her climb under the covers.

"Avery, I'm not sure what you heard, but ..." I shook my head, unsure of what I was going to say.

"Don't." There was no anger in her voice, just exhaustion. She stilled, her back to me.

I peeled off my shirt and then kicked off my shoes and jeans. When I slipped into bed, I was careful not to bounce her around. I wanted to wrap my arms around her, but I didn't want to make things worse.

"This was obviously before we met." She glanced over her shoulder and I closed my eyes. She'd heard it all.

I nodded in confirmation.

"Then hold me." I slowly wrapped my arms around her, pulling her back against my chest. Her body stiffened, but she didn't pull away.

She was silent for several moments. Seconds had never passed by so slowly. She breathed in, and then said the best thing I'd ever heard.

"I love you."

I pressed my forehead against her back. "I love you, too."

"We should probably talk about it … when you're ready."

I nodded. "I'm ready." I took a deep breath. "Her name was Brooke. A buddy from high school named Daniel introduced me to her one night at a party the summer after we graduated. Daniel went to an alternative school. He'd been held back twice, barely graduated, already had a kid somewhere—bad news all around. Brooke was Daniel's tutor through most of that. She'd just finished her freshman year of college, so of course I thought I was hot shit when she started flirting with me.

"Daniel broke it to me that she was pregnant a month later." I breathed out a laugh, still in disbelief. "We'd only spoken once since that night. Neither of us was interested in a relationship, but suddenly, we were attached for life. I never pressured her to get rid of it. I never even brought it up."

Avery tightened my arms around her.

"I was a scared kid, sure, but never once did I try to sway her one way or the other. Daniel was dying to swoop in and be her savior, constantly offering his shoulder to cry on. I went to her first appointment, and then ... I freaked. I needed space. She wanted me to be her rock, but I didn't know how. We got into a huge fight. We both said things we didn't mean. I left town for one night and turned off my phone.

"When I turned it on the next morning, she'd left me a message. She was going to a clinic. I tried to call her. I called her a dozen times, but she wouldn't ... she wouldn't fucking answer," I said, feeling suffocated by the memory. "I got stuck in traffic, and by the time I got there, she'd ... she ... it was over. It was done. She never spoke to me again."

The room was so quiet it hurt.

"Avery?"

"I love you."

My breathing faltered and my eyes burned. "There's more."

"I'll still love you."

I gritted my teeth, trying not to break down, and then told her everything about the day Kayla died, and everything after.

I spoke about my childhood and college and everything in between. Avery listened and loved me through it all. I talked until my voice felt like sandpaper, until I fell asleep with her in my arms.

When I woke, my hand roamed over cold, bare sheets. My heart sank at the sudden realization that I was alone.

Tossing off the comforter, I pulled on my jeans, tugging my shirt over my head. I nearly tripped while slipping on my sneakers. My legs wouldn't move fast enough as I tried to hurry from my room. Once I reached the living room, I froze at the sound of Avery's voice.

She hadn't left me. I spun around to see Avery and my mother sitting at the kitchen table, drinking coffee and chatting.

"Morning," Avery called out to me. She pulled one of her knees to her chest before taking a sip from her mug. "I made coffee."

I rubbed my hand hard against the back of my neck, struggling to process what was happening. Not only had Avery stayed, but she seemed to be having a pleasant conversation with my mother.

Walking across the room, I bent down and pressed my lips against her forehead, letting them linger for an extra second.

"How are you feeling?" I asked.

"Better." Her sweet smile put me more at ease.

I stood, glancing over at Mom. She looked everywhere but at me, trying to avoid eye contact. It was nice to know she hadn't lost her conscience.

Grabbing a mug from the cupboard, I filled it with steaming coffee and sat next to Avery. She explained to my mother what she did for a living. As Avery described nursing school and her shifts in the ER, Mom listened intently and seemed to actually enjoy it.

It was hard to pay attention to their words as I watched Avery in awe, wondering what I had done to deserve someone so understanding.

We would be different on the way home ... *our* home. The next step was to ask her to marry me. I just had to restrain myself from proposing the second we walked in the door.

CHAPTER FIFTEEN

Avery

An hour had passed since Quinn had radioed ahead that they were bringing a teenage boy in critical condition to St. Ann's. When the ambulance arrived, Quinn and Deb pushed the stretcher through the ambulance bay doors. Josh was straddling the patient on the stretcher, chanting numbers as he counted chest compressions. I helped Deb with vitals as Dr. Rosenberg rushed in.

Forty minutes after the patient arrived, I reached up and grazed a cloth across Josh's sweaty brow, noticing the green and red decorations on the ceiling.

"You need another break?" I asked, tending to the head wound.

Josh shook his head.

"You've only had one," I said with labored breathing. Sweat had glued my bangs to my face, and the room was buzzing with organized chaos.

Josh refused to give up, still on the stretcher, using his entire upper body to help his arms ward off muscle fatigue.

"He's gone," Dr. Rosenberg said. "I'm calling it."

"No, he's not!" Josh said, continuing.

The ECG picked up a single sinus rhythm, and then another peak blinked on the monitor. Everyone froze.

Deb held her fingers to the teen's neck. "No pulse."

"Resuming compressions," Josh said, placing the heels of his hands in the proper position and working even harder. "He's coming back. He's gonna come back."

"What are you doing, Josh?" Dr. Rosenberg asked. "It's a GSW to the head."

"It's Christmas!" Josh snapped, panting. "He's a fucking kid, and his mom's waiting on us to come tell her he's going to be okay!"

"Fine, one more," the doctor said, pointing to me. "Epinephrine."

I flicked the preloaded syringe twice and then stabbed the IV port with the needle, administering one milligram of epinephrine.

Josh continued compressions for three more minutes, and then Deb checked for pulse and rhythm.

Deb's brows pulled together. "Asystole, Doctor."

Josh leaned over the boy again, positioning his hands. "Resuming compressions."

"Enough, Josh," Dr. Rosenberg ordered.

The staff's eyes bounced between Josh and the doctor.

Dr. Rosenberg yanked off his gloves. "Time of death, one twenty-two a.m."

Josh's jaws twitched under his skin. He'd heard the doctor, but ignored him and continued compressions.

I glanced at Dr. Rosenberg, worrying that if he felt like he'd lost control of his ER, Josh would lose his job.

I reached out and touched Josh's arm, leaving a bloody handprint on his skin. "Josh, he's gone. Enough."

Josh leaned back on his knees, winded. Sweat poured from his hairline. He used his forearm to wipe his brow, smearing dark blood across his skin.

We all looked at the monitor, hoping for a miracle. Nothing but a flat line streamed across the monitor.

"Goddamn it! Stupid fucking kid!" Josh yelled.

"Josh," I said, standing with my arms out to my side, my scrubs covered in blood.

Josh kicked the tray table, knocking it over, his eyes wild. Everyone but me backed away. "Avery! Out!" I yelled.

Josh shouldered his way out of the room as the rest of the staff stood around the boy, just fourteen.

The X-ray tech backed out of the room with her portable machine, and the respiratory therapist followed. Deb printed out a final rhythm strip showing the flat line, and one by one, staff members removed tubes and began cleaning up the mess.

"I'll go speak with the family," Dr. Rosenberg said.

"Doctor," I said, stopping him. "Might want to change first."

He looked down, noted the mess on his coat, and then nodded.

"I'll finish up," Deb said.

I pulled off my shoe covers and gloves and nodded to her, wiping my face with the back of my wrist. I walked out of the room, down the hall, and turned the corner, looking for Josh. He was sitting on the break room floor, his back against the wall.

I knelt in front of him. "You can't do that."

"I know," he growled.

"Look at me," I said. His head snapped up. "You can't pull that in my ER, understand?"

His shoulders fell and he looked away, nodding. His jaw shifted to the side. "I'm sorry. It's just that it's ... it's fucking Christmas. He blew his brains all over the Christmas tree with his mom's new pistol."

"I know," I said, wishing I could say something more

comforting, but there was nothing rational about what had happened to that child.

He wiped his wet cheek and sucked in a breath, his face crumbling. "I feel like a fucking pussy."

"It's okay. Everyone deals differently."

"Baby," he said, reaching out to wipe my face.

I leaned away from him. "I've got it. I'm going to get cleaned up. Make sure you debrief at the station."

I stood, looking down at the large crimson splotches on my scrubs.

"Yeah?" I confirmed.

He nodded again, indignant. "Yeah, yeah, all right."

"See you at home."

Josh's bottom lip trembled for a moment, and then he sniffed, stood, and shook it off.

We all had our reasons for doing this kind of work. Josh's compassion ran deeper than even he knew. He didn't do it for the money or the glory. We had shitty hours and even shittier pay, but at the end of the day, Josh could go to bed knowing he had helped someone, and for him, there were few things more important than that.

The women's locker room was decorated in cheap red and green decorations. Most of the lockers bore pictures of the nurses' children or nieces and nephews. Mine was empty but for one black and white photo of Josh and me at Quinn's mom's house on Thanksgiving. I walked past the lockers and into the bathroom, pulling my scrub top over my head and tossing it into the red biohazard box.

In the mirror, I noticed dark spatters and smears on my face, and the blood that had bled through to my sports bra.

My eyes stared back at me, dull green with dark circles underneath. Pieces of blonde hair had fallen from my ponytail.

The rest of the staff was a mess, too. We had all worked hard the last hour to save that boy, but sometimes, no matter what we did, we couldn't fix everyone. Not even Josh.

I pulled off my scrub bottoms and then turned on the faucet, watching the sink turn red while I washed my face and arms. I dried off, feeling the weight of disappointment and heartbreak, knowing not even a fraction of what I was feeling could be compared to the loss felt by the boy's mother.

I gripped the sink, choking out a cry. After that first sob, my entire body shook, and I gave myself five minutes to grieve for the boy I never knew. My watch counted down the minutes, and then I washed my face again and dressed in fresh scrubs, ready to do my best to help the next person in need.

Michaels pushed through the door, her eyes puffy and red. "Good work, Jacobs."

"Thanks," I said, unable to make eye contact. I walked past the room, the doors closed and family present. Just as the mother began to wail, I grabbed another chart and pushed through the double doors to the waiting room. "Charles?" I called and smiled as a woman pushed her elderly husband's wheelchair toward me.

Josh was waiting for me after my shift. He stood, still in his navy-blue T-shirt with the white logo and navy-blue cargo pants, bundled in a matching puffy coat. He pulled his ball cap low over his eyes, huffing out a cloud of crisp air when I approached.

"Hey," I said, crossing my arms over my middle. "How long have you been out here?"

He shoved his hands into his pockets. "I had Quinn drop me

after we clocked out. Risking sounding like a huge vag again, I didn't want to be at the apartment alone."

I slipped my arms under his, pressing my cheek against his chest. The strong scent of whiskey assaulted my nose. I leaned back. "How many?"

"Just one, after work. It wasn't even my stash, it was Quinn's." He smiled and then shrugged when I didn't respond. "It's fucking cold out here."

I pulled out my keys. "Let's go home."

Josh opened the driver side door for me and swept his arm toward the seat. I smiled, sat, and then leaned across the seat to open his door.

He sat, rubbing his gloves together while I attempted to start the car. It whirred three times but didn't start.

"Shit," I groaned, slapping my palms against the steering wheel.

"Try it again. She's just cold. Don't pump the gas. Let her turn over a few times and then stomp it to the floor."

I did as Josh instructed, and the Dodge started right up, blasting icy air from the vents. I breathed out a sigh of relief and then turned to him, smiling. "Brilliant. You're brilliant."

Josh scrambled to turn off the fan and then rubbed his gloves on his thighs. "Home, baby! Shit, it's cold!"

I giggled, shifting the car into gear, pulling out of the parking lot, and making my way to the highway. Traffic was ridiculous, with last-minute holiday travelers. The Dodge inched forward, and I shook my head. "It was bad enough that we both had to work on Christmas. I just wanna get home already."

"At least the heater's working," Josh said, patting my knee and forcing a smile.

"It was a bad night," I said.

Josh nodded, somber. "I'm sorry I yelled. And kicked over the instrument table. And stormed out."

"Deb said she's seen doctors do the same thing. Doctors who give a shit. Not Doc Rose," I qualified.

Josh grinned at me. "You called him Doc Rose."

"So? *You* call him Doc Rose."

"As an insult. I've never heard you say it before."

I shrugged. "It fits."

"Do they still call me McPanties?"

"No. At least, not to my face."

Josh chuckled and leaned back. "One more mile 'til our exit. Sweet baby Jesus owes us a Christmas miracle."

"It's our first Christmas together," I said, smiling at him.

"It's our *second* Christmas together. Knowing now that we had to work, I'm patting my back for the first one."

"You should. It was perfect."

"I have something up my sleeve for this one, too. Don't you worry, baby."

"Oh yeah? Like what?"

"You'll see," he said, his grin growing wider with every foot we rolled forward.

Twenty minutes later, we reached our exit, and I pulled off. It only took another ten to reach our apartment building, and I parked behind Josh's Barracuda.

He hooked his arm around my neck, pulling my hair against his lips. "Are you excited?"

"I can tell that you are," I teased, bumping him with my hip while he unlocked the door. He chased me up the stairs, and then we paused in the hallway, panting and smiling.

He unlocked our door and I pushed him in. After saying hello to our furbaby and giving him a Christmas treat, Josh walked over to the Christmas tree and plugged in the lights, standing to face me. The rest of the apartment was dark, adding to the magical feel.

"Is it lame that it isn't technically Christmas anymore?" he asked.

"It's still Christmas in California," I said.

He looked at his watch. "No, no it's not. But we can pretend."

I flitted to the tree, sitting on the floor with my legs crossed. Josh sat next to me, handing me the first present. "You first." He ruffled the dog's hair, pure exhilaration in his eyes.

"Then you, right?"

"As you wish."

I giggled while I tore open the orange paper with green spiders. "Spiders?" I asked.

"It's one of the things on your list." He winked, and my heart melted at how thoughtful he was, and how much effort he still put into fixing our memories.

I peeled back the paper to reveal a cardboard box stamped *Amazon*. "Books?" I asked. He didn't answer, so I lifted off the top of the box, looking closer. There was another box, this one smaller. I raised an eyebrow. "Really?"

"Just open it," he said with a smile, taking a deep breath.

I opened one side and then pulled out clear plastic packaging. I looked up at him with a smile. "It's a watch!"

"It's not *just* a watch. Google says it's the number one nurse's watch. It has antimicrobial bands and backing, and the numbers and hands glow in the dark!"

"Ooh!" I said, squinting.

He grabbed it out of my hands and gave me another. "Next."

I set it down and pulled one of his presents from under the tree. "Your turn."

I wrinkled my nose and smiled as he tore open the paper,

not nearly as daintily as I had. He held it up with a huge grin. "It's a watch!"

I cackled. "Not *just* a watch. It's a freaking Rolex!"

"Baby." He shook his head. "It's too much."

"I saved. We're good."

He grabbed each side of my face and planted a firm kiss on my lips. "We really were made for each other. Open yours. I'm dying here."

"This is fun, isn't it?" I said, wiggling with anticipation. I picked up the box he gave me and opened it. I looked up at him, confused. "What is it?"

He smiled.

"Is this a joke I'm not getting? It's empty."

He reached over, plugging in another extension cord. The rest of house lit up. The doors, windows, and even the floorboards were aglow in every color of the rainbow.

He tapped his phone, and our song began playing from a speaker across the room.

I clapped. "*Ah!* I love it!"

"That present isn't actually yours," he said. "I just didn't have the heart to tell you."

"It's not?"

He shook his head. "It's the dog's. I got him a new collar."

"You did?" I squealed, looking out our baby's new bling. Something scratched my hand, and I turned the collar. "A new tag, too?"

"No." Josh chuckled. "Not a tag."

I tugged on it gently, and the whole collar came loose. "Oh, no!" I panicked until I saw the gold band with the small but perfect princess cut diamond between my fingers. "Oh, my Go— Josh?"

"Avery Jacobs," he said, shifting to get on one knee.

"Oh, my God," I breathed, unable to say anything else.

"I ..." he blinked. "I had this all planned out, and my mind just went blank." He laughed and then rubbed the back of his neck.

I laughed and covered my mouth with one hand. "Josh!"

"I'm so damn nervous. To hell with it, Avery ... Will you marry me?"

I stared at him, unable to move, unable to speak without sobbing.

"I know it's too soon. I tried to wait, I swear to God, but ... I love you more than anything, Avery. I mean that. More than *anything*. I haven't been able to think about anything else but putting a ring on your finger."

I threw my arms around him, tears streaming.

"Is that a ... is that a yes?" he asked while Dee jumped on his back.

"Yes!" I said, leaning back. "Yes."

Josh slipped the band on my finger while I wiped my cheek with the other hand.

"Don't cry, baby," he said, using his thumb to wipe my eyes.

"I love you so much," I said, sniffing. "I'm just so happy that you love me. And ... I'm going to be Avery Avery."

I meant for it to be funny, but he scanned my face in pure adoration. He took my cheeks in his hands, shook his head, and sighed. "The words just don't seem enough anymore." He pressed his lips to mine, kissing me under a thousand twinkling lights. *At last.*

CHAPTER SIXTEEN

Josh

Long after the last flake of snow had melted and the final patch of ice had evaporated into nothingness, Avery was still struggling to plan the perfect wedding. Our schedules never seemed to let up, making nailing down the details difficult. Avery insisted on a summer wedding, wanting to wear her dress without shivering. I just wanted to be able to call her my wife—*mine*.

Pinching the bridge of my nose, I tossed the estimate for the cake onto the kitchen table. "This is ridiculous, babe. No cake is that good."

Avery stood in front of the stove, the morning sun pouring in the through the window and casting a glow over her hair. "I've tasted her cakes. They're good, but it's not so much about the cake as the appearance."

"We can just have our reception down at Corner Hole."

She turned to face me from the stove, a spatula her weapon of choice. "You want to have our wedding reception at a dive bar?"

"A dive *what*? That's blasphemy! You *love* Corner Hole."

"Yeah, baby. I love it for an after work drink and to unwind. Not the place to celebrate the rest of our lives together. They don't even serve food."

"We can order from JayWok."

"JayWok?" Her eyes threatened to pop out of her skull. "You want Japanese takeout for our wedding? Really, Josh?"

"Another thing you love. Now it's not good enough? Who are you trying to impress? This day is supposed to be about us. No one else." I pushed up from my seat at the table and wrapped my arms around her waist from behind.

She shoved the scrambled eggs around the pan. "I'm sorry." She sighed as her shoulders sagged. "I don't know what this wedding has done to me. I've *never* cared about any of this kind of stuff. I just ... It's an important day. *Our* day, about us and the beginning of our marriage. I want it to be perfect."

Pushing her hair over her right shoulder, I pressed my lips to the back of her neck. "It will be perfect. Going into debt over a cake is not a good way to start our forever."

She sniffed once. "I would just hate to let anyone down, and—"

"What *asshole* is going to be let down by *our* wedding? You're too stressed out, baby. What can I do to fix it? Let me help." I turned her around to face me, wrapping my arms around her waist. She tucked her face into the crook of my neck and inhaled deeply.

She shook her head, her whining muffled against my skin. "You can't fix this."

"I can fix anything."

"I don't have anyone to walk me down the aisle, Josh," she confessed. "How are you going to fix that?"

I squeezed her tighter, hating that the best day of our lives had opened old wounds.

"Let me handle it."

"What?" she asked as she pulled back, eyeing me.

"You said you would *hate* to disappoint everyone. Put it on the list. I'll take care of it. Just like our dates."

"No." She began to shake her head slowly, uncertain. "You can't ask some random person to give me away at our wedding."

"I want to. Let me do this. You've been working so hard at everything else."

Her bottom lip pulled between her teeth as she slowly bit down, unsure.

I placed my hands on either side of her face, looking her in the eye. "Please. I *want* to do this."

She nodded as I pressed my lips to her forehead.

The sizzling in the frying pan snapped us from our tender moment as Avery whipped around to take the pan from the burner.

"Damn it," she yelled as the pan clattered on the counter. She rushed to the sink and pushed on the cold water, soothing her burnt hand under the stream.

"Jesus Christ, Avery!" I grabbed her hand, stretching out her palm so I could inspect it. The pink outline of the handle on her skin was already beginning to fade.

"Doesn't look too bad," I said, offering an encouraging smile.

Groaning, she looked up at me with her bottom lip jutting out. "I give up. I am going back to bed and will try again tomorrow."

"Hey." Rubbing the pad of my thumb over her lip, I pulled her back against me. "It's going to be all right. I promise."

Her head moved against me as she nodded.

"Go ahead. I'll finish up the eggs and bring them in to you, and we can both spend the day in bed."

"You're too good to me."

"I didn't say *what* it is we'll be doing while we're in bed." I patted her ass as she walked away.

She stopped in the doorway, a sexy grin on her lips. "Like I said, you're too good to me."

I'd spent the last two weeks doing my part, booking plane tickets and finalizing time off work. Even a simple wedding took some time to figure out. I still wanted our day to be special, regardless of how simple it was.

Avery didn't seem as stressed, but she'd stopped discussing the wedding. Every day, I worried more that she was having second thoughts.

"I said no, tit bag. Quit worrying," Deb said.

I pressed the phone closer to my ear. "Don't fuck with me. This is important."

"You know, I used to like you. Back when you were cool. Now you're like a weepy vagina all the time and trust me, those aren't fun. I miss when you were fun, Josh."

"Double D!" Quinn called in the background. "Get your hot ass in here!"

I rolled my eyes. "Can't you be serious, Deb? Just this one time? It's important."

She was quiet for a moment. "No. Can I go now? Your bestie wants a post-dinner hand job."

"Christ. Bye," I said, poking END and dropping my phone in my lap. I covered my face and groaned.

A noise across the room prompted me to look up. Avery was in her scrubs, leaning against the kitchen doorframe with her arms folded over her chest.

"Hi."

I did my best to pretend I didn't want to choke out her friend. "Hi, baby."

She hesitated. "Who was that?"

"Just last-minute plans for the wedding."

She nodded but didn't say anything.

"Is something wrong?"

She shrugged, pushing from the door and walking to the fridge. "I just thought we were going to elope ... quick and dirty. Now you're on the phone all the time, but I don't feel like there's been a lot of progress."

"Baby, it's only been a few weeks. I had to get some things together, but it is almost there."

"A few weeks? Do you know what today is?"

I wrinkled my nose. "Cinco de Mayo?"

"It's May, Josh. You chose June. You wanted to take over the planning because you felt it was too stressful for me. Now you're dragging your feet."

"Avery," I chided. I cleared my throat. My exasperation with Deb was bleeding into our conversation. "What is going on? First it was all happening too quickly and now it's not fast enough. I'm trying."

"Are you stalling?" She turned around slowly, a tear slipping down over the apple of her cheek. "Because you don't have to do that. You can talk to me."

She touched the penny at her neck, and I panicked and pointed at her. "Don't walk out on me."

She blinked. "I wasn't ... I ... was going to offer it to you. For your thoughts. Just asking doesn't work as well anymore."

I sighed. "We definitely need to talk. I can't keep wondering, but I don't want to upset you."

"About what?" she asked, shifting her weight.

"I'm nervous."

Her face fell. "About marrying me." It wasn't a question. She said the words as if she'd expected everything I was saying.

"No. Absolutely not," I said, walking over to her. I held her arms in my hands. "You've been quiet. You clam up when I ask you about the wedding. I'm okay. I don't want to wait, but if you do, I will."

She shook her head.

"You don't want to wait?" I asked, nearly allowing myself relief.

"There's been talk at work," she said, biting her lip.

"Talk? What kind of talk?"

"Michaels mentioned she saw you at Corner Hole the other night when you said you were at work. She didn't say it to me. Deb overheard her telling someone else."

I blinked. "I was."

She looked up at me. "I texted you fifteen minutes before you got home. You said you were driving home from work."

My mouth pulled to the side. *Fuck.* "I wasn't trying to lie. I didn't even think about it until now."

"Why didn't you tell me you were going by the bar after work?"

I shrugged. "You've never needed me to before."

She thought about that a moment. "Were you with a girl? A blonde?"

"No," I said, inwardly cringing. Going to Corner Hole was stupid.

"Avery," I said, squaring my feet, lowering my chin until she met my eyes. "I want to be with you, more than *anything*. There is no one else, I swear to God. There will never be anyone else but you. You're just going to have to trust me."

She hesitated, looking to the floor. I held my breath

"Is there something else?" I asked, a million horrible thoughts racking my brain.

"I hear you talking to her on the phone at night." Her voice was barely a whisper, but I heard it loud and clear over the hammering of my heart.

"What?" My head turned to the side to hear her more clearly, wondering if I'd dreamed it.

"I wasn't trying to catch you or anything. I just woke up."

I shrugged, trying to play it off. "I don't know what you're talking about, baby."

Disappointment shadowed her face. She watched me for a long time. "Is that your answer?"

"I don't have an answer. You know I've been making wedding plans. I told you I'd take care of it, and I meant it. That's the truth."

"I'm going to bed," she said, passing me for the bedroom.

"Baby." I reached out to her, but missed. "Aren't you hungry?" I called.

"I'm not hungry," she said from the bathroom. She closed the door, the light forming a halo around the edges.

I walked into our dark bedroom, standing alone. Frames holding pictures of us that we'd taken over the last year were scattered around the room, on the nightstands, and the corner table where I kept my emergency stash. Avery's apartment didn't have room for the hutch, so I sold it. Now I wondered if I should have found a smaller, locking chest. Opening a drawer was too easy.

The shower turned on, and I sat on the bed. I was stuck between telling her the truth to shield her from her imagination, and ruining everything.

I opened the door, seeing her perfect, naked silhouette blurred by the glacier glass. She kept her head under the water, letting it cascade over the hands that covered her face.

I had to tell her.

"Avery," I said, reaching for the door.

"Please don't," she said.

"We need to talk."

"No. I just want to stand in my shower and process everything."

"I can fix this."

She was quiet for a moment, and then she yelled. "Has it ever occurred to you that I don't want you to fix everything? Maybe I just want it to be right and good in the first place! Maybe I don't want something that has to be fixed!"

I stood with my mouth open. She'd never yelled at me before.

"O ... okay," I stammered. "I'm sorry. I'll, uh ... I'll leave you alone."

"Great," she snapped.

I backed out, closing the door, and then kicked off my shoes. The clock glowed in the dark bedroom. I had to be to work in five hours and had no fucking clue how I was going to sleep. I peeled off my shirt and jeans, crawling under the covers in my boxer briefs.

The shower turned off, and Avery went through her nightly routine. The door opened, and she fell into the bed, yanking on the covers and turning her back to me. Her wet hair slapped against the pillow, and she let out a long sigh.

We lay in silence for a while, and then I reached back for her, touching my fingertips to her hip. "I can't leave. I'm afraid you're going to change the locks tomorrow and have all my shit laying on the sidewalk."

She didn't respond.

"I swear to God, I've never cheated on you. I've never wanted to. Don't you know how much I love you?"

She sniffed. "Something doesn't feel right, Josh. I've felt this way for a while. I don't know what it is. Don't you feel it?"

"Sometimes," I said, trailing off. I thought about the times when I had to stop and take in the reality around me. Sometimes, sitting with Quinn, it felt like talking to a stranger. Some days I felt like I was at work, but most of my time between moments with Avery were just a blur. "You loving me has always been ... I dunno, a surreal thing to me. But that doesn't mean it's not right."

She sucked in a breath through her nose. She was crying now. I turned over. "Avery," I said, wrapping my arms around her body.

She pulled her knees against her chest. "Just don't lie to me. Ever."

"Can you think of anything that would warrant me risking the most important person in my life?"

"Stress does weird things to the best people. Look at Dr. Rosenberg."

I pushed up on my elbow, looking down at her. Her cheeks were wet. "I used to want to be like him, but that was only because of the way you looked at him. I don't wanna be anything like him, Avery. I'm going to cherish every second I have with you, and our kids, and our grandkids. We're going to grow old together, and I'll look back on all of this and know I honored what we had."

She reached up to touch my cheek, still unsure. "Tell me I'm imagining things. Tell me Michaels is imagining things."

I sighed. "I can't. I did go to the bar. I was talking to a girl. I couldn't tell you if she was blonde or not; I wasn't paying that close attention. But we were just talking. I did tell you I was driving home from work instead of the bar. I do talk to people on the phone late at night. But I only want you. Please trust me."

Avery's bottom lip quivered, and then she pulled me down to her, locking her wrists around my neck. I dug my hands between her and the mattress, holding her as if she were anchoring me to the earth.

The morning sun poured in through the windows, filling the room with light. Avery groaned. She'd covered for Deb the night before and had just trudged in at three a.m.

I stood, closing the curtains.

"It's no use," she said. "I'm awake."

I rushed back to lie beside her under the covers. "Try to go back to sleep. You must be exhausted."

"I can't. There are only ten days left of May."

I squeezed her tight. "Then it's June."

She looked up at me with weary eyes and a sleepy smile. "Then it's June."

"Still nervous?"

"I just hope no one is disappointed. It's just a tiny wedding, no reception."

"Hey," I said. "I suggested pizza."

She tilted her head, tucking her chin. "I'd rather not feed anyone than offer pizza for a wedding dinner."

I shrugged and smiled. "They are just going to be happy to be there, Avery. They want to share this day with us."

"I just don't want it to suck."

"You really think our friends and family are going to judge us based on if we feed them shrimp cocktails and have an ice sculpture?"

"No, but someone might."

"Who are these fictional assholes that you speak of and why would we invite them to our wedding?"

Her giggles filled the bedroom, and she finally relaxed. "You're right. I'm sorry. I can't figure out what this thing is hanging over my head, so I'm making stuff up."

"What do you mean?"

"You know," she said, twirling her hair around her finger and looking out the window. "That thing."

I wondered if she meant the same uncertain feeling that had been plaguing me. Clearly, neither of us was unsure about our relationship. It was something else, and she was feeling it too.

"How are you?" I asked, brushing her hair back from her face.

She smiled, amused. "I'm fine."

"You know what I mean," I said, nudging her. "How are you feeling?"

"Like the luckiest girl on Earth." She grinned against my lips as she slipped her hands around the back of my neck and pulled me closer. Moving the blanket from between us, I slid my body over hers, still wanting her just as badly as the first night we'd made love. Settling my hips on hers, her thighs fell open wider, granting me access.

Reaching between us, she gripped my length, positioning me at her entrance, skin to skin. I glanced over my shoulder at the nightstand, but Avery pulled me down, planting a deep kiss on my mouth. "I want to feel you." She bit her lip. "Just you."

Lifting my head to look her in the eye, she nodded before I pushed forward, filling her slowly as she gasped at the new sensation. Her eyes fluttered closed, and I pressed my lips to each eyelid as we began to move together, her nails biting into the flesh of my back.

"It's like you were made for me," I rasped.

She sucked in a ragged breath, releasing it against the shell of my ear, causing a shiver to run the length of my spine.

Her hips rose and fell as her gasps grew louder, increasing in frequency as her release began to build. Rolling over, I pulled her on top of me as she kept her chest pressed to mine.

She sat up, raking her hair back, arching her back so I could appreciate her full form. "Christ, you're beautiful," I said, running my hands over her soft breasts and down her middle.

Her lip was between her teeth, pressing into the delicate flesh as she adjusted. The movement nearly caused me to finish, and I gripped her hips to give me time to refocus.

A piece of her golden hair fell into her eyes when she looked down at me. For the first time in a long time, she seemed confident, and that thought alone made my dick harden inside her.

I reached up, running my thumb over her mouth. She kept her eyes on mine, pressing a kiss to my skin, and then opened those beautiful lips, sliding them down over my index finger, gently sucking as she pulled away.

My breathing faltered. "For fuck's sake, woman."

She smiled. "You like that?" Her tongue ran up my finger again, something new flickering in her eyes. I didn't dare question what, in case questions snuffed it out.

She pushed against my chest until she was sitting astride my hips, her nipples hardened into tight buds. My grip tightened on her hips as she slowly rose and fell, teasing me.

"I love you," I confessed for the millionth time, but it felt like it would never be enough. Her movements grew less controlled as her inhibitions lowered. I began to move her with my own rhythm, pulling her hips forward and rolling them back like waves in sync with the pulsing of her body around me.

"I love you," she whimpered as her hands ran down the ridges of my abs. "So much."

"Show me." With those words, she came undone in my arms, collapsing against me in the aftermath of our affection.

CHAPTER SEVENTEEN

Avery

"I'm suffocating," I panted, tugging the silky white material of my sundress.

"You look like a new pair of tits on a one-legged hooker," Deb assured me. "I'm jealous."

"Is that a good thing?" I asked as I stared at my flushed face in the mirror.

"That dress would look like a hand towel on me," she said—as if that clarified anything at all.

The heat was sweltering and it was only mid-June. We had arranged airline tickets for Josh's parents, and Mrs. Cipriani had graciously offered her spare bedroom and arranged to rent a vacant apartment in her building for cheap to help us cut down on costs.

"Why are you smiling like a pervert?" Deb's voice shook me from my thoughts as I fastened the back onto my pearl earring. "You thinking about Josh's wang?"

"I'm just ... happy." I shrugged as I slid my other earring in my ear. Deb twisted her face in disgust over my shoulder.

"Well, stop it. You're grossing me out."

I closed my eyes, behind them a blurry, horizontal peek of the hospital, as if I were looking into one of the rooms through blinds. I blinked them open.

"Whoa," I said, reaching out for the dresser next to me. "I need more sleep."

"What?" Deb said, leaning over to look into my eyes. "You're not going to pass out on me, are you?"

"No," I said, shaking my head. "I didn't sleep great last night."

"Typical. Your whole relationship is typical. I wanted an *oops* pregnancy and public fights and Josh to beat the shit out of Dr. Rosenberg for looking at you too long. Love is boring. No, thank you."

"Don't pretend you don't know what love feels like, Hamata. I see you looking at Quinn like you want to eat him."

"I'm a big girl, Jacobs. I'd eat just about anything you put in front of me." She winked, nudging me in the ribs with her elbow. "All right, fine. I love him. He's the yin to my yang. The lube to my anal."

"You make that sound so ... sweet." I made a fake gagging sound as she took my necklace from my hands and clasped it around my neck. "Thanks."

I felt the single pearl that dangled in the center of my chest. It was the necklace my grandmother had worn when she married my grandpa. Josh had my aunt ship it from Florida as a surprise. I tried not to be hurt that she couldn't make it to the actual ceremony, but I knew we were asking a lot and it was last minute.

Stepping out of the small community center, I looked up to the rays of sun shining through the branches of the oak trees.

As the light flickered from the leaves swaying in the breeze, a beautiful combination of sun and shadows danced across my skin. I knew it was silly, but I thought of my parents, feeling them reaching out and pushing me forward into the next chapter of my life. Although I had no one to walk me down the aisle, that image gave me a semblance of comfort, envisioning someone on my side, in my corner.

I smiled, looking across the courtyard and feeling silly. Josh had been that person for me for over a year, and after the ceremony, our promises would be a pact.

"You look incredible," a familiar voice called from behind me. I whipped around and my hand flew over my mouth. Aunt Ellen stood ten feet away, looking so much like my mother that I had to reach for something to stay upright. On either side of her were my cousins, Zane and Maggie.

"You look—" she took my hands, holding them out as she took in my dress "—just like your mother."

"So do you," I choked out.

Her smile beamed with pride. "She would be so happy.

"I wish they were here."

"They are," Aunt Ellen said, touching my cheek. "Maggie has been here once to finalize plans. Josh told me you found out, and that he had an awful time preserving the surprise. We've spent a lot of late nights chatting, trying to make this work." She touched my cheek. "Your parents should be seeing you in this dress. I know they're proud of how you've overcome everything that's happened to be the woman you are now." Her eyes glossed over.

My own tears began to form, clouding my vision. I looked to Deb. "It was my cousin at Corner Hole. It's my family he's been talking to this whole time." I covered my mouth, relief washing over me.

"Nope," Deb scolded. "None of that shit. I spent forty-five minutes on that face." She dabbed a tissue beneath my eyes, careful of my makeup.

I breathed out a laugh, looking at my aunt in disbelief. "I can't believe you're here," were the only words I could get past the lump in my throat. She was there, standing right in front of me, but it didn't feel real. I closed my eyes, and strange images filled my mind. I shook my head, feeling confused.

"Honey?" Aunt Ellen said. "Aren't you feeling well?"

"Sit," Deb said, guiding me to an ottoman. "I'm getting you some water. Don't forget to breathe."

Aunt Ellen kneeled in front of me, pulling me against her chest into a comforting hug. "Don't be nervous, sweetheart. Your future husband is a good man." She smirked. "A determined young man."

"Yes," I said with a knowing smile. "He loves to fix things."

Deb brought me a small bottle of water, and I took a sip while she fanned me and took my pulse. "Pulse is within range. Tell me how you feel."

"I don't know. It's weird. I think I have a headache coming on. I keep getting weird flashes."

"Anxiety," Deb said. "Your brain is in overdrive."

Aunt Ellen pointed at Maggie to fetch her purse. "I have Xanax."

Deb shook her head. "Thank you, Ellen, but I'm sure Avery wants to remember her wedding day."

Aunt Ellen chuckled, gesturing to Maggie again.

My cousin brought over a travel-sized bottle of Fireball whiskey. "If you ask me," Maggie said, "this is better than Xanax. You're relaxed without feeling sedated."

I grabbed it from her hands, twisted the lid open, and looked up at Deb.

She shrugged. "If you're going to drink that, I'm next."

I took a large gulp and then handed the rest to Deb, who finished it off.

After a few minutes, I began to feel more relaxed.

Aunt Ellen stood. "You look like you're feeling better, but I'm not a nurse. Deb?"

"I feel better, so I'm going to go ahead and take a guess that she does, too."

I inhaled deeply. "Much. Thank you. You're that aunt with literally everything in her purse."

She patted her oversize Louis Vuitton saddlebag. "A lesson taught to me by your great-grandmother Celeste: a lady is always prepared, whether it's a broken nail or a Saturday Night Special."

Deb narrowed her eyes. "Ellen, do you really have a gun in your purse?"

Aunt Ellen simply winked.

Zane sighed, annoyed with his mother. "Mom, she's gonna be late. Family reunion later, okay?"

I stood and hugged my cousins before walking out into the sunshine and across Myers Park. In the center of the expansive field was a large tree looming very close to where Josh had taken me on one of our stranger dates.

To help me overcome my hatred for coconuts, Josh had had Quinn help him secure a kiddie pool and an oversize sandbox. As I walked across the courtyard with my family, I suppressed a giggle, remembering my soon-to-be husband in a frighteningly high-cut yellow speedo, lounging next to a small plastic pool. He'd said that the date doubled for my hatred for overripe bananas, for obvious reasons.

It had turned out to be a surprisingly romantic getaway that we'd both needed during a time when vacationing would have been impossible.

Bouquet in hand, I felt my heart pounding, knowing at any moment, I would see Josh. I slipped away to the memory of our coconut date, relaxing to music and working on our tans. It had been worth being scolded by a police officer who couldn't keep from staring at Josh's banana hammock.

A laugh escaped me, and Deb bumped her shoulder against mine, sharing in my quiet happiness.

My mind flashed again to the hospital, and I blinked. "What the hell?" I said under my breath.

"Headache?" she asked. "I'll get you more water. Maybe ibuprofen will help."

"No. It's not a headache. I'm seeing things, Deb."

"You're hallucinating?"

"No. Just when I close my eyes."

Deb watched, mildly worried while the officiant came into view, standing under the center tree. White lights hung from the branches, and even though it was daylight, they shimmered and twinkled under the canopy of leaves, reminding me of Christmas when he'd proposed. A faint dusting of white along the base of the large tree that trailed down between some potted plants gave the illusion of a magical path in a forest.

It all felt like a dream I never wanted to wake from. I was aware of the ridiculous grin on my face as I saw the tree, the candles, the flowers, and our families, and then my gaze settled on Josh. He stood by the officiant, wearing dark-wash denim with a black button-up shirt and black blazer I had helped him purchase a few weeks before.

His brows pulled in, his eyes glossed over, and he mouthed one simple word: *beautiful.*

In the distance, the sound of children's laughter filtered through the chatter of our friends and family. Just like Josh had promised, our wedding was perfect. I positioned myself at the end of the makeshift aisle, nodding to the officiant that I was ready to begin.

Just before I took a step, Josh's father stepped to my side, offering me his arm. "Darlin'," Silas said. "I would be honored to escort you down this aisle to my son, so we can welcome you into this family."

Tears pricked my eyes and I nodded, unable to speak when I looped my arm in his. Silas watched me fidget with anticipation while we both waited for our cue to begin walking. My knees threatened to buckle as Etta James began to belt out *At Last* over the sound system, in place of the *Wedding March*.

Silas guided me toward Josh, surrounded by the people we loved, all there to celebrate the first day of our marriage.

When we reached the end of the path, Silas placed a kiss on my hand before placing it in Josh's.

Josh smiled, thanking his father as he gave my hand a gentle squeeze and sucked in a deep breath.

"Friends and family of Josh and Avery," the officiant began, but as he spoke, his words blurred together while I got lost in Josh's gray eyes.

"I, Josh, promise to mend you when you're hurting, and to make you smile when you feel like crying. I will hold you when you can't stand on your own, and spend the rest of my days making good memories with you. I promise to tell the truth—" he glanced at Aunt Ellen "—even when it's difficult. I promise to protect you, and respect you, and to love you and only you." He held up the penny necklace. "And I swear to *always* offer a penny for your thoughts."

Sliding the ring onto my finger, he mouthed *I love you* before taking the necklace and slipping it over my head.

The officiant turned his attention to me, letting me know it was my turn to speak.

"I, Avery, promise to hold your hand through trying times, to accept you for everything you are, to never pump the gas when the Dodge won't start." The crowd snickered with Josh. "I mean, I promise to be patient, to trust you even when I think it's difficult, and to always offer you a penny for your thoughts." My fingers shook as I slid the large gold band onto his finger. Once the ring was in place, I squeezed his hand tight.

"I now pronounce you husband and wife. You may kiss your bride."

Josh gently combed his fingers through my hair as he lowered his mouth to mine. His lips felt hard against mine at first, and then he relaxed, kissing me soft and slow. I squealed against his mouth when he bowed me backward, hearing the small group clap and cheer.

We stood upright, and the officiant held up his hands. "I'd like to introduce to you, for the first time, Mr. and Mrs. Josh Avery."

"I never knew exhaustion could feel so wonderful." I sighed, falling back onto the hand-sewn quilt atop a king-size bed.

Josh lay down next to me on his side, touching my waist with a grin on his lips. "We can sleep when we're dead, Mrs. Avery." Lacing his fingers in mine, he admired our wedding bands. "Right now, we are going to make love until the management of this place kicks us out." I giggled as he pressed his lips to mine, silencing my laugh with his tongue.

I didn't see the point of spending extra money to travel for a honeymoon when we both knew we wouldn't see the outside of the hotel. But Josh insisted we at least leave Philadelphia for a few days.

We compromised by heading over to Lancaster, breaking

from the reality of a fast-paced life in a big city hospital in exchange for a few days in the countryside.

The Altland farm was two hundred and nine years old. Fifteen acres of corn and blue skies spanned as far as my eyes could see. The home was no longer occupied by the Amish, but the family who lived here opened their property to others looking to experience a simpler life. Oil lamps offered a subtle, romantic glow to the rustic interior, and a converted one-room schoolhouse offered a honeymoon suite I'd never dreamed of.

"This is like being on another planet," I said. I was easily distracted while Josh's lips traveled across my collarbone.

"I bet I can make you see stars," he teased as he slid his hand under my skirt, trailing his fingertips up my thighs toward my panties.

A loud knock at the door caused him to pause, hanging his head as he laughed once in disappointment.

"Dinner is served in the main house," the man called from the outside.

Josh looked at me, hoping I would say no.

"I'm starving," I admitted.

Reluctant, Josh lifted himself from my body, pouting like a little boy banished to time out.

"That's okay," he grumbled as he ran his hand through his hair. "It's a little easier to live with, knowing we have the rest of forever."

I pushed against his chest and slid off the bed. The owner of the farm was standing on the other side of the door when I pulled it open. He greeted me and then extended a handwritten menu, and I smiled.

"We look forward to seeing you at our table." He grinned as he looked past me to Josh.

"We'll be right over," I said, chiming in when Josh didn't respond. I closed the door, leaning my back against it.

I narrowed my eyes at Josh, watching him shove off the bed, unbuttoning his shirtsleeves and rolling them up his arms.

He sauntered over to me, gliding his hand over my ass and then gripping my thighs. Lifting me into the air, he wrapped my legs around his waist and pressed my back against the wooden door.

He kissed me hard, reminding me of exactly what I was missing. I gripped his shoulders as Josh yanked up my skirt, his length pressing against the apex of my thighs. He knew what he was doing, and it was working. I wondered if I could ever leave a bed with him in it again.

As quickly as it began, his lips broke free from mine. I quietly panted as he lowered me to the ground.

He took a step back from me, looking smug. "And now we're even." He ran the back of his thumb over his lower lip, wiping away the remnants of my gloss.

I flattened down the front of my dress, scowling at him for getting me all hot and bothered. "That was cruel, *husband*," I sneered. I could pretend to be annoyed, but saying the word *husband* spawned a flock of butterflies in my belly.

"We have the rest of our lives to make it up to each other." He held out his hand as a peace offering. I only hesitated for a moment before weaving my fingers between his.

He pulled open the door to our suite, and I pressed a kiss to his cheek. I tugged him forward, but he resisted.

"What are you waiting for?" I asked. "Let's go start our forever."

Josh lifted me into his arms, kissing and carrying me the whole way.

I covered my mouth with my hands, muffling my gasp as we stepped inside the main house. The many smiling faces of our friends and family peppered the room.

"How?"

Josh lowered me to my feet, taking my hand in his and guiding me to our seats.

"We couldn't have them come all this way and not spend time with them." He shrugged as he pulled out my chair.

I sat, still in shock. "But the logistics of getting them all here, and the money ..."

"Don't worry about it," Aunt Ellen said. "Just enjoy your day."

Josh pressed his lips to my hair, and then he took the seat next to me.

Aunt Ellen was beaming. Sitting down to eat, surrounded by everyone I loved, felt like Christmas dinner. I scanned the small group, shaking my head.

"What?" Josh asked.

"I just ... I guess I don't understand. This just seems impossible."

"Stop," Maggie said with a grin. "We all wanted to do it. It's not like Josh had to organize the mass exodus of three hundred guests from Philly. We rented a car and drove Josh's parents."

"That was fun," Zane grumbled.

Aunt Ellen jabbed her elbow into her son's ribs, still smiling wide.

"Ow!" he said, rubbing his side.

Maggie lifted a flute of champagne. "To Josh and Avery."

Everyone else followed her lead, except Zane. Aunt Ellen smacked his hand away when he reached for her glass.

"To Josh and Avery," our family and friends said in unison.

I glanced at Mary, who lifted her flute and then set it back on the table, pushing it toward Silas. He nonchalantly placed it on his other side.

"Did you see that?" I whispered to Josh.

"She just finished thirty days of sobriety. I think she wants to start over with grandchildren."

I looked up at him. "Then let's give her some."

CHAPTER EIGHTEEN

Josh

I paced the floor until my feet ached, nearly biting my nails down to the bone.

"You're going to wear a hole in the floor," Quinn said with a yawn as he rested his head against the doorframe. We'd been working all night during a full moon, and I had barely dragged my tired ass through the door when my cell phone chimed.

"You should come," she said, trying to subdue the excitement in her voice.

"Really?" I asked, blinking to keep my eyes open.

"Really."

I hurried to the hospital lab. The elevator was taking too long, so I ran up the stairs two at a time and pushed open the door.

Avery sat in the waiting room wearing her scrubs, her stethoscope still around her neck.

"Have you gone in yet?" I asked.

She shook her head, too excited to talk.

I scanned her face, taking in how beautiful she looked in that moment. "You are absolutely stunning, you know that?"

Her eyes softened, and she opened her mouth to speak, but a phlebotomist opened the door. He looked at the chart twice before calling her name. "Avery Avery?"

Avery smiled and stood, but when I did the same, the phlebotomist pointed at me with his pen. "This will be super quick, so if you could just wait here, that would be fabulous."

"Uh ... sure," I said, frowning at the sight of Avery disappearing down a short hallway.

I ran my hands through my hair and bobbed my knees up and down while I waited. I played Angry Birds on my phone, shot out a few sarcastic tweets, and then looked at the clock.

"Fuuuuuck," I hissed under my breath. My eyelids felt like sandpaper as they raked over my bloodshot eyes.

"We'll call you with the results, Mrs. Avery."

My beautiful wife stepped into the waiting room, gorgeous in her purple scrubs and a matching tourniquet wrapped around her elbow. I closed the distance between us, gripping her waist as I planted a kiss on her forehead.

"It will be a few days," she reminded me with an easy smile.
My face fell. "A few days?"

"You act like you haven't done this before."

I frowned, unhappy about the reminder. "Not this part."

I kept my palm on the small of her back as we walked into the hall toward the elevator. Avery looked so happy, grinning at everyone who passed. A heavily pregnant mother waited with us, pressing on her back with her hand.

I leaned over, whispering in Avery's ear, "It's happening this time. I can feel it." I pressed my palm against her stomach as her hand covered mine.

"I don't want to get my hopes up just yet," she said.

"I will. They're up. This is it. I'll bet my paycheck on it."

She leaned against me. "Stop," she said, sounding like a mother already. She lifted her wrist and frowned at her watch. "I have to get to work."

I nodded even though I didn't want to let her go. "I'm already looking forward to your maternity leave so I can see you once in a while."

"You love your job just as much as I love mine," she said, stepping inside the elevator.

The doors opened, and she walked toward the ER while I headed for the parking lot.

"Love you," she said, waving good-bye.

I reluctantly let her go, watching as she made her way down the long white corridor. Her bright purple scrubs abruptly disappeared behind the large double doors at the end.

I gripped my keys in my hand, smiling at the idea of a little Avery running around.

"Please, let this happen," I whispered. I thought I couldn't want anything more when I had asked Avery to marry me. Now, all I wanted was for her to be pregnant with my child.

I only turned on the red lever and left the blue one alone, but the water still wasn't hot enough to soothe my aching muscles.

I turned off the shower and reached outside the stall to grab a towel, allowing heat to escape so I could breathe. The mirror immediately fogged, the tiny bathroom filling with thick steam.

Dax was waiting outside the bathroom door, his tail wagging wildly as I stepped out onto the linoleum floor.

"You're going to have to wait a minute," I warned. I wasn't looking forward to dragging my ass down the two flights of stairs to let him go to the bathroom.

His head cocked to the side, and I laughed. The thick white cotton of my towel collected water droplets from my skin, immediately leaving goose bumps in their place from the slight nip in the early morning air.

Fall was my favorite time of year, and this fall was going to be the best yet. The sweltering heat had let up enough for Avery to once again drown in my oversize hoodie. I loved the look of her bare legs under my sweatshirt when she woke in the morning to make coffee. Unfortunately, our schedules had shifted again, and I was working mostly nights.

Dax yelped as I wrapped the towel around my waist, shaking my head at how short it was. I would have to get some more of those oversize ones Mrs. Cipriani had given us as a wedding present. Avery used the only two we had and left the tiny ones for me.

"Do you see this?" I pointed to the small pile of towels in the corner as Dax's tail began to whip harder. "I am not married to you. You can't tell me what to do." I padded my way to our bedroom, leaving wet footprints in my path. Grabbing a pair of basketball shorts from the clean laundry basket, I tugged them up over my hips, rolling my neck to the side and closing my eyes as it popped loudly.

"Let's go." I followed him from the bedroom, grabbing his leash from the counter and clipping it to his collar before leading him downstairs.

Our newest neighbor was shoving her key in the lock to her apartment, a baby car seat in the other hand and the straps of her wristlet purse between her teeth. She'd only moved into the apartment below us a few weeks before, and her colicky son's room was directly below our bedroom.

"Let me help you with that," I said, hurrying to her side. I took the seat handle from her hand, smiling down at the chubby baby inside.

"Thank you." She batted her faded pink hair from her face and let out a loud, exasperated sigh as her key finally found its way into the lock. She shoved the door open with her shoulder and stepped out of the way so I could enter.

Her place was laid out exactly like mine and Avery's, but with baby furniture and paraphernalia. It looked like a Babies "R" Us had exploded.

Hope called over her shoulder as she put her purse on the kitchen island. "Thank you so much, Josh. You can just set him down next to his playpen, if you don't mind."

I set the carrier on the floor and began to unbuckle the little boy. "How you liking this place?" I asked, smiling down at him.

"It's a quiet neighborhood." She laughed. "Well, I guess I'm the loudest one around here. Sorry about that. Toby doesn't sleep through the night yet."

"No worries." I pulled the boy from the seat and stood with him in my arms.

Hope watched me.

"Oh," I said. "I hope this is okay."

She smiled. "He likes you."

I bounced him a bit. I had no clue whether that was the right thing to do or not, but it felt right. "It's good practice. We hope to be adding a baby to our family soon, too."

"Oh," she said, surprised.

"What?" I paced the floor with Toby, bouncing slightly.

"Oh, nothing. I just thought you guys were a casual thing. I don't see her around much and she's always running out in the morning." Her cheeks darkened, embarrassed by how much she knew.

"She works days and I have the night shift at the moment. But Avery's definitely not casual. She's my wife."

"*Wife?* Congrats."

"I know. She's way out of my league," I said.

"Don't sell yourself short." Crossing the room, Hope pulled Toby from my arms. "I just meant you look too young to be married."

"Ah ... well, when you know, you know."

"Yeah ... I mean, I guess." Hope set her son in his swing and turned it on. It swayed and chimed a nursery rhyme tune while Toby became mesmerized by the lights. "Best invention ever." She turned to me. "You know, Josh ... I thought I knew once, too. Believe me, it was never my plan to be raising this little man on my own."

Dax pawed at my leg, anxious to continue downstairs. "All right, furball. Let's get you to the grass."

"Thanks, Josh. You're my favorite neighbor." Hope stood and held the door open for me.

"Anytime. If you guys every need anything ... we're just upstairs."

"I just might take you up on that." She called to me as I left her apartment.

The morning chill was beginning to subside as Dax wandered down the narrow walkway between apartment buildings to the small yard in the back. My thoughts went to Avery and the possibility of us having a child of our own. We'd need a place, something bigger with a yard where he could run, and big enough for a tree that could hold a swing. The oak in the center of the yard offered the only shade on the property.

I wasn't certain the landlord would allow us to hang anything from the branches like the old plank swing my father had hung out back for us ... *us*. My gut twisted and I shook away the sad memory of my sister.

My father had always tried his best to make our childhood perfect. All the hours we'd spent tearing down and rebuilding motors wasn't to line our pockets, but to heal our souls. Still, it kept us afloat, and it was something I was good at. I blinked. *Something I can easily do now and be able to spend more time with my wife.*

Reaching up, I pulled a scrap of bark from the old tree. We'd need a home of our own, one with a large yard and not just *a* tree, *lots* of trees. I could already see Avery outside, soaking up the sunshine and working on her garden as our children ran around her, playing.

It sounded like Heaven. "Josh?" Hope called from the strip of grass between the apartment buildings. A plastic ivory box was in her hand, an antennae sticking out the top.

"Yeah?" I asked, dividing my attention between her and Dax.

"Toby is sleeping. I was wondering if you'd like to come in for a glass of wine, or a beer ... or formula, if that's your thing." She giggled quietly.

Hope was an attractive woman. Before the accident, I would have led Hope to my apartment and had her flat on her back the first night she moved in. But now, I could look at her, notice she was attractive, but not feel attracted to her. It was weird, and just one more thing that assured me how in love I was with Avery.

"I can't," I said. "Thanks for the invite."

Hope nodded, smiling to me before turning around. She stopped, trying one more time. "I don't know a lot of people here. It would be nice to make a friend."

I thought about her words. I was once the transplant, too. I knew how she felt, and loneliness was definitely not a good thing for a single mother.

"I'll talk to Avery. Maybe we can stop by this weekend?"

Hope laughed once and looked down. "Yeah, I've got to work this weekend, but another time. What's your schedule like?"

"I work nights, Tuesday through Saturday. For now."

"And Avery works days?"

I nodded, tugging on Dax when he pulled against his leash. "Mostly."

Hope nodded again. "See you later."

I waved at her, turning to Dax, who was bent in a C, creating a smelly mess I was going to have to clean up.

I rolled my eyes. "Maybe Hope will let me borrow some diapers."

I'd slept away the afternoon, hoping to be awake when Avery finally finished her shift. Four and a half hours wasn't nearly enough. Seeing each other outside of work was becoming impossible.

I scratched my head and crawled out of bed, pulling on my gray sweatpants. Avery would be home in twenty minutes. I couldn't shake the excitement of owning a home, watching Avery pick out where we would raise our children.

I picked up my phone, dialing Dad's number. We chatted for two hours before deciding that selling my Barracuda could possibly net me enough for a down payment on a home. We'd have to move farther out of Philadelphia, into the suburbs, but it was doable. I fantasized about a big garage. I would need a vehicle with four doors once we started to expand our family anyway.

I wasn't sure what Avery would think about me restoring cars for some extra money, and maybe, if all went well, I could turn it into a business and a full-time career. It was a gamble, but if we were patient and did things right, we would get to spend more time together, and later, with our children.

I padded into the kitchen, pulling ingredients for fettuccini Alfredo, Avery's favorite.

It was a full moon, and Quinn had said Deb was complaining about back-to-back multi-car accidents. Avery would be exhausted. Adding the stress of waiting for her test results would be too much for her.

I set our table with the nice dishes with the swirly patterns and flowery shit the nurses had gotten us for a wedding gift. I smiled at myself. Avery was going to love it. Just as the Dodge rumbled outside, I finished stringing up a few white Christmas lights for ambience, a subtle reminder of the day I'd made her my wife. Part of me hoped the occasion would be more than trying to cheer Avery up, and she would come home to tell me for sure that she was pregnant.

After several minutes and no sign of Avery, I looked out the window. It wasn't her Dodge I'd heard, but the Mustang from the guy in 14B. I frowned. I had more work to do on the Dodge if I could mistake it for that pussy Mustang.

As the sun sank down behind the buildings across the street, the subtle hues of the orange and blue sky faded into blackness, broken up by millions of tiny, twinkling specks.

I looked at the watch Avery had gotten me for Christmas. The memory brought a smile to my face, but it faded when I took in the time.

Pulling my cell from my pocket, I dialed her number. It rang four times before her voice filled my ear, rushed and overwhelmed.

"What's going on, baby?" I asked.

"Have you been watching the news?" she asked.

"No, baby, I've been cooking you dinner."

She groaned. "I'm starving."

"I can bring it to you? I'll put it in that hot food keeper thing your aunt bought you for a wedding present."

She sighed. "Thank you, really, but I won't have time. A busload of senior citizens is overloading the ER right now. There was a massive fire down at Oakridge Home."

"You need me to come in?"

"No, no. We have things under control, but I won't be home anytime soon."

I turned around, glancing at the twinkling lights. "It's fine. Just keep me updated."

"I will."

The phone disconnected as the *I love you* I was about to say died in my throat.

"Perfect," I mumbled, sliding the phone back into my pocket.

"It's no big deal," I whispered to Hope.

She still looked frazzled even though Toby had finally passed out.

I'd listened to his pained cries for over an hour before deciding to knock on her door and offer help, even if it was just to take him off her hands for a few minutes before she lost her mind.

I swayed back and forth while he drooled on my sleeve, worried he would wake up if I stilled.

Hope spoke softly, refashioning her bun and then pulling her robe belt tight. As she adjusted the terrycloth, I got a glimpse of her short black nightgown and her bare legs. "You're an angel, Josh. Really. I don't know what I'd do if you weren't home."

"You know," I whispered, "my friend Cinda lives across from my old apartment three blocks down. She's a professional babysitter. She even watches Dax for me sometimes."

Hope's expression fell. "Unless she takes state assistance, I can't afford her."

"Maybe she'll give you a deal."

"I'm sure the whole building hates us anyway," she said, tearing up as she looked at her sleeping son. "Avery is probably sleeping with ear plugs."

"Avery's still at work. She had to work a double. He didn't wake her."

"I just don't know what to do anymore. I mean, there has to be something wrong with him, right? No baby should be freaking out at three in the morning."

I shrugged. "I think all babies cry at night. Right?"

"Not like that. He cries like I'm killing him."

"Avery would be much better at this stuff than I am. You should ask her."

"Why? Because she's a woman? I don't have a clue what I'm doing, and I'm a mom."

"No, Avery works with babies and kids all the time."

"Avery is always working," Hope said. "I don't think I'm going to be getting advice from her anytime soon."

"I know," I said, feeling bitterness seep into my thoughts.

"I'm sorry. It must be hard for you."

I ignored her. My marriage wasn't Hope's business. "Maybe he's teething." I glanced into his open mouth.

"You can put him in his crib in my room," Hope said.

I cringed. "What if I wake him?"

"I'll help," she said, walking down the hall and opening her door.

I bent over his crib illuminated by a small heart-shaped nightlight.

I placed him gently on his back. He stirred, and Hope and I froze and held our breaths. After he rubbed one eye with his chubby little fist, he relaxed and his breathing evened out.

I walked back out to the living room, laughing to myself as Hope sat and shoveled Alfredo noodles into her mouth. When she caught me watching, she hurried to wipe her mouth with the back of her hand.

"I'm so embarrassed. I probably eat like a rabid animal. I can't believe how good of a cook you are."

I sank down on the couch beside her and lifted my plate. "I'm just glad someone is enjoying it."

CHAPTER NINETEEN

Avery

When my eyes finally peeled open, Josh's side of the bed was empty. I reached for my phone on the bedside table, holding it up to my face to see that it was ten in the morning.

"Josh?" I called out before kicking off my covers. The heat was set too high and I was roasting.

My bare feet slapped against the tile in the kitchen, and I looked around. He wasn't home. I squinted as I checked the thermostat. Josh slept best when it was cold. The heat must have woken him up.

I opened the fridge, seeing a half-eaten Tupperware bowl of Alfredo. I pulled it out, noticing maybe only a small helping was left.

After spooning cold sauce, noodles, and chicken onto a plate and popping it into the microwave, I tapped on my phone to text Josh. It wasn't like him to leave without a note.

The microwave beeped, but just as I reached for the handle, someone knocked on the door.

I smoothed back my wild bun but gave up after one look at my wrinkled tank top and pajama pants. I peeked through the hole, seeing the new neighbor, Hope, holding an empty dish.

The chain complained against the track as I slid it open, matching the whine of the door hinge.

"Hi," Hope said with a bright smile. She scanned me from head to toe, surprised. "I figured you'd be at work.

"I traded. Can I, um … what's up?"

She shoved the plate at me, and it was then that I recognized the design.

"I'm just returning your dish."

I held it in my hand, confused. "Thanks."

She waited for a moment and then spoke again, "Tell Josh the Alfredo was amazing. You are one lucky girl."

"I will," I said, watching her turn on her heels toward the stairs, a bounce in her walk.

I shut the door and carried the plate to the sink. *What. The. Fuck.*

My phone rang, and I lunged for it. Instead of seeing Josh's name on the screen, it was the hospital. I held the phone against my forehead. "No, no, no," I whispered. "Please don't call me in."

I slid my thumb right across the screen. "Mrs. Avery?" the woman on the other end said.

"Yes?"

"Hi, it's Evelyn from Dr. Weaver's office. We've got your test results. Are you ready?"

I looked around at my empty apartment, and then at the empty plate. "Y-yes."

"Congratulations! You're pregnant. By the counts, it looks like you're six to seven weeks along. Can you schedule an ultrasound today, or would you like to call back?"

"Um," I said, scratching my head. "Let me talk to my husband, and I'll call you back."

"Great. Talk soon."

She hung up, and I stood in the kitchen alone, still holding the phone in my hand. The apartment was quiet.

I rushed over to the window, seeing Josh's Barracuda resting in its spot. I lifted the phone and called him. Instead of ringing, his voicemail answered.

Hi, this is Josh Avery. I'm probably at work or with my wife. Call back. I don't check my messages.

"Hi," I said, my voice sounding quiet and unsure. "This is your wife. You're not with me. Where are you? Call me back."

I set the phone on the kitchen counter and looked down, placing a hand on my belly. "I'm pregnant," I said to no one. My bottom lip trembled. "I'm pregnant."

The bolt lock clicked, and the front door quietly opened. Dee's tiny nails clicked across the floor as he scampered in.

"Shh, buddy," Josh whispered as he snuck in. He froze when he saw me standing alone in the kitchen.

His expression thawed, and he closed the door. "Hi, baby. I figured you'd still be sleeping."

"I'm pregnant."

He dropped the bag in his hand. "Really?"

"Really."

He stepped toward me. "How ... how do you know?"

"My period was late. I took a home test, but it was negative."

"What? When? Why didn't you tell me?"

I shrugged, feeling more nervous than I'd expected. "I wanted to be sure. I didn't want to get your hopes up."

"But you are?" he asked, still in disbelief.

"Dr. Weaver's nurse just called me. The blood work came back. I'm pregnant. She wants to schedule an ultrasound."

Josh took three wide strides across the living room and knelt in front me. He wrapped his arms around my hips, holding his cheek to my belly. "They're really sure? Like, *sure* sure."

"They're sure. She says I'm around six to seven weeks. The ultrasound will give us a better idea."

He kissed my belly once, and then three more times, standing to hug me. His arms were so tight and he was so happy, I could almost forget about the plate by the sink. "Say it again," he said, his voice breaking.

I breathed out a small laugh. "I'm pregnant." No matter how many times I said it, it didn't feel real.

He pulled back. Noticing my expression, his brows pulled together. "Aren't you happy?"

"Yes," I said, nodding once. "Yes," I choked out, "of course I'm happy."

Josh hugged me again. "Just when I think it can't get any better, it does. I'm so happy, baby." He took a step back, holding his fists in front of him. "I'm so fucking happy!" He ran to the window, and yelled, "I'm going to be a father!" Then he ran to the door and jerked it open, yelling into the hall. "I'm going to be a father!"

I smiled and shook my head as he slammed the door and strode over to me, his chest puffed out. He wrapped his arms around me again, lifting me up and twirling me around. When my feet touched the floor again, he planted a hard kiss on my lips.

His smile faded. "You're not telling me something, I can tell. Did the doctor's office say something?" He blinked. "Is the baby okay?"

"Yes. I mean," I said, looking down. "They didn't really say anything except for how far along I might be. They want me to call back to schedule an appointment, but I wanted to talk to you first."

He swallowed hard. "About what? Them asking for an ultrasound. Is that normal?"

"Yes." I looked up, scanned his eyes, trying to see if I could read something more—guilt, innocence, fear. I only saw Josh, *my* Josh, the man who loved me. That hadn't changed.

"Where've you been?" I asked.

Josh let me go to jog across the room, picking up the white sack he'd dropped. It was from JayWok. "You said on the phone last night that you were craving noodles."

"For breakfast?"

He gestured to the leftover Alfredo on my plate. "Looks like I was right."

I breathed out a laugh. "Touché."

He shrugged. "I think it's kind of romantic."

I fought a smile. That was the first thing Josh had said to me after the crash, the response that had started it all. "But they're not open for another hour."

"I called in a favor."

"They owed you a favor?"

"We're good customers. What did you want to talk to me about?"

I glanced at the plate, and then back at him. On our wedding day, I had promised to trust him, just like he'd promised to love only me. He was happy about our baby. I couldn't jump to conclusions.

"I just wanted to talk to you about your schedule, to see when a good time was to schedule the ultrasound."

"I work nights, baby. You schedule one, and I'll be there."

I hugged him tight, pressing my cheek against his chest. "We're going to be parents, Josh."

He exhaled. "No, we're going to be *amazing* parents. I was thinking that maybe ... maybe we should look into buying a house."

I leaned back. "We can't afford a house."

"If I sold the Barracuda, we would have most of the down payment for something small in the suburbs. We'd get a tax break. It's doable."

"How would you get to work?"

He shrugged. "Quinn."

My nose wrinkled. "Quinn is going to drive to Haddonfield?"

Josh twisted his face, unhappy. "Haddonfield? I was thinking more like Devon or Blue Bell."

I glared at him.

He held out his hands and let them slap to his thighs. "Okay, Cherry Hill."

"You want to move to *Jersey*?" My voice rose an octave, and I rubbed my temple, feeling another headache coming on.

"Okay, don't stress. We don't have to talk about it right now. But if I find a nice house in a nice neighborhood ... will you think about it?"

I sighed. "I'm already working fifty to sixty hours a week, Josh."

"I know," he said, unhappy.

"We don't have enough saved up, not even if you sell your car, and the stress of only having one vehicle for a family of three ..."

"Okay," he said, gently holding my arms. "Deep breath. I'll make a list and crunch numbers. If it doesn't make sense, we'll stay put."

"I know you want all the best things for the baby. I do, too. But can we not change everything on day one?"

"Right. You're right. Too soon. I'll take care of it. You don't have to worry about anything."

I nodded. "Thank you." I looked down at my cold plate of food, placed it in the microwave, and closed the door.

"Sorry there's not more left." He held up the sack with a small smile. "But you have noodles."

"Oh yeah," I said, reaching for the sack. I looked at him, unable to stop my mouth from forming the words. "So, Hope liked your Alfredo?"

He shrugged, pulling out the box of noodles from the sack. "She scarfed it down like a starving mule. It was kind of gross."

"When? Did you take her some?"

He slid the box toward me, handing me the long plastic package of chopsticks. "Her baby was wailing. The guy in 2E was screaming *shut up* down the hall. It was bad. I felt sorry for her. I'd made a whole pan, and you were still at work, so I brought her some and rocked her baby. He cried for like … I dunno, two hours. I wasn't sure if I was going to get home before you did."

I raised an eyebrow. "Before I did?"

He sighed, thinking. "Yeah, I went over there at like three and finally got home around four."

"You were in her apartment at three in the morning?"

He cringed. "Well, yeah. I was up. You weren't home. Toby had been crying for an hour. I thought I could help. He likes me."

"He likes you."

Josh looked around, confused. "Yeah."

"How do you know he likes you? Did he tell you?"

He chuckled. "No, baby, he's five months old. Hope told me."

I lifted my chin, my jaw moving to the side. "Of course she did."

"I promise it's not like that. Not even close."

"It's inappropriate for you to be in a single woman's apartment in the middle of the night. Don't you see that? And you brought her my favorite meal? Really? Neither of you even leave any for me!" My head began to throb.

"Avery," Josh began, watching me massage my forehead. "I'm sorry. I wouldn't have eaten any if I knew—"

"That's not the fucking point!"

"Okay," he said quickly.

I took a deep breath and then picked up the empty plate. "She brought this by today. She thought I would be at work. I'm a woman, Josh. I work with dozens of women. I saw it in her eyes. She's not your friend. She is looking for a baby daddy."

"C'mon, Avery, that's not fair."

"You're a daddy. But Toby isn't your baby."

"Exactly," Josh said, reaching out for me. "We're having a baby. I don't want her," he said, frowning at the door. He touched my belly, running his hand over the fabric of my tank top. He kissed the corner of my mouth and then leaned down, kissing my neck. "You have the day off."

"Until five."

"Eat, and then let's go to bed."

My lips formed a hard line and I looked away, trying to stay mad. I knew he wasn't cheating, but going to her apartment had been stupid. "No."

Josh ran his tongue up the skin of my neck, stopping on my earlobe, taking it gently in his teeth. He pulled away, kissing the skin he'd left behind. "I want you. Only you, since the first time you were in my arms."

I looked up at him, and he kissed me, opening his mouth. I did the same, allowing his tongue inside. I touched each side of his face, feeling his hand under my tank top, holding his palm against my belly.

"You're my family, Avery. This baby is our family." He shook his head. "There is nothing more important than that."

I smiled, and he turned to the box of noodles, opening the lid. Steam rolled up into the air, and my stomach growled.

I unwrapped the chopsticks, pulling them apart, and then tore into the noodles. "Oh my God," I hummed. "I didn't realize how hungry I was."

"Feed that baby," Josh said with a smile. "He's going to be a tank."

"Or she. Dr. Weaver wants an ultrasound scheduled around thirteen weeks. We might be able to find out then," I said with a mouthful.

"That's hot. I'm not sure I can wait to get you in bed until after you finish," he teased.

"If you try to take this food away from me, the least of your worries will be hearing me talk with my mouth full."

Josh held up his hands, taking a step back. "It was a joke, baby. I can help you if you want." Josh picked up a few noodles, and I leaned my head back, opening my mouth wide. I giggled while he missed more than twice, and then finally lowered the long strips into my mouth.

Once I finished breakfast, I washed my face and brushed my teeth, and then I crawled into bed next to my husband. His body was at least ten degrees warmer when he was in bed, and every inch of my skin touching his formed a thin sheen of sweat.

"We've got to turn on the air conditioner," I said.

Josh lifted his head, looking at me in disbelief. "Really?"

"Really. Can you? Please?"

"You know I'm not going to argue with that. I'm going to enjoy your pregnancy. I can already tell."

"Pregnant," I breathed as he hurried to the thermostat. He dialed to the right, the AC kicked on, and he jogged back to bed, snuggling with me under the sheet.

"Yes, pregnant. We created life. That's nuts," Josh said, in awe.

"Not as nuts as it will be trying to raise a child. Most of the time I still feel like one myself."

Josh smiled and nuzzled my neck as I stared up at the ceiling, fantasizing about our baby.

The ultrasound tech ran the transducer over the slimy gel she'd slathered on my barely protruding belly moments before, and smiled. The room was dim, but I could still see the brown curls that formed a bushy helmet around her head. "Do you have any names picked out, yet?"

"Yes," I said, resting my arm behind my head. I leaned toward Josh, trying to get a better look. "Joshua Todd if it's a boy." I smiled at Josh. "We'll call him Todd, after my dad."

"Can you see, Avery?" Josh asked, engrossed with the black and gray images on the screen.

The tech pressed a few buttons on her keyboard, and then smiled. "And if it's a girl?"

"Penelope Anne," Josh said. "We'll call her Penny." He watched the screen, running his fingers through my hair.

The tech touched her finger to the screen. "Well, there she is ... your lucky Penny." She smiled at us, and Josh laughed out loud.

"A girl?" he asked, grabbing my hand. "You can already tell?"

"Definitely a girl," the tech said. She turned to freeze the image, then typed BABY GIRL PENNY in big white letters next to what looked like girl parts.

"Is that ...?" I asked.

"Looks like a hot dog ... or a hamburger, depending on the direction," the tech teased.

Josh used his thumb and index finger to quickly wipe his eyes.

"Aw, baby," I said, squeezing his hand.

He lifted my fingers to his mouth and pressed his lips against my skin.

"This is so surreal," I said. "Did you see that?" I squinted my eyes toward the tiny black and white image as I watched our daughter kick and twist.

"What is it?" Josh looked back at the screen, worry marring his handsome face.

The technician laughed, waving her hand. "These things are like a moving Rorschach test. Your daughter looks great."

I smiled back at her. "I'm just so tired. I think it's getting to me." I yawned, but Josh still looked concerned.

"Any morning sickness?" the tech asked.

I shook my head. "Nothing. I feel perfectly fine."

"Lucky you," she said while she worked, finishing the exam.

I looked up at Josh, his face partially shadowed in the small, dark room. He was watching the screen so intently, I hated to interrupt.

"The other nurses keep telling me it's odd," I said. "I'm getting a complex."

The tech shook her head. "It's uncommon, but count yourself lucky. Once in a while, I get a mama in here that has energy, never experiences the morning sickness, and you'd never know she was pregnant until she started to show."

I looked down at my stomach. "I just have a pooch."

"She's a wiggly little thing," the tech said, pointing and chuckling.

Josh laughed out loud, amazed.

"It's so weird, seeing her move around so much on the screen, but I can't feel it."

"You will," the tech said, hanging up her transducer. The screen went black, and she used a cloth to clean off the gel from my skin.

Josh helped me up. "Everything looked okay?"

The tech smiled. "I'm going to send the images to the doctor and he'll tell you all about it."

"But..." Josh said, his voice tinged with worry. "Is she okay?"

The tech looked around. I wasn't sure for whom; we were alone. She leaned in. "She looks perfectly healthy to me."

Josh sighed and then helped me sit up, kissing my temple. "Thank you."

"Congratulations."

The tech showed us out, and as we made our way to the ER, Josh's cell phone rang. He glanced down, rolling his eyes and pressing the speakerphone button.

"Hello?"

"Josh? It's Hope. Are you working today?"

"At an appointment with Avery, what's up?"

She hesitated. "Oh. Never mind."

I narrowed my eyes at him. "She has your phone number?" I whispered.

He held up a finger to me. "Did you need something?"

She sighed. "Toby's running a fever and fussier than usual. I was wondering if you wouldn't mind picking up some diapers on your way home. Size three."

I made a face.

"Uh ... sure, I can do that. Any brand?"

"Luvs, please. Thank you so much."

Josh hung up the phone, and I eyed him.

"What am I supposed to do, baby? He's sick and she'll have to drag him into a store screaming if I don't help."

"He's not screaming. Did you hear him screaming? Strange for a sick baby who already had colic."

Josh's eyes softened. "I'd want someone to help you if I weren't around."

"You think Hope will help me?" I asked, sardonic.

251

Josh opened my door. "Yeah, I do. She's actually a nice person, Avery. You'd like her if you got to know her."

I sat in the passenger seat, waiting for Josh to jog around to his side. "If she were interested in getting to know me, I'd be friends with her, too. Don't you see it, Josh? You can't be that blind."

"She works the late shift, Avery. I'm off when she's off. Otherwise, she'd be bugging you to run her errands for her."

I frowned. "Is this the first time she's called you for something?"

"Er ... no. But sometimes I'm busy."

"Josh, you are not her husband! Stop letting her order you around!"

"Okay, Avery. Don't get upset. I'll fix this."

"You'd better," I said, settling back into the seat.

CHAPTER TWENTY

Josh

Tipping the longneck to my lips, I let the beer slide down my throat, soothing the itch that had been forming. Winter had come and gone. The March air was warm, but I still wore my old hoodie. It smelled like Avery.

"Shots no longer doing it for ya?" Ginger ran her bar rag over the wooden surface. She was smiling, but her eyes showed how long of a day she'd had.

"Needed a change of pace," I replied, leaning the bottle back to read over the label.

"Everything okay with you and the old lady?"

I nodded, chuckling at her terminology. Ginger had recently been seeing Bear, a meathead biker who rarely showered. He was already rubbing off on her.

"She's a little stressed," I said.

"Hormones."

I nodded and took another swig. It was more than the baby on the way. In fact, Avery loved every minute of being pregnant, even with all the aches and pains that came with being thirty-one weeks along. As time passed, she'd grown more agitated. She'd even begun to suffer from hallucinations, and they'd been happening more frequently.

It was scary as hell, but we'd been to the doctor, taken as many tests as being pregnant would allow, and our only option was to try meds she couldn't or wouldn't take.

"It's not just hormones, Ginger."

"How did the tests come out?" she asked.

I shrugged, taking another swig. "With her fluctuating hormones, the doctor is reluctant to diagnose her. The MRI didn't reveal anything, either." I was beginning to worry it was all just in our heads.

"Is she still working so much? That can't be good."

"No," I said simply. I'd convinced her to cut back at work because the stress seemed to make things worse. At first, Avery was resistant, until she saw how terrified I was that something may happen to her and our daughter.

My mind went to Kayla and how she may have looked today, on her twenty-third birthday. A black cloud had always hovered over March sixth, but today it seemed worse knowing that soon I would have my own little girl to look after. I couldn't help but worry that just because Avery hadn't experienced the extent of my bad luck, Penny might.

I wondered if she would take after me, dark hair and light eyes, reminding me of Kayla. Maybe even curly tendrils like the ones I used to tug on and laugh when they sprung back into place.

A chill ran up my spine, thinking of those curls being wet and sprawled across the grass.

"You stalking me now?"

I glanced over my shoulder as Hope slid onto the stool next to me, pulling her pink hair up into a high, messy ponytail. It was now fuchsia instead of Pepto-Bismol. She was still wearing her white T-shirt and black slacks for her waitressing job.

"I was here first. That's not how stalking works."

I held up a finger to Ginger, letting her know I needed another beer. She noticed Hope and arched an eyebrow.

"I'll get her drink, too," I said, feeling the alcohol burn through my veins. "That doesn't mean this is a date."

"Of course not. Thanks," Hope said, flicking her hair behind her shoulder.

"What are you doing here?"

"I needed a break, and I remembered this place when you told me the story about how you started dating Avery." She sighed. "I love that story."

"Where's Toby?" I asked.

"Cinda has him. That woman is a godsend. Thanks for the heads-up. Toby loves her."

I bobbed my head in agreement, peeling back the label of my beer. "She's great with kids."

"And thanks for letting me use your dryer. I think I'm going to have to try to find another one at the secondhand. It's a huge pain in the ass lugging all our wet laundry to the laundromat with Toby in tow."

"No problem."

"Is it weird that he has more clothes than I do? I have five white shirts for work, two pairs of jeans, six T-shirts, two pairs of cotton shorts, two nightgowns, one bar shirt, one black dress, four pairs of socks, two bras, and ten pairs of panties." She made a face. "You're officially poor when you have an exact count of every article of clothing you own."

"I prefer to call it frugal."

"What's wrong?" Hope bumped her shoulder against mine. I swayed slightly on my stool. "You worried about being a daddy?"

I shook my head, looking down at the wooden surface in front of me. It wasn't me I was worried about. My gut twisted, feeling like I was betraying Avery just by my thoughts.

"I've seen you in action under pressure, Josh. You're going to do just fine. And if you need help ... well, I owe you one or fifty."

Hope's words didn't help, and the tightening in my chest was becoming vise-like.

Ginger placed two shots and a fresh beer in front of me, her eyes darting back and forth between Hope and me.

"Josh," Ginger said, warning in her voice. "Maybe I should call you a cab."

I ignored her. I wasn't doing anything wrong. Didn't even plan on it. I glanced over at Hope, who smiled at me the way Avery used to.

Ginger left us for the opposite end of the bar, glancing at me once in a while between tending other customers.

"So, if you're not anxious about parenthood, what is it?"

"Do you believe in curses?" I asked, taking a sip from my Budweiser.

"I curse all the fucking time," she joked, causing me to laugh.

"I'll drink to that."

Hope held up her tiny glass and waited for me to do the same. Clinking them together, I tilted my head back and poured the liquor down my throat, no longer flinching at the harsh flavor.

Hope's face screwed, and she waved her hand in front of her nose. "So ... did you steal some treasure you shouldn't have touched, and now pirates are out to get you?"

"Something like that." I took another sip. "I dunno. It just feels like no matter what I do—"

"Stop doing this to yourself. You have everything, and you feel like you don't deserve it. Am I right? So now you're looking for some defect, some flaw that you can blame when you run to St. Louis."

"St. Louis?" I cocked an eyebrow, taking a long pull from my bottle.

"Isn't that where *all* the deadbeat fathers run off to?" She twirled her empty shot glass in a circle, resting her chin on the heel of her hand. "I'm sorry. You're not him. Far from it. I'm not sure you're appreciated for that."

For a second, I didn't feel like such a fucking outsider in my own life.

"That guy was a moron," I said.

"You don't have to tell me. I lived with him." She giggled as she took the bottle from my hand and finished it off.

My laughter died in my throat when I glanced past Ginger, seeing a familiar face at the end of the bar. Carissa Ashton was watching me intently.

"Fucking great," I grumbled, nodding in her direction. Her smile spread as she made her way around the bar.

"Who's that?" Hope asked in a hushed tone.

"Stage five clinger."

"Didn't expect to see you here, Josh," Ashton purred as she eyed Hope. "Who's your *friend*?"

"Hope, this is Carissa Ashton. Ashton, this is Hope, my neighbor."

"Oh." Ashton held out her hand to Hope, who reluctantly shook it. "I work with Josh's *wife*, Avery."

"Neat." Hope shrugged as she picked up her shot glass and held it up for Ginger to see.

"Yeah, how is your wife, Josh? She looks like she's ready to pop any day now."

"Nine weeks," I mumbled, hating that I had to make small talk with her. The moment Avery began to show, Ashton took every opportunity to make little digs about Avery's marginal weight gain.

Ashton smirked as she tipped her martini glass to her unnaturally pink lips. "Tell Avery I said hello ... if you happen to see her tonight."

My nose wrinkled. "Why wouldn't I see her tonight?"

Ashton shrugged innocently, looking to Hope. "You just look sort of busy."

I sighed, the whiskey erasing any patience I usually maintained with Ashton. "Fuck. Off. And when you get there, fuck off again until you come back. And you *will* because you'll never leave me the *fuck* alone!"

Ashton turned her back to me, pretending it wasn't her I was yelling at. She retreated to her side of the bar with a satisfied grin.

Hope's eyebrows shot up. "That was—"

"Stupid," I said. "Carissa Ashton is a vindictive little bitch." I stood from my stool. "I'd better get back home."

"Did you drive?" she asked as she gulped down her newest drink. I dug my wallet from my back pocket, tossing cash on the wooden surface. "Yeah."

Hope stood as she looked me over. "I took a cab here. I should drive you home. You need to make it back to Avery in one piece."

I thought about it for a moment and then nodded. "Go ahead. I'll tab out." I slipped Hope the keys, knowing Ashton was clocking our every move. Even if Avery heard the truth, it would hurt her. Between the pregnancy, the headaches, and flashes, she had become fragile.

I shoved open the door to our quiet apartment, slipping inside and pushing it closed behind me. The moon was hidden behind clouds and all the lights were off, making it hard to navigate. The sound of Dax's claws making their way across the linoleum gave me pause. I bent down, running my hand over his head and letting him lick my fingers.

"Where's Avery?" I stopped just outside the bathroom when a shuffling sound caught my attention.

The bathroom door was slightly ajar. I pushed it open the rest of the way and flipped on the light. My eyes adjusted, and Avery came into view. She was sitting on the floor, her knees pulled up against her belly and her face streaked with tears.

"Ashton didn't waste any time, did she?" I said, kneeling in front of my wife.

"Just leave," she sobbed, wiping her cheeks with the back of her hand.

"I wasn't there with Hope." I hunched over until I was eye level with her, noticing her cell clutched in her left palm.

"Late night chat?" I asked, reaching for her phone.

"Don't," she warned. Her eyes wide and wild as they met mine, wet mascara smeared beneath.

"Okay." I held up my palms and settled onto my knees.

"Avery—"

"I said don't."

"I just want to talk."

"Sounds like you've been talking quite a bit already this evening."

I laughed once, trying to lighten the mood. "Yes, I talked to her. You talk to other guys all day long, but I know you love me. And you are the only woman I have ever—*will* ever—love."

"Yeah." She nodded, swallowing hard before she looked up at me again. "I know you didn't love any of those women before me either, but that didn't stop you from sleeping with them. Why would it be any different now?"

"Because I have *you*."

Avery's long hair fell into her face, blocking me from getting a good look at her. "Getting upset isn't good for the baby."

A sob racked her body as she banded her arms around her knees, hugging herself tightly.

"Whatever it is, I can explain. Please talk to me, Avery. What did Ashton say? Ginger was there and saw the whole thing. I was drinking at the bar. Hope showed up. We chatted. Ashton came over to stir up trouble, I told her to fuck off, and then I left. The end."

A knock at the door got my attention for half a second, but I quickly focused back on Avery. "Baby ..."

"Avery?" Deb's voice echoed in the apartment as the front room illuminated.

"Back here," Avery called out. She glared at me while she yelled, as if she could see betrayal in my eyes.

"What are you doing?" I asked. "Why is Deb here?"

My pregnant wife pushed up to her feet, and panic pushed through my veins.

"Avery?" Deb said, stopping when she saw her friend. "You ready?"

"Okay," I said, trying to remain calm. "Take some time and think about this. Call Ginger. She can explain."

"I'm not interested in whatever story you and Ginger concocted. She's your friend, Josh. Not mine."

I heaved, her words knocking the breath out of me. "I should have known. It ruins everything."

Avery narrowed her eyes, her fury building. "*It*?"

"I'm fucking cursed, Avery," I blurted out. "I should have told you, but I'd hoped if I did right by you, if I changed ... It destroys everything I touch."

"*Cursed?* Do you think this is funny?"

"My sister, my parents, Brooke, the baby ... I'm being punished for what I did to Kayla."

"You're not being punished, Josh," Avery spat. "You were a kid."

"I thought if I did this right, if I didn't fuck around, that just maybe we ..." I shook my head, unable to finish.

"Bad luck is an excuse used by cowards who don't want to take responsibility for their actions."

"You don't understand, Avery," I said, reaching out for her. "It sounds crazy, but I've lived it. Bad things happen to people I care about. I'd stopped trying until I met you."

"Bad things happen, Josh. You can't just give up on making the right choice."

Avery awkwardly bent over to pick up a bag I hadn't noticed sitting by the bedroom door.

An overwhelming sinking feeling came over me. "Don't leave," I begged. "I can fix this, Avery. Just ... don't leave me."

Avery covered her mouth, and with a sob, turned for the door.

Deb seemed sad, curling her arm around Avery's shoulders and walking her outside.

I slid down against the wall, knotting my fingers in my hair. "I can fix this," I whispered to myself. "I'm gonna fix this."

The living room light reflected off a silver chain on the coffee table. Avery's penny necklace was lying on the glass. My heart began to pound against my rib cage, and I closed my eyes tight. "I'm gonna ... what the fuck do I do?"

I stood and stumbled toward the necklace. Beneath it was a pair of coral lace panties, ones I was sure didn't belong to Avery. I picked them up, turning them in my hand. "What the fuck?"

After a knock on the door, I ran across the room and yanked

it open. Avery wouldn't be knocking, but at the moment, I didn't care why. I just wanted my wife to be standing on the other side.

"Hey," Hope said. She noticed my expression and then poked her head in. "Are you alone?"

"I can't talk right now, Hope," I said, turning and closing the door.

It didn't close. Instead, I heard Hope's footsteps behind me.

"Um … that's my, um … in your hand."

I stopped and turned around, looking at the thin fabric. I tried to keep my voice even. "Why are your panties in my apartment, Hope?"

She shrugged, looking embarrassed, but not surprised. "I must have dropped them on the way out after I finished my laundry."

I held up the lace in my fist. "My wife found these. She fucking left me, Hope."

Hope took a step toward me. "I'm so sorry. I can try to call her if you want." She touched my arm. "She's been so irrational, Josh, even for a pregnant woman. She's … I didn't want to say it before, but she's so mean to you. I hate to see you beat down over and over again. You're so good and so loving. Avery doesn't see it. I'm not sure she ever will. Do you want to come over and talk about it? Toby's asleep."

For the first time, I saw the desire and intention in Hope's eyes.

"I just want to make you feel better," she said softly. "We can hang out on the couch, or … we can do whatever you want, Josh. Sometimes we just need one night not to have to think about or feel anything."

I looked down at her.

Her gaze fell to my lips. "I can make you feel better."

Just as she leaned closer, I shirked my arm from her grasp. "You scheming bitch. You did it on purpose."

"What?" she said, feigning surprise.

"You told me earlier you knew exactly how many pairs of panties you had." I threw the lace to her, and she caught it against her chest. "You left them here for Avery to find!"

"Josh," she said. "You're upset. You're being ridiculous."

I pointed to the door, feeling rage boil in my blood. "Get out. Get out before I throw you out."

"You're crazy," she said, backing away. She stopped in the hallway, indignant. "You and Avery belong together."

"Yeah, we do," I said, slamming the door in her face.

My spine ached from sitting so long on the floor, but it felt right to suffer. Avery had been gone for three days, and I'd been drunk for about the same amount of time.

My bloody hands shook as I tipped the fifth of Jack to my lips, closing my eyes as the burn scorched a path from my lips down to my stomach.

The amber liquid was barely a trickle now that I'd sucked the bottle dry. Tossing the glass to the side, it clattered and banged along the floor, coming to a rest against the kitchen island.

I looked down at my hands, flexing them and feeling the bloodied skin of my knuckles pulling open. A few hours before, after I'd left Avery yet another voicemail, I'd taken Dax out for a walk and decided to punch the tree in the back courtyard.

It took me two tries to push myself to my feet, stumbling to my right while struggling to keep my balance. The world around me blurred and spun as I blinked back tears.

I'd gotten everything I'd wanted. I had Avery, the woman I never deserved, and a child on the way. Somehow I'd managed to destroy everything.

I pulled keys out of my pocket belonging to a black Dodge Durango and choked out a laugh. I had a family vehicle and no family.

I'd managed to sell my Barracuda for a profit, but after the down payment for the Durango and the cost of preparing for the baby, we didn't have enough to buy a house like I'd hoped.

I'd picked up extra shifts to build up our savings. Instead of having more time together, we saw each other less. Even when the choice was made to make our future better, it ended up being wrong. I'd fucked up everything, no matter how hard I'd tried to hold it all together.

A sharp knock at the door caused me to jerk my head up, wondering if Avery no longer felt like this was her home. *Had she left her keys?* I looked around, but couldn't focus.

"Come on, man," Quinn's voice called out from the hall. "Open the door."

My heart sank. I needed to hear my wife's voice. I had to know she was okay.

Stumbling across the room, I twisted the lock on the handle and pulled it open.

Quinn walked past me. "You look like shit," he scolded.

"Where is she? I need to see her."

He shook his head. "You really fucked up this time, Josh.

"No, I didn't. I swear to God, Quinn."

Quinn's expression twisted into a combination of aggravation and disbelief. "Avery found the neighbor's panties by your nightstand. You can't explain that away."

"The nightstand?" I cringed, imagining Avery's reaction

when she found them, and how hurt she must have been. "I'd let Hope use our machine earlier that day."

"Your washer and dryer stack are over there," Quinn said, pointing to a closet next to the refrigerator. "How did the panties end up in your bedroom?"

I rubbed the back of my neck. "Avery warned me. She tried to tell me Hope was up to no good. I didn't see it. I didn't see it because I'm so in love with Avery."

He still didn't look convinced.

"Hope did it on purpose, Quinn. She left the panties here knowing Avery would find them."

Quinn shook his head. "God knows I love ya, Josh, but that's pretty convenient. I get it. You got caught screwing Strawberry Shortcake and lost the best thing that's ever happened to you. But it's time to come clean."

"I never fucking touched her! You have to believe me. I swear on my unborn child. I've never cheated on Avery, I've never even thought of Hope in that way."

"Don't swear on your baby, Josh, Jesus Christ."

"It's the truth."

Quinn stared at me for a long time, and then his face and shoulders fell. "I believe you."

I breathed out a sigh of relief. "Thank you. I need to explain to Avery. Can you make that happen?"

"No."

"Quinn, please—"

"You need to back off, man. Deb's really worried about her. So am I. She isn't in a good spot. She needs some time to think."

"She can have time. She can have everything she needs, but I have to know she's coming back. I'm going fucking crazy here, Quinn," I said, my voice breaking.

The muscles worked under the tight skin of Quinn's jaw.

I began to panic. "She is … isn't she?"

Quinn pulled a duffel bag from his shoulder. "I don't know. Deb hasn't slept in twenty-four hours trying to keep an eye on her."

"She wouldn't hurt herself. She has headaches and flashes, Quinn. She wouldn't hurt our baby."

Quinn unzipped the bag. "You haven't been around. She was hysterical for a solid three hours. We couldn't calm her down. She was talking nonsense about the hospital and nothing being real. It was fucking weird."

"I need to see her. I need to tell her the truth. The stress is making her worse."

"Worse? She's been this way for a while, Josh. I tried to tell you. We all have. You can't keep ignoring it. Avery needs help."

I tried to fight against the whiskey fog that was making it all difficult to process. I was angry with myself all over again.

"You should clean yourself up, man," Quinn said, disgusted. "She would be devastated to see you like this." He made his way to a laundry basket of clean clothing across the room.

"She can't hate me any more than she already does."

Quinn shoved a few of Avery's shirts into the duffel bag. "Not as much as you hate yourself, I'm guessing."

"Deep down, Avery knows I wouldn't cheat on her. She's just … having a hard time."

"I hate to say it, brother, but all signs point to a different conclusion. She might be having 'a hard time,' but women without a head injury have suspected worse with less evidence."

"She *is* having a hard time."

"And you're not helping her by making excuses. She doesn't need you defending her mental state to the world. She needs medication, Josh."

"I'm not defending her. She hasn't done anything wrong," I snapped.

Quinn hung his head, pinching the bridge of his nose. "I know she hasn't, Josh. But this—" he waved his hands at the overturned tables and empty beer bottles "—isn't good for her."

"I know. I'll fix it." I sank down on the edge of my bed, my head hanging as my entire world crumbled around me. "If I just knew how." My voice was barely a whisper as I thought back to Kayla. I couldn't help her either.

Quinn's stern expression softened. "You sober the hell up, first. She's not going to listen to a raging drunk."

I nodded.

"Give her some time, and when she's ready, you go to her. Explain about Hope. Then you need to get her an appointment with a neurologist."

"She won't. She's scared of what they'll say." I let my lashes fall closed, sending the tears that pricked my eyes cascading down.

"She's scared because she doesn't understand what's going on with her health, and now her marriage is falling apart. She might be mad as hell, but she needs you."

I nodded, swallowing back the lump in my throat.

"I'm gonna ... I'm gonna shower and sober up. Make a pot of coffee, would ya?" I looked up at Quinn, who was now standing in front of me with the bag hanging at his side.

"Sleep it off. She isn't going anywhere." He cupped my shoulder in his hand and then walked away, disappearing out the bedroom door. A few seconds later the apartment door slammed closed, and I fell back on the mattress, letting my sadness take over.

Despite my drunken stupor, it was almost impossible to sleep. I drifted in and out of consciousness, dreaming of Avery coming home and having nightmares that she never would.

When the sun finally cast shadows on the walls, I grabbed my phone. The screen read 7:04 a.m. It wasn't too early to head over to Quinn's. Avery would be awake, and hopefully she'd missed me, too.

I showered, shaved, and brushed my teeth, feeling the way I had before our first date. I looked for the shirt she loved and spritzed on the cologne she always said made her unable to keep her hands off me. If I was going to win her back, I'd need all the help I could get.

I slipped on my jeans and shoes, grabbed my wallet, phone, and keys, and headed for the door. I swung it open, feeling mildly confident. If Quinn believed me, Avery could, too.

My keys dropped from my hands when I recognized the woman standing in the hallway, puffy and red-faced from climbing the stairs.

"Avery," I breathed.

CHAPTER TWENTY-ONE

Avery

My purse slipped when I snatched it from the kitchen counter and it toppled to the floor. I crouched, picking up sticks of gum and pennies, groaning when it was time to push back up to my feet.

"Let me help," Josh said.

"I've got it," I growled.

"Can we talk?"

"I just came back for my vitamins, and no, I don't have time. I picked up a shift today."

"Picked up a shift? Avery, your anxiety is through the roof. Did Deb check your blood pressure this morning?"

"It's a little high," I said, wiping my hair from face. "Let's not pretend you care."

"Just hear what I have to say." He looked so exhausted, so desperate, it was all I could do not to fall into his arms. But I had to be strong for Penny. I had to walk away from a man I couldn't trust, who didn't respect me and the promises he'd made, even if that man was Penny's father.

I walked past Josh into the bedroom, searching in the closet for a pair of scrubs that still fit.

Josh stood in the doorway, watching me change out of my maternity jeans into scrub pants. I slipped the blouse off over my head and pulled on a matching top over the stretched skin of my belly. I reached down, feeling my belly button through my shirt.

Josh smiled, and his bloodshot eyes filled with tears. "I love you."

I sighed, looking down at my baby bump since I couldn't see the floor anymore. "Please, don't. You're making it harder on me. This was your choice, not mine."

"You trying so hard not to cry is making me want to hold you even more."

"I have to be to work in an hour. I can't do this right now." I hesitated, knowing I was about to say words that, if Josh obliged, would be the beginning of the end. "I need you to ... Penny and I can't live with Deb. I need you to have your things out by the time I get home."

He bristled. "What? No, Avery. You're not even giving this a chance."

"I gave this a lot of chances."

"I'm not leaving. You're not leaving," Josh said, pacing. "If you'd just let me explain ..."

Tears finally spilled over my cheeks. "You can't. And honestly, I don't want to listen to you try." I stood, grabbing my purse off the bed and holding it to my chest. Receipts and my wallet tried to climb out through the zipper, and with trembling fingers, I stuffed them back down.

My eyes felt raw and swollen, and when I stood, cool air kissed the bottom of my burgeoning belly. I yanked down my too-small scrub top.

Josh reached for me, his eyes desperate. "I'll leave. I go over to Quinn's, and you can stay here and think. You can't drive like this, baby, it's not safe."

My patience fizzled, and my temper flared. "Oh, *now* you care about Penny and me?" My face crumbled. "You ruined everything, Josh. I loved you!"

"I don't know how to make you believe me. I know it looks bad. She came over because her dryer was on the fritz. I mean ... she said it was. I don't know if even that's true."

Pressure began to build in my head, and I closed my eyes. "Stop. I can't hear this. I don't want to know."

"You'll accept the lies you see, but you won't you accept the truth you hear? Fine, Avery. Look at me. Look at me, and tell me you believe I could ever cheat on you. You don't believe that. I've never touched another woman since I fell in love with you, and I've loved you since the beginning. You've known all along what Hope's been up to. If you're going to leave me, at least do it for something I did. Not over a fucking misunderstanding. I just need five minutes. Just give me five minutes to explain."

Everything in me wanted to believe him, but I had to trust what I knew, which was the evidence of his past and the lace panties next to our bed. My lips trembled as I spoke, "There comes a point, Josh, where I have to start listening to myself. I can't stay with you just because I'm in love with you. I have Penny to think about now."

"Okay," he said, fidgeting. "I don't want you to drive upset. We can talk later. I'll go."

"You would just love that, wouldn't you?" I sneered. "To run to her while I'm sitting at home, growing our baby, and she's feeling so sorry for you for having a crazy wife." I felt my strength and anger falling away. My chest caved as I sobbed.

"You're not crazy, Avery. As far as you know, you have a smoking gun. I can see why you're upset, but Hope left the panties here on purpose. When she came over after you left—"

I sniffed, anger consuming me. "She's been here since I left?"

"Yes, but—"

"Oh, fuck you and your explanations." I snatched the keys off the counter and waddled toward the door.

Josh stepped in my way. "I can't let you leave like this." He tried to cup my shoulders, but I slapped his hands away. "Okay. Okay, I won't touch you. Give me your car keys, and I'll leave."

"You don't *let* me do anything," I said through my teeth. "And you definitely don't pretend to give a shit about us when you've been fucking the neighbor! Everyone warned me to stay away from you, but I ignored them." Twin rivers streamed down my cheeks. "Now I'm pregnant, weeks away from having your baby. You had everything you said you've ever wanted, Josh! You can't take this back!"

"You know it's dangerous for you to drive," he said, trying to stay calm. He shifted his weight, squaring himself in front of me. "Think about this for a second, Avery. Something's off. This isn't right. Reach down deep in your heart and tell me you truly believe I am even capable of fucking everything up that bad." He watched me, hoping I'd change my mind.

I shook my head, emotionally exhausted. I rubbed my temples.

"Headache?" he asked, sweeping my hair away from my face. Once he realized I wouldn't fight him, he slowly brought me into his chest. "Let me get you something."

I shook my head. "No. We've talked about this. It's not good for the baby."

"Avery. The OBGYN said acetaminophen is fine."

I shook my head. "No."

"I'll get you some water." He left me for the kitchen, opening the fridge and pulling out a clear bottle. He returned and held it out to me.

I looked down at the water, and then back up at him. "I have to take care of myself now."

He tilted his head to the side. "Avery. You can't go to work like this."

I nodded. "You're right." I picked up my phone and called Michaels. She was always willing to take shifts.

"Thank you," Josh said when I got off the phone.

"I didn't do it for you. I'm going to Deb's. I want you gone by the time I get back."

His expression changed. "I'm not leaving. I didn't do anything wrong. I'm not quitting."

"This is *my* apartment."

"This is *our* apartment."

I sighed, my head hurting too much to argue any more.

"Move in with Hope. At least then you and Penny can be close," I spat. I froze, mortified at my own words. "I didn't mean that. I'm angry and it just came out."

Josh's cheeks flushed.

"It doesn't matter where you live. You can see Penny whenever you want."

Josh balled his hand into a fist, slamming it down on the counter. His already battered knuckles split open, spraying blood on the Formica. "You're not a fucking single mom, Avery. You're my *wife*. We're not doing this! Nothing happened! You're not thinking straight; you haven't been for a while. I've tried to ignore it, but this is too much. If you leave me, I'm calling the doctor. I'll tell them about your hallucinations. They're not going to let you have custody of Penny in the state you're in."

My mouth fell open, feeling slapped in the face. "You're blackmailing me?"

"Whatever it takes," he said without apology.

"You are a selfish bastard."

His eyebrows pulled together and he sucked in a breath. A single tear fell down his cheek. "I'll do whatever I have to do to keep this family together. Once you get some rest, you'll think this through. You were right about Hope. We can confront her together, if that's what you want. I can fix this, Avery."

"No, Josh. This is one thing you can't fix."

I turned around, walking toward the door. Josh rushed around me, pressing his palm flat against the metal. "Please?" he begged. "Please, don't do this."

"If you hadn't snuck around with the building whore, I could have asked you that, too, and none of us would be here right now."

I yanked on the knob, and Josh stepped back, unwilling to physically restrain me. After I slammed the door, Josh opened it again, walking out into the hall. "I'll be here when you get back. I love you. Be careful."

I trotted down the stairs, wiping my eyes and shoving through the lower door. I stood on the stoop, looking around, watching the world go on as if mine hadn't ended.

The Dodge started right up, growling before I shifted into drive and pulled away from the curb. Our neighborhood fell away, and I turned up the music, flipping channels until something sassy and empowering came through the speakers. I drove through Philadelphia until the streetlights flickered, until the gas light dinged, and my back began to ache. I rubbed my belly and turned toward home, hoping to God Josh had gone to Quinn's with most of his things.

The sky was dark, and the stars had begun to poke through the blackness when I slowed to a stop, waiting on a red light to turn. I could see the top floors of St. Ann's looming above the tree line, and then looked down when I felt Penny move inside me. When I realized where I was, I choked out a sob. The sign for Holly Road sat above the sign for Jackson Avenue, the intersection where it had all begun.

I could go back to Josh, but I couldn't forgive him. I couldn't trust him. That wasn't a marriage I wanted Penny to witness. I had a responsibility to my daughter to show strength I would want her to have.

My head began to throb behind my eye, and I wondered if Josh had meant what he'd said about taking her away. I'd lost my parents, then Josh, and I could lose Penny, too. Letting go had been so easy for me, but in that moment, I recognized that I hadn't let go of the people I loved. They were taken from me.

Josh's theory about curses might not have been so farfetched after all.

"This isn't happening," I cried. The flashes, the hallucinations, the headaches—it had all started since the wedding. "This is just a bad dream," I said, sucking in several breaths. A new cry ripped from my throat. "I just want to wake up." I slumped over, touching my head to the steering wheel. "I just want to wake up."

I closed my eyes, seeing flashes of the hospital room, and I blinked, looking around the Dodge. Maybe Josh was right. Maybe I was going crazy. Everything had felt off since the accident. Maybe I was imagining things. Crazy people didn't know they were crazy.

My blurred vision came into focus, and I noticed a small copper circle at my feet. I reached down, picking up the dull penny and clenching it in my palm.

My breathing faltered, and a wail bubbled from my chest, piercing the night. Two bright lights came closer, and I held my breath, closing my eyes.

I woke up panting with fear, gripping handles on either side of my hospital bed. Beeps surrounded me on every side, and

I looked down. My scrubs were gone, and I was dressed in a hospital gown. I reached down to feel my flat stomach. Penny was gone, too.

I cried out, covering my face, and Michaels ran in. "Avery?"

I could only cry.

Michaels called frantically down the hall. "She's awake! Avery's awake!" Michaels ran in, checking my vitals. "Do you know where you are?" she asked, her voice smooth and soothing.

"The hospital," I said. "Is the baby okay?"

Michaels' eyebrows pulled in, and my heart broke.

A female doctor rushed in, with shiny dark hair that barely brushed her shoulders and a large mole on one side of her chin.

She flashed a pen-sized light in my eyes, from one to the other, and then turned it off, plugging her stethoscope into her ear. "Can you tell me your name?"

"Avery ... Avery," I said, wincing from the light.

"It's nice to finally meet you, Avery. I'm Dr. Weaver. You've been in a car accident."

I frowned, confused.

"We've been waiting for you to come back to us." She rubbed the diaphragm of the stethoscope on her white coat and slid it under my gown against my chest. "Can you take a deep breath for me?"

I did as she instructed.

"Is Penny ... is the baby okay?" My voice faltered, afraid to even speak her name aloud.

Dr. Weaver pulled the stethoscope from her ears. "Avery, we still have some tests to do, but we need to have a conversation. It could be shocking."

My bottom lip quivered, and then I covered my face, feeling tears slip between my fingers. "Can someone call my husband?"

Dr. Weaver glanced back at Michaels and then touched my shoulder. "Avery ..." she said, her voice thick with concern. "You're not married."

I looked up and blinked. "Yes, I am."

Michaels frowned and looked at Dr. Weaver.

I pointed to Michaels, the IV tugging on my hand. "Call my husband. Please. He's probably worried sick. I have to tell him about Penny. I have to tell him what I've done," I said. I began to wail, and Dr. Weaver patted my leg.

"Give her a mild sedative. I need a full blood work-up and another CT. I want to see how the bruising has healed."

"Bruising?" I asked as Michaels left the room. "Is that what's been wrong with me?"

Dr. Weaver offered a comforting smile. "You've been asleep for quite a while, Avery. Your body has been healing."

I looked at her, feeling something dark and frightening weighing on my chest. "Please find my husband."

She pressed her lips together, empathetic to the fear in my eyes. "I'll do my best."

I sat in the dark room alone, the same room I'd seen so many times in the flashes. The same wallpaper that covered the rooms in Step-Down, the same room I'd woken in after the accident. I looked around for my phone, my purse, anything. All that surrounded me were monitors, machines, and ugly wallpaper.

Michaels stood in the doorway, her silhouette outlined on the floor. "Avery? Do you remember Deb?"

I wiped my face. "Yes, can you call her?"

"She's here. Can she come in?"

I nodded, watching as Deb stepped into the room. She covered her mouth and then rushed to kneel next to me.

She grabbed my hand in both of hers. She had lost weight, and her hair was a bit longer.

"Jesus Christ, partner, you took the longest nap ever."

"Please call Josh for me," I said. "I don't have my phone, and I know he's worried sick."

"Josh?" Deb asked, shaking her head.

"Yes, Josh. Why is everyone being so *weird*?"

"Josh Avery?" she asked, watching me with concern in her eyes.

"Deb, stop! I'm freaking out here."

"Avery," she said, her voice uncharacteristically soothing. "Josh is down the hall."

I sat up. "Then tell him I'm awake! Why won't anyone go get him?" I thought for a moment, and then sat back. "He doesn't want to see me. He told me not to leave, and I lost the baby. He hates me, doesn't he?"

"Honey," she paused, clearly trying to find the right words. "Josh is in his own room, down the hall."

I gripped her arm. "He's hurt? Deb! Take me to him!"

Michaels injected my IV port with the sedative Dr. Weaver had prescribed.

"No!" I said, fighting her.

She finished pushing the meds and stepped back, looking both sad and confused.

"No!" I looked to Deb. "I need to see him."

"Rest, honey," she said, running her hand over my hair. "Rest. You can see him when you wake up."

"I've been resting! I want to see my husband!"

Deb gasped and looked up at Michaels. Michaels shook her head and left the room.

My eyes grew heavy, and then I fell into darkness. I didn't cry, I didn't feel, I didn't dream. I only slept.

When I awoke, I could only recall a moment of panic before I had been sedated. Deb was sitting in a chair, flipping through the pages of Cosmopolitan.

The sheets slid against the mattress when I sat up, and Deb dropped her magazine, hurrying to help.

"Morning, sunshine," she said. "Want me to open the blinds?"

I nodded.

She walked over to the window and twisted a long, horizontal rod, letting in the bright sun and revealing a large billboard for J.C. Penney.

I squinted until my eyes adjusted, and reached for my necklace. "I left it."

"What?" Deb said, sitting next to me on the bed.

"My penny necklace Josh gave me. We fought. I left it behind when I stormed out on him."

Deb seemed uncomfortable and searched for something else to say. "Dr. Weaver was in this morning. All of your tests came back great. They're going to move you to the second floor today."

"To rehab?" I asked.

Deb pulled her mouth to the side. "You need to build back muscle in your legs, Avery. It won't take long. Water?" she asked, pouring some into a large mug before I answered.

I looked out the window, feeling emotion weigh down on me. I had been so quick to walk out on my life with Josh the day before. Now I would do anything to find my way back.

I touched my stomach, feeling more alone than I ever had. I had lost my parents. I had lost friends. This was much, much worse. Tears filled my eyes and spilled over my cheeks.

"Dr. Weaver has scheduled Dr. Livingston and Dr. Brock for this afternoon."

"Who are they?" I sniffed.

"Dr. Livingston is the neurologist." She hesitated. "Dr. Brock is a psychiatrist." When I began to protest, Deb held my hand in both of hers. "No one is judging you, Avery. Your little body has been through so much. It's really a miracle that you survived at all. Your brain had to do what it had to do to distract you while you healed. There is so much about the brain that we don't know. It's important that you tell them everything."

"I just want my husband." I pulled my hands from hers, covering my face. My chest and face hurt from the hours of tearfully mourning my daughter.

Deb only nodded, sympathy in her eyes.

"Deb," I said, warning her with my tone. "Will you take me to see Josh?"

"I can," she said, sad. "But it will upset you."

"Take me," I said. Josh would be the only thing to calm me down.

Deb brushed my greasy hair and braided it, and then she held a cup of water while I brushed my teeth.

"Here," she said, handing me a warm washcloth. "Wash your face while I get a chair."

I rubbed the warm terrycloth over my face, feeling it evaporate and cool while I worked it over my skin. I wasn't going to look in the mirror. I didn't want to.

Deb wheeled in my ride, pressing the brakes down and lifting up the foot pedals. She used her upper body strength to lift me up and pivot, and with incredible control, she lowered me back into the seat.

"All set?" She unplugged my IV and held it in one hand, gripping the handle of my chair in the other.

I nodded, feeling her push forward. When we cleared the threshold of my room and broke into the hallway, something inside me clicked into place. The feeling that something was out of place or missing was gone.

Deb passed four rooms and then paused. "Are you sure, Avery? I really think you should give yourself more time. You're confused, and ..."

"I'm sure," I said, reaching for the doorjamb.

With some difficulty, I pulled myself through the doorway and into the room. All the wind was knocked out of me as I scanned over Josh's body. He was on his back, hooked up to as many tubes and machines as I had been, his eyes closed, his chest moving up and down only by the ventilator.

I reached for his hand. His fingers felt foreign in mine, and the gold band I'd given him on our wedding day was missing. I held up my own hand, which was also bare. *Why couldn't I have just listened? He wanted to tell me more. That Hope ...* A sinking feeling overcame me. Hope had done her laundry at the house. She had wanted Josh all along. She had planted the panties. That's what he was trying to tell me.

"I'm so sorry," I whispered. I glanced back at Deb. "What happened?"

"You were both on your way home from work. You pulled out into the intersection in front of a semi, and your car was knocked back into Josh's. The cars were a mangled mess."

"No, Deb, what happened *this* time?"

"That *is* what happened this time, Avery. His partner, Quinn, said when he arrived on the scene, you were both unconscious, but your vehicles were mashed in such a way that your fingertips were touching."

"His partner Quinn," I said, scanning over Josh's sleeping face. "You mean your *boyfriend*, Quinn?"

Deb looked down at me, amused. She pulled my braid over my shoulder. "No, honey. Ew."

"What do you mean no? You've been dating Quinn for almost two years."

Deb chuckled, but when she realized I was serious, her brows pulled together. She shook her head slowly.

"Yes," I said, leaning forward, holding Josh's hand tight. "Josh, wake up. You have to tell them. I'm not crazy."

I looked up at Deb. "What happened to Penny?"

She shook her head and shrugged. "Who's Penny?"

"Our baby. Josh's and mine. I was thirty-one weeks pregnant, Deb."

Deb tried to back out my wheelchair, but I gripped Josh's blanket in my hand. She knelt down beside me. "Avery, you weren't pregnant. You weren't married to this guy," she said, pointing to Josh.

"Stop it," I said, feeling panic building.

"You two were in the same accident, and you've both been in comas."

I shook my head and tucked my chin. "You're lying."

"Avery," she said, touching my arm. "Why would I lie about something so hurtful? You've been unconscious for seven weeks."

"Seven weeks?" I said. "I've been with Josh for two years. We were dating. We got engaged. I remember the wedding and the day we found out we were pregnant. It wasn't a dream, Deb. I would know the difference between a dream and a memory. It happened." I looked at Josh, desperate. "Please wake up. Please wake up and tell them. I'm so afraid."

"Avery ... Avery, we have to get back to your room. You need to try to eat something. You need to rest."

I held Josh's hand to my cheek and then closed my eyes. "Wake up, Avery. This is just a bad dream. Wake up. Wake up!" I screamed.

"Okay, honey," Deb said, backing me away from Josh. "Visit's over."

I reached for him until she spun me around, and then I turned, reaching for him again.

"Josh! *Josh*!"

CHAPTER TWENTY-TWO

Josh

"I know you said you'd take her shift, but she hasn't come home. Where else could she be?"

"I haven't seen her all night," Michaels assured me. I muttered a thank-you and hung up my phone, my mind reeling with worry.

I quickly dialed Quinn, pacing the floor as it rang three excruciatingly long times.

"Are you guys fighting again?"

"Quinn, Christ, Avery left for a drive to clear her head and she hasn't come back. It's been four hours and she won't answer her phone."

"Calm down. I'm sure she's just driving around and lost track of time."

"You saw how she was. What if she got a flat tire and her cell is dead? What if she got in an accident?"

"Did you call the hospital?"

"Yeah." I chewed on my thumb, continuing to pace. "Michaels took her shift, and she would have told me if Avery got brought in."

"What about the police?" His voice was more cautious.

"And tell them I got in a fight with my wife and now she won't come back to me? They'll laugh in my face."

"Tell them ..." His voice lowered. "Tell them about her mental state. Tell them you have reason to be concerned for her safety."

I sank down on the couch, my head resting in my palm. "She's not that bad," I lied to myself.

"You can't protect her if you continue lying for her, Josh. It may upset her, but it is what's best."

I nodded even though he couldn't see me, and swallowed against the lump in my throat.

"You have to do this, Josh. It's what's best for Penny."

"I know," I whispered. I lowered the phone from my ear, hitting the END button with tears in my eyes. Everything was falling apart so quickly.

Avery would never forgive me for this, but I had to choose between her safety and our marriage, and her safety had to come first.

My fingers shook as I dialed the emergency number, pacing the floor once more. Explaining the situation to the operator, I prayed I was overreacting and Avery would walk through the door. As we spoke, my phone beeped, and I pulled it from my ear to see Avery's name and a picture of her face splash across the screen.

"I have to go. It's my wife," I huffed out in a panic and switched the call. Avery's voice sounded distant and muffled as if she'd called me by accident, and I couldn't make out what she was saying.

"Avery? Can you hear me? Where are you?"

"What happened?" she asked.

Another voice responded but faded in and out. "You pulled out into the intersection in front of a semi." The call broke up. "The cars were a mangled mess."

"Avery? Baby? I'm coming. I'll be right there." My body was on autopilot while I hurried around the apartment, grabbing my shoes and slipping them on before hurrying down the stairs and out the front door.

"You have to tell them. I'm not crazy!" Her voice was panicked and I felt helpless not being by her side.

"Don't worry, baby. I'm on my way. I won't let anything happen to you," I reassured her, pressing the start button on the Durango.

"What happened to Penny?"

"Who's Penny?" the other voice asked.

"Our baby. Josh's and mine. I was thirty-one weeks pregnant, Deb. Did I lose her? Did they take her away?"

"Avery? Answer me. Did you say Penny?" I mumbled, tears now blurring the road ahead.

"Avery? Can you hear me? I'm coming!" My stomach twisted again. She was with Deb, but where? I slammed on the brakes as the light on the desolate road turned red. My fingers readjusted their grip on the steering wheel while I waited for it to switch back to green. She had to be at the hospital.

"Stop it!" she said. Her voice was panicked, and I was praying I'd get to hold her in my arms soon. "You're lying!"

When the light changed, I stepped on the gas. Rain began to fall in a fine mist. With little traffic on the road, I was able to speed through the hills.

"Tell them. I'm so afraid," she cried.

"Don't be scared, baby," I yelled out as I pushed down the gas pedal. "I'm coming. I swear I am coming to get you!"

"Josh! *Josh!*"

The line went dead, and I clutched the phone in my palm, praying she would call me back.

Just a few minutes later, I was pulling into the emergency room, parking my SUV near the ambulance bay. I rushed through the doors, barely able to catch my breath.

The lobby was filled with old men and sick children, but I didn't see my wife. "Avery?" I choked out.

The receptionist waved to me from behind her desk. "Josh? Everything okay?"

"Angie," I said, relieved to see a familiar face. "Avery called me. I think she's here. I think she's hurt. Is she here?"

"Take a breath, Josh," Angie said. Her voice was too calm, only making me more afraid.

"Josh!" I spun around to see Ashton holding a clipboard in her hand. "I was just about to call you. Avery's here."

"Is she all right? What happened?"

"She took a turn too fast and rolled her car. She was wearing a seat belt, but ..."

I only waited a couple of seconds for her to find the words. I didn't care about tact; I wanted to know if my wife was okay. "But what? Ashton, fucking tell me!"

"She's stable. Dr. Weaver just left, but she'll be back. Dr. Rosenberg has ordered her something for the pain.

"What about Penny?"

"Who?"

"The baby," I snapped. I followed her through a double set of doors to the exam room hallway.

"I'm so sorry, Josh." Ashton stopped, turning to me. "We did the best we could."

I nodded, my knees threatening to give out under the weight of the sadness. *We did the best we could.* The words played on an endless loop in my mind. *Did we?* Was there more we could have done? I should have stopped her from walking out on me. I should have listened when she told me she was upset instead of dismissing her as irrational. My life with Avery was everything I'd ever dreamed of, and I had let it slip through my fingers.

My feet stopped shuffling, and I realized Ashton had guided me to one of the doors that lined the hallway, each hiding a tragedy behind it.

"It's going to be all right," Ashton reassured me.

I nodded, knowing it was a lie. I'd uttered that phrase to so many fathers and husbands. They were just words staff felt compelled to say to relieve our own guilt. It wasn't easy to feel helpless when helping was the primary function of our jobs. If we couldn't help, what good were we?

I pushed open the door to where Ashton had led me. Words wouldn't change the outcome.

Avery lay on the bed looking as if she'd fallen asleep. Her blonde hair splayed against the white pillow, a purplish bruising marring her skin just below her hairline.

Monitors beeped around me in a steady rhythm as I wrapped my hand around hers, squeezing her fingers gently as if she were so fragile, she would crumble and slip from my grasp. The first of many sobs racked through my body as I let my tears fall onto the white blanket covering her.

"I should have never let you leave."

I pressed my lips to the back of her hand before holding her soft skin against my cheek, letting my eyes fall closed so I could picture her smiling on our wedding day.

"I hate seeing you like this. I hate seeing you in pain. I'm going to add it to the list, okay?" I attempted a smile, feeling as broken as the rest of me. I combed away a few wayward hairs from her face.

My life with Avery had slipped from a dream into a frightening nightmare, one from which we couldn't wake up. It was as if we were in limbo, suspended in purgatory. Her eyes moved behind fluttering lashes that never batted open. Her heart rate spiked at whispered *I love yous*, but never jolted her from her deep slumber. I couldn't let go of us. I refused to walk away.

I went to her every day and waited. Waited for the impossible, for a sign, for her to look at me ... hoping sinners were granted miracles, too.

CHAPTER TWENTY-THREE

Avery

My eyes felt puffy and raw as I stared out the window. My lunch sat on the table uneaten, and Deb sat in her chair, pretending to read a magazine.

After a knock on the door, two women in white lab coats walked in, attended by a skinny male nurse.

Deb stood. "Avery, these are the doctors I told you about." She pointed at a brunette with shoulder-length, kinky hair. Her full lips were glossed with a nude shade, complementing her dark, warm skin. "This is your neurologist, Dr. Livingston."

"Nice to meet you," I said.

Deb gestured to a short, squat woman with warm hazel eyes and silver hair. "This is Dr. Brock."

Dr. Brock was the first to speak, her smile lighting the room. "I'm so happy to meet you, Avery. I'm sure your situation has been very upsetting, but if you don't mind taking the time to explain, we're hoping maybe we can help."

"You can't help me," I said, sullen.

Dr. Livingston stepped forward. "We'd like to try."

Deb checked my monitors and then nodded to me once.

"Yes," I said to her, waving her away. "You've been here for hours. Go find Quinn." As soon as I spoke the words, I bit my lip.

Both doctors looked over at my monitors and traded glances.

"I mean," I said, trying not to cry, "take a break."

"Who is Quinn?" Dr. Brock asked.

I shook my head, unable to answer.

Deb returned to my side, holding my hand. "Quinn was Josh Avery's partner before the accident. She remembers Quinn and me having a relationship."

"Have you?" Dr. Livingston asked.

Deb shook her head and spoke quietly. "No. Never."

Something about being in a hospital made anything personal impersonal. Bad breath, sexual partners, foot fungus, vaginal odor, gastrointestinal noises, even past relationships and bad habits were no longer private, they were *health history*. In a hospital, doctors were priests, and anything less than cleansing your soul was an act of aggression against your wellbeing. Or, in this case, Deb must have felt she would be acting against mine.

Dr. Livingston gestured to her nurse. He left for a moment and then returned with two chairs. The doctors took a seat at the end of my bed.

"It would be interesting to ask her questions during a MEG," Dr. Livingston said.

Dr. Brock nodded, still staring at me with that deceivingly warm smile. "And your memories of Josh span back nearly two years?"

"Yes," I said, feeling more like an experiment than a patient.

Dr. Brock was trying hard to seem interested in helping me, but I could see them planning their articles in *The New England Journal of Medicine*. I had been guilty of the same excitement and curiosity the doctors had in their eyes. We were healthcare professionals, and day in and day out, we saw many of the same ailments. Seeing something atypical was exhilarating. That interest didn't mean I couldn't empathize, but it was a struggle to balance one against the other—a struggle the doctors were losing.

Dr. Brock crossed her legs and settled into her chair, readying her pen and notebook. "How did it make you feel when you saw Josh?"

I pointed to her paper. "I haven't agreed to a session. I'm not comfortable with notes."

"I understand," Dr. Brock said. "I can easily dispose of any notes at the end if you decide you don't wish to continue."

Deb glanced at me.

"But," Dr. Brock said, "this has clearly been traumatic for you. It would be overwhelming to try to process this loss of time and mourn Josh and the life you led while unconscious and still navigate today, or tomorrow, or the next day. Have you thought about what you'll do when you leave the hospital?"

"She has a week of physical therapy," Deb said. "They're moving her to rehab tomorrow."

"And after that?" Dr. Livingston prompted.

"I ... I don't know. Josh was living with me in my apartment. I'm not even sure I still have my apartment."

"You do," Deb said, squeezing my hand.

"Tell me more about your memories," Dr. Livingston said, "and the physiology that accompanies them."

I frowned.

Dr. Brock stiffened. "Dr. Livingston, if you don't mind, I think we should concentrate on Avery's emotional state for the first session."

"Or not mix two completely separate health fields," Deb grumbled. "What was Dr. Weaver thinking?"

"Excuse me?" Dr. Livingston snapped.

"This is a train wreck," Deb said. She looked at me. "You both approached Dr. Weaver, didn't you?"

Dr. Brock breathed out a small laugh. "Hamata, Avery's recovery will happen in many different facets. We just want to help her readjust to reality."

"I'm very interested in—" Dr. Livingston began, looking to Dr. Brock instead of me.

Deb held up one hand. "We know you're very interested. We think you should both leave, and come back when you can stop talking like Avery isn't in the room."

The male nurse smiled.

"Hamata," Livingston began.

Deb walked over to the door, opened it, and smiled politely. The doctors traded glances and then stood, nodding to me. The nurse picked up the chairs and did the same.

"Feel better, Jacobs," he said.

"Thank you."

Deb began to shut the door behind the doctors, but a nurse pushed through, rushing around the room, checking monitors, pulling the EKG strip, and writing in my chart.

"Look, Jacobs. It's the new girl," Deb said.

"Hi," the nurse said back, barely looking up. Her voice instantly made me angry, but I had no idea why.

"New?" I asked.

"I started in the ER just before your accident," the nurse said. "Do you remember me?"

The tawny beauty reminded me of someone, but I couldn't quite place her. I didn't remember knowing her at all from the hospital. Something told me she was bad news.

"No," I said simply. I wanted her to leave. Her presence made me want to throw things.

"You look tired, Parsons," Deb said.

"Yes, I'm swamped. Michaels called in. Pretty sure there's a Bruno Mars concert tonight."

Deb chuckled, but I narrowed my eyes.

Parsons smiled at me. "Sorry for not introducing myself first. I assumed because we've met before ... but I shouldn't have. I'm Hope Parsons. I actually just moved into your building a few weeks ago." She leaned over and offered her hand to me.

I didn't take it.

Parsons stood, slow and awkward. "Um ... okay, it was nice to meet you again. I have to get back to Josh's room."

"I bet you do," I murmured.

She glanced at me and then spoke to Deb. "I'm assisting Dr. Weaver with a procedure."

"On Josh?" I asked.

Parson's eyes grew large. "I shouldn't have said that. I can't discuss his care with—"

"You can discuss it with me," Deb said. "I'll be his nurse tomorrow."

Parsons shook her head. "I can't, Hamata. Not in front of Avery. I need this job."

I sat up. "Why? Because you're a single mom?"

Parsons hesitated. "Yes. Why?"

"When did you move into my building?"

Parsons was confused, but I could see she was counting in her head. "A few weeks after your accident."

"Have I met your son?" I asked.

"No."

I bit my lip. I was either going to be crazy for being right, or being wrong. "Is his name Toby?"

Parsons offered a cautious smile. "Yes? I must have been talking about him when I came in to check on you. We've had a few one-sided conversations," she said, her cheeks pink. She scribbled a few more things on my chart and then hooked it to the end of the bed. "I really have to go. Glad you're okay, Jacobs."

She hurried out, and Deb frowned at me. "What was that about?"

"You don't think it's weird that I know her son's name? That I even know she has a son?"

Deb shrugged. "She admitted to talking about him. You know loved ones are encouraged to speak to patients in comas. You heard her. That's all."

"Call Quinn," I said.

Deb winced. "I'm not calling Quinn. He's had a rough time, and ..."

"Deb, are you my friend?"

"Yes, but ..."

"Then call him. Tell him I want to see him. I have questions."

She stood, gathering her things. "Fine." She pointed at me. "But if you don't stop, one of those doctors is going to commit you just so they can do whatever tests they want. Be careful."

I smiled at her, watching her leave. "Thank you."

"To be honest," she said, pausing at the door. "I hope you're right. Quinn is hot, and I wouldn't mind getting pummeled by him every night."

"In a better life, he's in love with you."

Her grin was half sad, half hopeful. "Maybe they'll let me live there with you."

CHAPTER TWENTY-FOUR

Josh

It had finally happened. Brooke had called me a selfish bastard. Years later, Avery had called me one, too. Hope was likely thinking it. They were all right. I was like poison, yet I had pursued Avery anyway.

I'd hoped if I did it the right way, if I was honest and treated her with respect, treated our relationship with respect, that maybe whoever had cursed me would give me a second chance.

I looked down at Avery, surrounded by machines, tubes, and steady, irritating noises that meant she was alive, but she was too far away for me to reach. I took her frail hands in mine, unsure if she would take me back when she woke. *If* she woke.

The door creaked as it opened behind me and footsteps sounded. It wasn't the sound of a nurse's sneakers, but Quinn's heavy boots.

"How's it going, partner?"

I sighed. "Still no change."

"You want me to wait with her? Get yourself a decent dinner."

"No."

"Breathe some fresh air. Take a shower."

"No."

"Josh, you need to—"

"What if she wakes up for two seconds and I'm not here?" I snapped.

"What if she wakes up for two seconds and you smell like old salami? She'll go back to sleep just so the smell will go away."

I shook my head, my eyes feeling raw and heavy. "I can't leave her, Quinn. I can't ..." My head fell, and my breath caught. I gripped the blanket, my knuckles turning white.

Quinn gripped my shoulder. "I'm so sorry. I can't imagine what you're going through. But she's going to need you to take care of her when she wakes up." He exhaled. "You can't take care of her like this, man. You need rest."

I took Avery's hand in mine and kissed her fingers, closing my eyes. "Okay," I said, standing. "You won't leave her?"

Quinn sat in my seat and held her hand. "Not even for a second. Not even to go to the bathroom. I'm right here until you're back. Don't forget to shave and brush your teeth. Seriously. This is the grossest I've ever seen you."

I nodded, trying to laugh at his joke. If Avery didn't wake up, I wasn't sure I'd ever laugh again.

CHAPTER TWENTY-FIVE

Avery

I picked at my fingernails, nervous about seeing Quinn. The last time I'd seen him wasn't the last time he'd seen me, and I wasn't sure how to greet him. It was confusing trying to decide how well we knew each other.

I thought back to my time in the ER before the crash. Quinn and I had traded a few smart-ass remarks. He'd flirted with me a handful of times until he'd partnered up with Josh. After that, he didn't speak to me as much. I had to treat him as if we barely knew each other, and that was going to be difficult. Quinn was practically family.

A quiet knock sounded on the door. Deb walked in first, followed by Quinn. He looked nervous, too, and strangely, that made me feel more relaxed.

"Hi," I said simply.

"Hi, Jacobs," Quinn said, his voice sad.

"You can call me Avery," I said.

He was wearing his paramedic uniform, the navy-blue T-shirt and matching cargo pants with boots. I wanted to reach out and hug him, if just to feel that fabric against my skin again, but I continued picking at my nails.

Quinn's knee bobbed up and down, and he cleared his throat. "I was glad to hear you woke up. Gives me hope for Josh."

"He'll wake up," I said, unsure where the confidence came from.

One corner of Quinn's mouth twitched. "I heard you had quite the dream."

"Weird news travels fast."

"Josh would love to hear that. He was into you. He talked about you a lot before ..." Quinn sighed. "I knew he liked you, but ... when I rolled up on that wreck—" he shook his head and lifted his hands, pressing against an invisible ball of metal "—your driver's side hit his driver's side, and your open windows were welded together. The damnedest thing I've ever seen."

"I shouldn't have pulled out before looking. That was stupid," I said.

Quinn switched between expressions, unsure of which to use. "He called me from the scene. He sounded confused and out of breath. The last thing I heard him say was *get her*, and *help Jacobs*."

"He called you? From the scene?"

Quinn nodded. "I called nine-one-one, but I got there a few minutes before they did. I was still at the hospital, trying to score a date with Nikki Liberty."

I smiled. "She's pretty."

Quinn frowned. "When I pulled up, I ran up and had to look through your back window to see you both. His arms were around you, Avery. He held you until he was unconscious. I still can't figure out how your Prius was thrown back into his car—on that side—in that way. It doesn't seem physically possible."

My eyes burned, and I nodded. None of what happened was possible, yet it had happened. All of it.

"So, I think it's nice that you dreamed of him. I don't think it's weird at all. Matter of fact, I bet he's dreaming of you, too."

I blinked, letting tears fall for only a second before wiping them quickly away. "Have you heard any news? They won't tell me anything."

Quinn sighed. "His dad wanted to try to take him off the ventilator today. He has brain function, but he didn't do well off the machine. They're considering how much longer to keep him going."

"They're going to pull the plug?" I asked, sitting up.

"They don't have a lot of money, Avery. Josh had minimal insurance. They'll keep him alive as long as they can. I know. It makes me furious. The guys have started a fundraiser."

I bit my lip. Desperate times ... "Quinn? Mind if I ask you something incredibly weird?"

"Sure," he said, amused through his sadness.

"Is your last name Cipriani?"

He nodded.

I looked at Deb. She shrugged. "You could have heard that or seen that, Avery. You know I want to believe you, but that doesn't prove anything."

"Doesn't prove what?" Quinn asked.

"Does your mom make really, really great pie?"

Quinn stiffened, hesitating before he spoke. "She's Italian. Everything she makes is amazing. Josh loved her pies."

I breathed out, smiling.

"Avery," Deb warned.

Quinn narrowed one eye. "What are you trying to say, Avery?"

"It wasn't a dream, Quinn. I need you to believe me."

Deb walked over to the opposite side of the bed and touched my shoulder. "Quinn, Avery's very tired. Maybe you should head out."

I pushed her hand away. "I can describe your mom's apartment. I can describe the way her pies taste. I can tell you about Josh's parents."

Quinn stood, staring at me as if I were suddenly dangerous. "I don't know what you're doing, Avery, but it ain't right."

"I know what you're thinking. I'm not a crazy stalker, Quinn. I'm married to Josh. We spent time together, a lot of time together, and I have memories of things I couldn't possibly have memories of. It wasn't a dream. It was another life, and I want to go back."

"I'm sorry, Avery. You haven't been to my mom's house."

"House?" I asked, swallowing.

"Avery, stop," Deb begged.

"What do you want me say?" he asked.

"I want you tell Dr. Weaver that you believe me. I want you to convince her to put me back under."

"Avery!" Deb said.

I looked down, resolute. "Medically induced comas are done all the time. You can sell all of my things and put me in a nursing home."

"Avery, enough," Deb said, getting angry.

"He's probably worried sick about me!" I yelled. "I have to get back to him somehow!"

Quinn took a few steps back, and Parsons rushed in. "Is everything okay in here?"

I looked at Quinn. "You were in love with Deb. You were so happy, Quinn. You were going to ask her to marry you."

Deb's face flushed bright red, and she gestured for Parsons to escort Quinn out of the room.

Quinn complied, turning around to look at me once before Parsons closed the door behind them.

Deb shook her head. "Why didn't you tell me this was your plan? I do a favor for you, and you lie to me?"

"I'm sorry." I wiped my cheek. "I just have a few days left, and I don't know how much longer they'll leave Josh on the ventilator. It was a last-minute decision."

Deb sat, digging her elbow into my mattress and resting her head in her hand. "Tell me more."

I sniffed. "Really?"

She nodded, sincere.

"We'd just finished hanging the last painting on the wall of the apartment."

"Really? I thought you didn't like to put holes in the walls."

"Because it didn't feel like mine. Josh didn't understand why it made me so happy to watch him hammer holes into the paint." My breath caught. "Because it was ours. We'd made it into a home."

Deb nodded, resting her chin in her hand.

"Josh had just finished setting up the crib. He wanted to decorate her nursery in fire and rescue stuff." I made a face. "So we compromised. Pink and gray firetrucks and ambulances." I touched my flat stomach. "He was such a proud father. Now he'll never be able to hold her. I'll never be able to hold her. I might never be able to hold him."

"You really love him that much? You'd go back into a coma?"

"This isn't my life, Deb. I know it sounds absolutely insane."

"I believe you."

"You do?"

She nodded. "But you can't go back. We'll just have to make sure Josh wakes up."

"How?" I asked.

She shook her head, her hand pressing against her cheek. "I'll take you there every day after PT. You talked him into marrying you once. Talk him into waking up."

It had been ten days since I awoke from what I had thought was my life. Physical therapy was grueling. Even after just seven weeks, lying in bed motionless had made my muscles weak and scrawny, but I was determined to make progress. Every day, my body grew stronger, and even though I aspired to walk out of the hospital with my husband, my will to move forward diminished. My heart was broken. The love I'd felt had been very real.

Deb wheeled me into Josh's room every day after PT. His body still lay unmoving, a shell of his former self. It was painful to see him so gaunt and weak, but I spoke to him for hours, telling him about our other life, and how we could have it again if he'd only wake up. I held his hand, knowing full well the rumors floating around the hospital, but Dr. Weaver had ordered another round of tests, seeing some change in Josh's brain activity when I was in the room.

"I will be so glad to be able to take you home and feed you a decent meal." Aunt Ellen slipped her hand over mine and gave it a gentle squeeze. "You are getting so thin."

I smiled at her, hoping it looked convincing. I was grateful for her help, and I knew she had spent her savings to be by my side.

"I'd like to see Josh again. Could you tell Deb when she gets back?"

"You've spent two hours with him today, sweetheart."

I tried to hold my smile, feeling I may come undone along my tattered edges if I didn't get to see his face. The uncertainty in her eyes was obvious.

"I'm getting discharged tomorrow. It's my last day."

"So come back when you start your shift," Aunt Ellen said, tucking my hair behind my ear.

"I won't be cleared to work for a while. I don't have a car. I don't know when I can come back."

"You'll find a way."

Like everyone else, Aunt Ellen didn't understand. She was hoping I would forget my other life. She thought if I had enough time and space away from him, my love for him and my memories of our marriage would fade away. It wouldn't.

"I should go now, before lunch," I said, knowing I was pushing my luck. Aunt Ellen had no doubt heard the whispers around the hospital. "This whole thing is my fault," I explained. "It only feels right that I offer him some company."

She reluctantly held out her hand, but I waved it away, pushing myself to my feet. My body was stiff and ached from physical therapy, but nothing compared to the crippling pain in my heart.

My eyes teared as I gripped the handle of the muted silver cane that helped me to keep my balance. Every step was a struggle, but I made my way out of the room and down the hall. Physical therapy was difficult, but it was a relief not to have to depend on anyone else to take me to see Josh.

My chest heaved as I paused in front of Josh's door to rest.

Quinn stepped out into the hall, pulling the door closed behind him.

"Any change?" I asked, hopeful.

Quinn's head shook infinitesimally. "Nothing. Not a goddamn thing except for your visits. The second you leave, his brain activity slips right back."

I looked down at the ridiculous slippers Deb had brought me. Pink bunny heads shook above my toes. "He will," I choked out before sliding my hand over my cheek to wipe away a stray tear.

"Avery, I should probably tell you something. His dad got in last night." He shoved his hands into his pockets. "He's decided to..." He took a step forward, pausing when my aunt touched my shoulder.

"Hi, Quinn. Nice to see you again," Aunt Ellen said.

"Mrs. Collins," Quinn said, nodding.

"Avery is being discharged in the morning. She'd like to say good-bye to Josh."

"Not good-bye," I said.

"Good-bye for now," Aunt Ellen qualified.

Quinn glanced at her face before swallowing whatever information he was about to offer. "Good luck with your recovery, Avery. I hope to see you back at the hospital very soon." He turned in the opposite direction, hurrying through the double doors.

Forcing myself to continue, I pressed my palm against Josh's door, saying a silent prayer before pushing it open. A man was hunched over, sitting in the chair next to Josh's bed. His head snapped up at the sound of my cane on the floor. When he turned, I saw the essence of a man I'd come to love in my other life.

"Hello, Mr. Avery. I'm Avery ... Jacobs," I stammered, the name sounding foreign.

He pushed from his seat and rounded the foot of the bed, holding out his arms. "I'm so glad you're okay. I'm glad ..." His voice caught in his throat as he struggled to contain his emotions. He pulled me in, and I let him, finally feeling something familiar.

"I am *so* sorry," I whispered as Mr. Avery pulled me against his chest.

He looked a little different from what I remembered, but the scent of motor oil and grease was the same. A few sniffles turned into tears, and soon, his body was shaking around me.

I pressed the palm of my free hand against his back and let my eyes close, struggling to keep us both from crumbling into a heap of despair.

We broke apart as Dr. Rosenberg knocked on the open door and stepped inside. He smiled at me, looking tan and rested. "Hi, Avery. Your aunt told me you would be in here. I'm sorry I haven't been in sooner. I took the family to Fiji for vacation."

"It's' fine," I said, trying not to recoil.

Dr. Rosenberg read over Josh's chart before he turned his attention to Josh's father. "Mr. Avery, I've spoken with Dr. Weaver about your decision. We can discuss it later." The doctor nodded at me with a friendly smile.

He was trying to hint for me to leave, but I stepped forward. "What decision?"

Mr. Avery looked even more devastated.

My eyes danced between the two of them, and then I looked down at Josh, afraid. "What decision did you make?"

"Avery," Dr. Rosenberg said, putting a gentle hand on my shoulder. I shrunk away from him.

Everyone froze when Josh's monitor picked up.

"See?" I said, hobbling over to sit in his bedside chair. My cane fell to the ground, and I took his hand in mine. "He can hear us. He knows we're in here with him. He just needs more time. I woke up. When he's ready, Josh will, too."

Dr. Rosenberg looked down at me with sad eyes and reached for the call button.

"How can I help you?" a nurse squawked over the intercom.

"I need to speak with Mr. Avery in private. Please escort Miss Jacobs to her room." He stepped back. "I'm sorry, Avery. You're too upset."

"You're damn right I'm upset," I said, shaking my head, looking up at Josh's father. "Don't do this, please," I begged, tears streaming down his face. "He just needs a little more time. Just a little more time."

Parsons and Smith came in, picking up my cane and me, and gently guiding me toward the door.

I turned around. "Please!"

His face was red and blotchy, his cheeks wet.

"It's okay, Avery, shh," Parsons said. "Let's get you back to your room."

"A light sedative, Parsons," Dr. Rosenberg ordered, no inflection or emotion in his tone.

"No," I wailed. "Please let me stay with him!"

Aunt Ellen met us outside my door, helping the nurses to tuck me into bed. I was limp with despair. It made no sense for Josh and me to have gone through the accident, for me to have the memories I couldn't forget, for Josh's brain activity to increase at the sound of my voice, if it was all just a dream. Love was something we couldn't see, an intangible variable to the equation of life. Who were any of them to say what I felt wasn't real? Separating us may have been sentencing him to death. Josh was the one person I couldn't let go.

"It happened," I bawled. "We love each other. We had a life together."

Parsons leaned down, caressing my hair while Smith pricked my skin with a syringe, pushing the sedative into my veins. My mind fogged over, my body becoming too heavy to fight against them.

"Just rest, honey," Aunt Ellen said.

Once again, my eyes closed, but I didn't dream. I remembered only sinking into darkness, sadness pulling me further into the deep. I wondered if I would ever see my husband again.

I waited in a wheelchair for Aunt Ellen, watching the various cars and minivans load and unload patients and passengers.

The leaves on the trees were already beginning to turn, and the fall breeze blew through my light sweater.

Brakes whined as a yellow cab came to a stop, and the driver side door opened and closed. My breath caught when I saw the cabbie approach.

"Need a cab?" he asked.

My eyes glossed over. "No, thank you. I'm waiting on my aunt."

"Is she on her way?"

"She's just coming from the parking lot."

"I have a card," he said, digging a creased rectangle from his pocket. He placed it in my hand as if it were an inconvenience. "Call if you need a ride."

I looked down and sucked in a tiny gasp. "Thanks, Mel."

Mel hobbled back to his cab, waving once without looking back.

Once the dirty cab pulled away, Aunt Ellen swerved her rental toward the curb, parking next to me. She hopped out, rushing to help me into the passenger seat.

"Who was that?" she asked.

"That was Mel," I said, holding his card to my chest.

She watched me for a moment, curious, and then shut my door and rushed around the front of the car to her side. "And we're off," she said, merging into traffic.

With every mile we traveled closer to my building, I felt emptier.

"I bet you're excited to get home," Aunt Ellen said.

"Not really."

"No?"

"Not without Josh."

Aunt Ellen pressed her lips together. "That was some dream you had."

She exited the highway, taking a detour to the pharmacy before parking in front of my building.

"Here we are," she chimed, twisting off the engine.

I pushed out of Aunt Ellen's rental, stepping across the leaf-covered ground.

She rubbed her hands together. "Dear Lord, it's cold for this time of year, isn't it? It can't just be that I'm a Floridian."

I nodded. "It's colder than usual." My cane clicked against the sidewalk in a slow, defeated rhythm.

"I did a little shopping. I'm going to make you some spaghetti." She chuckled. "It's the only thing I can remember that you like. At least, you did when you were eight."

"I still do." I tried my best to smile, but failed.

Parsons stepped out onto the stoop, the automatic lock clicking behind her.

She beamed, her nose already red from the chill in the air. "Avery! Great to see you back. I was just on my way to work. How are you feeling?"

"I'm ... I'm good." It was difficult to speak to her in a civil tone. I was relieved for a moment that Hope trying to seduce my husband had just been a dream, but then silently cursed myself. I would keep the painful parts if it meant I could keep the good.

Hope patted me on the shoulder. "Glad to hear it. I have a lasagna I'd like to bring up for you later if that's all right."

"Of course," I said. "That's very thoughtful of you."

With a nod, Parsons hurried down the porch steps. I watched her pull out her keys and make her way to her car. I shook my head. Part of this was her fault, and she didn't even know it. It was confusing, hating her for something she hadn't done.

I gripped the railing, pulling my weight upward with slow, agonizing steps. Inside wasn't much easier, but I was happy to be out of the chilly air.

My apartment smelled of bleach and artificial flowers. "I hope you don't mind. I tidied up a bit." She slid my purse from my shoulder and placed it on the kitchen island.

My gaze drifted over the empty space that should have held a table. I looked away. That was from my other life, the one I preferred.

"You're a minimalist," Aunt Ellen joked as she pulled a pot from the cupboard. "That will make it easier on us during the move."

"Move?" I asked, sinking into the small couch in the living room.

I would miss the new pots and pans, the kitchen table, the new mattress, the new comforter, and shams. Most of all, I would miss Josh.

I waited for the scamper of tiny puppy nails against the floor and then covered my mouth. "Dee," I whispered, mourning the loss of him as well.

"Oh, honey," Aunt Ellen said. "I can't stay here forever." She laughed as she continued to rummage through the groceries she'd purchased.

"I'm confused."

"I've been meaning to discuss it with you, but you've been so upset. I just thought it would be easier for me to look after you in Florida."

"I don't need you to look after me."

Setting a jar of sauce down on the counter with a loud clank, she gave me a hard stare before sighing. "You have physical therapy, your car was totaled, and you can't go back to work yet. You can't be here alone."

"I have some money saved up, and I have Deb. I'll be okay for a little while."

"What about hospital bills, rent, utilities? They didn't get put on hold just because you were unconscious, sweetheart. Life went on."

Life went on.

My chest ached, and I wished it were me who hadn't woken up. I touched my chest, feeling palpable pain in my heart. I needed Josh. I needed our daughter. I would give anything to fall back asleep and be lying next to Josh in our bed, his hand on my belly as Penny kicked.

"I need to use the restroom," I mumbled as I slowly limped my way past the kitchen. The smell of diced onions turned my stomach as it mingled with the odor of cleaning supplies.

Flipping the light switch, my line of sight lowered to the floor where I had once curled up and cried, knowing my life with Josh was ending.

I let the cane fall to the linoleum floor with a clatter, gripping the edge of the sink. My eyes rose slowly to meet my own reflection.

"Avery? Are you okay, honey?"

"Fine," I called back.

It was the first time I had seen the aftermath of what the accident had done. A few yellow-gray bruises marred my skin. A deep purple streaked under my sunken eyes. My cheeks were hollow, like my chest felt. I raised my hand, letting my fingertips slide against my skin. I barely recognized myself; I hardly recognized anything. I was stuck two years in the past, with no hope of the same future. I folded into a sobbing mess on the ground, my body unable to support the horrible reality.

"Avery!" Aunt Ellen shrieked as she lunged toward me, lifting my chin to look into my eyes.

A million thoughts flickered in my mind before I rose to the surface. I looked up, expecting to see Josh above me, devastated all over again to see Aunt Ellen.

"No!" I cried, pulling into the fetal position on the floor.

Aunt Ellen sank to her knees, wrapping her arms around me and holding me to her chest. "Should I call Deb?" she asked.

"No, she's at work. I just passed out," I said, reaching for my wrist. I counted. "I'm fine. Just weak. I should rest."

Aunt Ellen helped me up, guiding me to the bed. "Is there someone else you want me to call?"

My husband, I thought, feeling my face crumble.

CHAPTER TWENTY-SIX

Josh

I rushed through a shower, unable to look away from the spot on the floor where Avery had sat, her knees pulled against her belly, looking betrayed. I couldn't get her expression out of my mind. Guilt consumed me, knowing the pain I had caused her, and the inevitable pain that awaited her when she woke up.

My eyes burned as tears streamed down, mingling with the hot water from the shower. The gravity of the situation had finally hit me. Even if Avery woke, I could still lose her. Placing my palm against the wall to hold my weight, I let the pain and anger roll through me until I was too exhausted to support my own weight.

"Why couldn't it be me?" I choked out as my forehead fell against the cold tile. I would have given anything to be the one in that car, to be the one in that hospital bed, lost in an eternal dream state.

The house phone beeped from down the hall, letting me know the answering machine had been overloaded with messages. I ignored the noise. Talking about it with someone else would make it all too real.

Turning off the water, I wrapped myself in a towel and stepped out onto the tile, glowering at my own reflection in the mirror. Purple half-moons bruised the skin beneath my bloodshot eyes, my heartache manifesting itself in my appearance. I looked away, rubbing the fluffy towel over my face, wiping away the water and tears that came flooding back. Avery was all around me, in the pink toothbrush sitting in the holder, the perfume bottle behind the faucet, even the fluffy towel around my waist.

The house felt so empty. Calling it a home without her in it was wrong. The heels of my hands turned white against the edge of the counter. The odds of her coming back to me were slim. I was stuck in a nightmare. Tears trickled down the bridge of my nose, dripping from the tip into the sink.

My head snapped up when Dax pawed at the door, and when I pulled it open, he danced around, needing to be let out.

I sniffed and then rubbed my face with both hands. "Give me a minute, okay?"

I padded to the bedroom and hurried to get dressed. I passed the kitchen, barely giving it a second glance. My stomach growled in protest, but I couldn't imagine sitting down to a leisurely meal knowing Avery was still in the hospital.

Exhaustion and skipping meals were beginning to take their toll. My body felt weighted by sand as I dragged myself around our small home. I patted my pockets and turned on my heels to search the bedroom for my wallet. I passed Penny's nursery on the way and froze in her doorway. A sinking feeling overwhelmed me. My selfishness had hurt her, too.

I backed out into the hallway and trudged down the hall. After finding my wallet, I made my way back to the front door. Dax panted as I latched his leash to his collar. His nails tapped against the wooden flooring as he walked with me outside.

I stood in the grass, waiting for Dax to do his business. Cinda had been coming over to help out with him, but he was alone in the apartment all day. I looked down at him. "I called Cinda, buddy. You're going to stay with her for a while. How does that sound?" The sound of my voice was even more depressing. I couldn't even pretend for the dog.

With his back legs, Dax scratched at the grass and then shook his entire body.

"Good boy," I said, reaching down to pat his back.

My cell rang in my pocket and I pulled it out, fumbling to answer Quinn's call.

"Is she awake?" I blurted out, prepared for disappointment.

"You need to get back here, man."

"What happened?" I said, sounding more accusatory than I meant.

"She's awake ... I just ... Get back here, Josh. Leave now."

I could hear voices in the background. Crying. Shouting.

"I'm sorry, Avery. You're too upset," a voice called out in the background.

"Is that Doc Rose?" I asked. "What's going on?

"You're damn right I'm upset! Don't do this! Please! *Please!*" Avery begged. My heart hammered against the wall of my chest at the sound of her voice in the distance.

"She's awake. Thank God," I choked out in relief. I held the phone to my ear, raking back my hair with the other hand.

"He just needs a little more time. Just a little more time." Her fear was palpable.

"Is she ... is she okay?" I asked Quinn, tugging Dax up the steps to our front door. "Did she wake up confused?"

I scrambled to find the right key and then shoved it in the lock, opening the door just long enough for Dax to run in, still attached to his leash.

I ran to the garage, holding the phone to my ear with my shoulder while I twisted the ignition. "You still there, Quinn?"

"Yeah. Yeah, but ..."

"But what? I'm in the car. Does she not want me there?"

"Yeah," he breathed out. "She definitely wants you here. That's the only sense she's making."

"Tell her I'm on my way."

"I can't."

I dropped the phone into my lap, tapping speakerphone. The SUV revved as I backed out of the drive and onto the street. "What do you mean you can't?"

"She's not listening to anyone. She's combative. She's saying weird shit."

"Like what?" I asked, pressing on the gas. My eyebrows pulled together. I had feared so much that she wouldn't wake up or wouldn't come home if she did. It hadn't occurred to me the millions of other problems she could have. "Has the doc ordered a CT? Maybe there's swelling," I said, swallowing hard. "It could be a brain bleed. He needs to run tests. Now."

"He's not going to take orders from me, Josh. You know that," Quinn said, sounding half worried, half frustrated. "She's … she keeps asking you to wake up."

"What?"

"She keeps saying it over and over. She wants you to wake up." He began imitating her. "'*Wake up, Josh. Listen to my voice. Come back to me. I need you to wake up.*' Her eyes are wide open, man. It's like she's talking to you, but you ain't here. It's … you just need to get here."

"Wake up?" I asked. "She's asking me to wake up?"

"*Wake up,*" Quinn said, over and over. "*It's time for you to wake up.*"

CHAPTER TWENTY-SEVEN

Avery

I clicked my nails on the table, staring out the window at the street outside. A Buick was parked in place of Josh's SUV. Quinn said Josh wouldn't be able to drive the Barracuda. It was bent and crumpled in a salvage yard next to the Prius.

There were a few lucky, blissful nights I dreamed of Josh, but it was nothing like before. His face was blurred, his voice not quite as comforting as I remembered.

"Avery?" Deb called from the kitchen. She brought me a bowl of steaming soup, setting it on the table. "Avery," she chided, "if you get like this every time I bring news about Josh, I can't keep doing it. It's not good for you."

"No," I said, snapping out of my stare. "It's okay. I want to know."

"I thought you'd be happy. Helping people is what he does. His dad donating his organs just makes sense out of all this."

I swallowed. "Planning for his death before he's dead is wrong. He's not dead. However you look at it, Josh protected me. Now he's spare parts." I thought about my Prius and shivered.

"I can take you to see him tomorrow."

"Yes," I said, nodding.

"I think he likes it when you come."

I smiled, swirling a spoon around the beef and vegetables. "He doesn't like it enough to wake up." My mood plummeted. "If he doesn't soon, his father won't have a choice but to take him off life support."

"That won't happen. You woke up. He will, too."

I tried to smile, but I'd forgotten how.

"Maybe you should … maybe you should visit your aunt in Florida? I know you two got closer while she was here."

"She wants me to move."

"I can't agree to that, but the sunshine would do you some good."

"There's sunshine here," I mumbled.

"Not like Florida. She lives a block away from the beach, right? Imagine being able to swim in the ocean whenever you want. That would be epic."

"I'm not leaving Josh."

Deb poured me a glass of orange juice, and then one for herself. "This would be much better with vodka."

"Don't tempt me."

"What were you thinking for dinner tonight?" she asked. "I can make something quick or grab something for you, and then I have to go."

"Don't worry about me, Deb. I appreciate you, you know that, but I'm not helpless. Go do whatever. Are you going to Corner Hole?"

"No. I don't know," she said with a coy smile.

I set down my glass and arched an eyebrow. "What are you up to, Hamata? Are you holding out on me?"

She shook her head. "I can't tell you. I would be a huge dick if I did."

"I'm your best friend. Do not think for a second I can't be happy for you."

"I have a date," she said, immediately cringing.

I smiled for the first time in weeks, grabbing her hand across the table. "Deborah Keiko Hamata! With who?"

She hesitated, then looked down at her glass. "Quinn."

"What?" I squealed.

"If I'd known you were going to actually show a real smile, I'd have told you a week ago."

"You've kept this from me for a week?" I said, a little hurt.

"I'm sorry."

"No. It's okay. I understand why you did."

"No. I'm sorry I have a date with Quinn. It might not even happen. He's been texting me nonstop, and then today ... nothing."

"Don't be sorry. It gives me hope," I said, looking out the window with a smile. The world was going on with me—without Josh. The branches were almost bare. Halloween was just a few days away. I closed my eyes, wondering how I would make it through the first snowfall, through Christmas without Josh. "And don't worry. Quinn's probably just busy at work. It's a full moon tonight."

"So ... dinner?" Deb asked.

"I was thinking Japanese. JayWok is right down the street."

Deb nodded. "You sure? I really don't mind."

"I'm sure. I've been craving it all day, actually."

"I can get takeout, or I can call them and have them deliver." She raked back her dark hair, looking guilty.

"I'm really fine," I said. "I feel like I need to go in. Sit down and have a meal. I've missed Coco and Jeremy, and ... it'll be good for me to get out."

"You're right. You need to walk and breathe in that fresh fall air. I just ... I just want you to be okay."

I made Deb leave early so she could get ready for her date. She waved to me from the street before she slid into her car and drove away.

I walked across the room to the bathroom, slow but without a limp. All traces of the accident were gone, the bruises had faded, my bones had healed.

I spent the day cleaning my apartment, running the vacuum, folding laundry, and hand-washing the few dishes in the sink. I showered after Bobbi, my physical therapist, said good-bye. We only had a few appointments left. If nothing else felt stronger, my bones and muscles did.

My stomach gurgled, and I reached down, realizing I'd skipped lunch. I made my way to the bathroom, feeling the strange sensation of excitement bubbling in my chest.

I dabbed on a bit of makeup, brushed my hair and teeth, and pulled my hair up into a messy bun. My face was beginning to fill out again, and although I still had a way to go, I was beginning to look like my old self.

The bolt lock on my door clicked when I twisted the key, and I turned, reaching for the railing to carefully navigate the stairs. I tried to leave my cane behind more and more, forcing my body to acclimate to walking without one.

I pulled my jacket around me, realizing too late and too many stairs later that a heavier coat would be more appropriate. My gaze instinctively pulled toward the curb where my car would normally be parked behind Josh's.

I took my time crossing the street, soaking up the sun, and waving to the motorists waiting patiently for me to reach the other side.

JayWok smelled of soy sauce and memories, and I inhaled as deeply as I could. My legs were shaking from muscle fatigue, but I was determined to make it all the way to my favorite booth in the back. My stomach rumbled when I reached my destination, sliding all the way across the seat, next to the window. I lifted my face to the sun, breathing in, trying to remember what it was like to be happy. All my best memories were with Josh. I wasn't sure I wanted to make new ones.

Coco approached my table, beaming. "I was wondering when you would get your fanny in here. How've you been?"

"Healing," I said. "Better."

"Good. The usual?"

I thought about it for a moment. "Yes."

She nodded once and disappeared into the back, emerging moments later with a drink in hand. I thanked her.

I took a sip, listening to the chatter, the door chime as customers came and left, the muted honking and dogs barking in the street. It was a regular day for anyone else. For Deb and Quinn, tonight would be the first of many dates. I wondered if it would play out the way I'd imagined, or if they would make their own path to happiness.

Coco placed a plate in front of me, spice and savory rolling up to my nose with the steam. "Oh, my God. That smells so good. Thank you, Coco."

"Of course. Hopefully it will clear out soon. I'm dying to catch up."

"Yeah. That would be really great," I said, grateful for the potential company. It had been a long time since I'd had to eat alone. At least, it felt that way.

I absentmindedly poked at the rice with my fork, watching the world carry on outside the large window. Traffic splashed into view, disappearing just as quickly.

A white sack hit the table in front of me, crinkling in the grip of a man's hand. I startled, and then my gaze traveled up to the wrist, stopping on a loose hospital bracelet. The tiny letters compiled a lot of information: date of birth, blood type, but it was the name that left me frozen.

Avery, Josh.

I sucked in a sharp gasp and held it, hoping if I had somehow drifted back into unconsciousness, I wouldn't wake from this moment.

"Eating alone?" he asked.

My eyes followed the arm up to the shoulder, the neck, the gaunt, but familiar eyes. Josh. *My* Josh. He was looking down at me with an exhausted but sweet half smile, flattening his other hand on the table to steady his weak legs.

His eyebrow rose as he waited for me to respond.

I looked down at my rice and back to him, terrified for half a second that he wouldn't be there. But he was. He moved as a customer accidentally bumped into him, muttering an apology before moving on.

"I'm sorry?" I asked.

"Eating alone?"

My heart throbbed at the sound of his voice. It was exactly as I had remembered. I pressed my lips together, and then smiled as tears clouded my vision.

"Pathetic, isn't it?" I asked past the lump in my throat.

"Oh, I don't know. I think it's kind of romantic."

THE END

Jamie McGuire was born in Tulsa, Oklahoma. She attended Northern Oklahoma College, the University of Central Oklahoma, and Autry Technology Center where she graduated with a degree in Radiography.

Jamie paved the way for the New Adult genre with the international bestseller *Beautiful Disaster*. Her follow-up novel, *Walking Disaster*, debuted at #1 on the *New York Times, USA Today*, and *Wall Street Journal* bestseller lists. *Beautiful Oblivion*, book one of the Maddox Brothers series, also topped the *New York Times* bestseller list, debuting at #1.

Novels also written by Jamie McGuire include: apocalyptic thriller and 2014 UtopYA Best Dystopian Book of the Year, *Red Hill*; the *Providence* trilogy, a young adult paranormal romance trilogy; Apolonia, a dark sci-fi romance; and several novellas, including *A Beautiful Wedding*, *Among Monsters*, *Happenstance*: A Novella Series, and *Sins of the Innocent*.

Jamie is the first indie author in history to strike a print deal with retail giant Wal-Mart. Her self-published novel, *Beautiful Redemption* hit shelves in September, 2015.

Jamie lives in Steamboat Springs, Colorado with her husband, Jeff, and their three children.

Find Jamie at www.jamiemcguire.com or on Facebook, Twitter, Google +, Tsu, and Instagram.

Teresa Mummert grew up in a small town in Pennsylvania where she began dating her husband when they were only sixteen years old. They married at eighteen and soon moved to Louisiana as her husband began his military career. They are the proud parents of four children that they are raising in Georgia.

Teresa began writing when her husband was deployed to Afghanistan as a way to cope with him being away at war. She soon became a *New York Times* and *USA Today* bestselling author. Her work includes, the word of mouth bestselling, *White Trash Trilogy* which landed her a three book publishing deal with Simon & Schuster. She has also written the *New York Times and USA Today* bestselling novel *The Note,* the *USA Today* bestselling novel *Safe Word, Perfect Lie, Pretty Little Things,* the *Honor* series, *Rellik, The Good Girls, Something Wicked,* and *Crave.* Find Teresa at www.TeresaMummert.com.

Made in the USA
Middletown, DE
03 November 2015